The Man Wh
and The Three Wild Men

TWO CLASSIC ADVENTURES OF

DOC SAVAGE

REG. U S PAT. OFF.

by Lester Dent
writing as Kenneth Robeson

plus new historical essays
by Will Murray

SANCTUM BOOKS

This Sanctum Books edition is an unabridged republication of the text and illustrations of two stories from *Doc Savage Magazine,* as originally published by Street & Smith Publications, Inc., N.Y.: *The Man Who Fell Up* from the July 1942 issue and *The Three Wild Men* from the August 1942 issue. These are works of their time. Consequently, the text is reprinted intact in its original historical form, including occasional out-of-date ethnic and cultural stereotyping. Typographical errors have been tacitly corrected in this edition.

ISBN: 978-1-60877-089-2

First printing: August 2012

Series editor/publisher: Anthony Tollin
anthonytollin@shadowsanctum.com

Consulting editor: Will Murray

Copy editor: Joseph Wrzos

Proofreader: Carl Gafford

Cover art restoration: Michael Piper

Doc Savage cover circle designed by Kez Wilson (miscmayhemprods.com)

The editors gratefully acknowledge the contributions of Jack Juka, and Elizabeth Engel of the Missouri State Historical Society for research assistance with the Lester Dent Collection.

Published by Sanctum Books
P.O. Box 761474, San Antonio, TX 78245-1474

Visit Doc Savage at www.shadowsanctum.com.

DOC SAVAGE
VOLUME 61

REG. U S PAT. OFF.

TWO AMAZING ADVENTURES OF THE MAN OF BRONZE AND HIS IRON CREW!

Thrilling Tales and Features

Cover art by Emery Clarke

Back cover art by Robert G. Harris, Charles De Feo and Emery Clarke

Interior illustrations by Paul Orban

They were later to come upon happenings even more mysterious. But, at first, Doc Savage's adventuresome crew thought nothing could be so fantastic as

THE MAN WHO FELL UP

A Complete Book-length Novel
by Kenneth Robeson

Chapter I
THE ONE WHO FELL

THE word "concerned," says the dictionary, means to be affected, disturbed, troubled or anxious.

One of the men was concerned.

The other man was just grim. So grim that his cheek muscles stood out in hard knots in front of his ears, making him look like a large gopher with two walnuts in its mouth.

They stood on a street corner. The city was New York. There was nothing distinguished about the street, except that George Washington had once stayed in a house in the next block. The street looked as if nothing in the way of upkeep had been done to it since.

The green building had been built since the

days of George Washington, of course, because it was a skyscraper of sorts. Sixteen stories and a water tank high. It still had most of its windows, except for the first three floors above the ground. Three stories was about as high as the brats in the neighborhood could pitch a stone. They were not very strong brats in this neighborhood. A surprising percentage of them ended up in tuberculosis sanitariums, and some of the survivors graduated to the stone walls at Dannemora or Sing Sing. One had even gotten as far as the little island in San Francisco Bay. It was neither a healthy nor a wealthy neighborhood.

The concerned man and the grim man were gazing at the tall green building.

"You will go to your death!" said the concerned man.

The concerned man had lean strength and power and range. Timbre in his voice. Character in his face. Muscles on the backs of his hands and in his neck. His suit was blue and good, and his face was shaved, his hair cut.

There was, however, something hard and sharp about him. Not a criminal look. Just hard and sharp. Like a gleaming knife that had cut, and could cut again, and still be polished.

"I cannot help it, Strand," said the grim man. "There is nothing else to do. Nothing."

The grim man was small and compact with the look of a bull pup. And his attitude toward the other was somehow that of a well-trained bull pup toward its master. Master and servant, perhaps. Certainly, at least, employer and servant.

"There may be some other way, Rod," said Strand.

"Name it."

Strand could not name it. He was silent, baffled, uncomfortable and worried.

"I'm going in there," Rod said.

Strand pulled a deep breath. "I order you not to," he said.

Rod looked at him strangely. Rod was thinking of something to say and wondering whether he should say it. Finally he did say it.

"You are not in the Army now, Strand," he said.

Strand got very white, like a man who had taken a needle through his stomach in a way that would make a man very sick. He did not say anything.

"You will be going to your death," Strand repeated.

Rod swallowed. The trouble he had with his swallow showed he was scared as well as grim.

"It's the only thing left to do," he said. "Shake hands, Strand." He took Strand's hand and shook it gravely. "I'm going in. If it is to death, that is the way it will have to be."

And with that, Rod walked into the green skyscraper, walked in to his death as he had been warned!

DEATH, however, came to Rod Bentley in a fashion which was not immediate but which was startling.

Several things happened first, but one of these things was more important than the others, as is often the case with incidents.

The important thing was Tottingham Strand's inability to get into the green building. He tried. He stood there for a few seconds, fighting his impulse to save his friend or at least share his friend's danger, until he lost the battle. Then he rushed forward to the door through which Rod had gone. The door was locked.

Strand wrenched savagely at the knob. He was incredulous; he stepped back, scowled. He leaped forward and kicked the door.

"Open up!" he bellowed.

Echoes of his kick on the door and his shout came back from inside the building with about the sound a pebble makes when dropped in a large cavern. He tried it again.

Strand's anxiety became a kind of frenzy. Sweat stood like hot grease on his forehead. He ran back from the door. He stood and stared up at the building, and the building was like an old green skeleton. Nothing moved. There was no life anywhere.

The sweat kept coming out on his forehead. He started trembling, the calves of his legs first, then his knees. And finally, when he tried to wipe the perspiration off his face, it was as if his hand were patting against the skin.

He stood there for minutes. Then he began running along the side of the building, leaping to get at the windows. There were boards nailed inside the windows. The glass was broken out almost everywhere. But the boards were too solid for him to burst inside.

He ran back in desperation to look again at the building, and it was then that he saw the man on the ledge.

The ledge was high up, one floor down from the roof. It was not wide, probably two or three feet.

The man there was Rod Bentley. There was no doubt of that. He was backing away along the ledge. He had gone out on the ledge, fleeing from something.

There were shots, then! Two rapping reports. Then three more. Rod Bentley slumped down as if hit!

In order to see better, Strand wheeled, raced back to the opposite side of the street, then stopped and stared upward.

Down the street, a couple had stepped out of a doorway to stare. A man and a wife, probably. They had heard the shots. The woman leveled an arm at the high ledge and began screaming. She screamed twice, with a quick intake of breath between. Then she stopped shrieking with her mouth roundly open, a cavity of surprise.

Strand became rigid, as if all his muscles were tight strings.

The figure above had fallen off the ledge. Possibly, the term "fallen" was not applicable, because the figure, although coming off the ledge, was going upward! It fell *up!* It fell up and up until it was small in the sky, finally a dot, eventually nothing that was visible. The form that had been on the window ledge became, in plain, unvarnished fact, if evidence of the eyes was to be believed—and there was no reason to disbelieve them—an upward-falling object that fell out into space.

This, of course, was not easy to believe, even if seeing is believing. The two people, the man and wife who had come out on their doorstep to see what the shooting was about, stood there gap-jawed for something like five minutes before they thought of anything to say to each other.

Strand had started running and had run out of sight by that time.

Chapter II
IN A GREEN FOG

TOTTINGHAM STRAND did a hard job of thinking. He walked streets. He got in a subway and rode to the end of the line and back again. He stood at the stone wall near the Soldiers and Sailors Monument on Riverside Drive and looked at the placid Hudson. He stood there for a long time.

While he stood there, Strand saw a man snatch a woman's purse. Actually, the man eased the purse off the bench where the woman had placed it at her side. The fellow zipped open the purse, made a scoop at the contents and put them in his pocket, then returned the purse to the bench. The man arose idly and strolled away from the bench, then stopped abruptly near Strand and stood looking out over the river.

The reason for the man halting, Strand saw, was the approach of a blue-coated policeman.

An impulse hit Strand. He thought it was a rather silly idea. But something impelled him to go through with it.

MONK

Strand arose, approached the man, spoke out of the corner of his mouth. "Savage is after you," Strand said.

"Huh?"

"Doc Savage," said Strand, wondering why he was doing a silly thing like this, "is on your trail."

The sneak thief turned completely white except for shades of green around his mouth. For a stark minute, he said nothing. Then he vaulted the stone wall, dropped a wild fifteen feet or so down the slope on the other side and lit running.

Strand watched him disappear. Then Strand climbed on a downtown bus, rode it to the midtown district, got off and entered the tallest building. He was calling on Doc Savage. The thing he had done on impulse to the sneak thief had decided him. He could not have explained exactly why, unless it was because there was suddenly no doubt in his mind but that Doc Savage was a nemesis of evil.

He did not meet Doc Savage, however.

He met two other fellows, and they were in a fight when he found them. Or practically. One of them was a dapper man with splendid shoulders, was smartly dressed, and was holding an innocent-looking black cane. The other was a wide, short man with a coating of hair that resembled rusty shingle nails and a face that was something to stop clocks.

Tottingham Strand stepped forward. He cleared his throat to get attention.

"I beg your pardon," he said. "Could you tell me where I can find Doc Savage?"

Neither Monk nor Ham paid him any attention. The two had been having an argument. Monk stood glaring at Ham.

"Ham, where do the flies go in the winter?"

"Search me!" Ham snapped.

"Oh, I won't bother," Monk said smugly. "I was just wondering."

Ham glowered and lifted the black cane.

"Gentlemen!" Strand said sharply. "Please, may I have a minute?"

Monk turned his head. He saw the tight glacial expression on Strand's face, and forgot their quarrel.

"You can't see Doc," Monk said. "It is impossible!"

Strand wet his lips. "It is important. Very important."

Monk shrugged. "I can't help that," he said. "You can talk to us."

"Who are you?" Strand inquired.

"We help Doc," Monk explained. "I'm Monk Mayfair. This guy with the fancy clothes here is Ham Brooks."

Strand thought for a while. The desperation in his mind moved across his face like grim reflections in a mirror. "I … I would like to talk to you, then," he said.

MONK and Ham conducted Strand to an elevator. They had met in a small office in a lower floor of the building, an office which the elevator starter had informed Strand was used to interview persons who wished to see Doc Savage. They rode to the eighty-sixth floor. They crossed a corridor, opened a plain bronze door which bore the name "Clark Savage, Jr.," in small print.

HAM

Strand found himself in a reception room furnished with a few comfortable chairs, a safe big enough for a bank and an inlaid table that was really an unusual piece. He was shown a seat.

"What's got you looking like that?" Monk asked.

"I … looking like what?" asked Strand, surprised.

"As if the Indians were coming."

Strand tried to be nonchalant and lighted a cigarette. His first impression of Monk and Ham had been that they were a pair who had some bolts loose. But now he was not so sure. They were as direct, now, as two roosters after a worm.

Ham said, "What is worrying you? What is this trouble you want Doc Savage to help you out of?"

Strand, startled, said, "I have not mentioned any trouble."

"Sure," Ham said. "But you would not be coming in here with that look on your face unless that was it."

"I see," Strand said. "You are accustomed to this sort of thing?"

"Somewhat."

"I see."

Monk, who was no diplomat and had never yearned to be one, said, "What you had better see is that we haven't got all day to sit around and listen to you stall. Did you come up here with something to say?"

Strand frowned. "If you wish me to be blunt, I will be that," he said. "I want help. I want you to get something. It is very valuable."

"Does this thing," asked Monk, "belong to you?"

"It certainly does."

"Where is it?"

"Some men have it."

"Where are they?"

"I can show you where they are," said Strand.

"What is this thing?"

"I'll show you."

"What shape is it?"

"We can handle it all right, once we get our hands on it," Strand said.

Monk pointed a finger at him.

"Friend, you'd better be more definite than that," Monk said, "if you want us to show much interest."

Strand began talking then. His voice was deep and smooth, his delivery faultless, and his words seemed to have power and persuasiveness. Monk and Ham, who were skeptical fellows, found themselves listening and nodding thoughtfully. Monk, in particular, drank it in, while Ham was a little more slow on the upbeat. Ham was a persuasive orator himself, but he was up against such a master in the person of Tottingham Strand that it did not occur to him that he was being talked into something.

Strand told them that he had a friend named Montgomery and that the friend had left a chest with him. Strand did not know what the chest contained, but it must be of valuable content, because Montgomery had been very concerned over its safety. Then—as Strand explained it—strange things had started happening: People watching him, an attempt to burglarize his house, and, finally, the chest had been stolen.

"It happened an hour ago," finished Strand, "and I came straight to you for help."

Ham nodded. He was to find out later that he had just listened to as smooth a cloth of lies as anyone had ever woven before his face. But he now thought every word that had been told him was the truth. He had been taken in!

Ham said, "Really, the thing to do is call the police. You can tell them the story, and they can do more than we can. Monk, telephone the police."

In alarm, Strand held up a hand.

"No," he said. "Unfortunately, my friend Montgomery said I must not, under any circumstances, involve the police with the box."

Ham frowned. "We want nothing to do with anything crooked," he said sharply.

Strand smiled grimly.

"Neither do I," he said. "Suppose we do it this way: You help me. I let you look at the contents of the chest, whatever they may be. If you think the police should be informed, we will do so, and they can arrest Montgomery."

"You would double-cross your friend?" Monk asked.

"That," said Strand, "would not be double-crossing. If the man involved me in something criminal in giving me the chest, he is no friend, and deserves none of the treatment of one."

That appealed to Ham.

"We'll help you," he declared. "Just a minute, until we get our equipment together."

BY equipment, Ham meant some of the gadgets which Doc Savage had developed. The bronze man's inventive genius had turned out numerous unusual—"unusual" was a mild word for some of them—devices for use in their profession. The gadgets were unorthodox. The bulletproof undergarments, made of a chain-mesh alloy that was not much heavier than a suit of long, winter red flannels, was an example, and probably the most commonplace of the devices they were in the habit of using.

Monk said, "You know something?"

"Where flies go in the wintertime?" Ham sneered.

"No. No, I'm not kidding," Monk insisted. "You know what? I think that guy talked us into something."

"He told a very convincing story."

"He sure did," Monk said strangely.

Ham scowled. "You mean he sucked me in? Ridiculous. Listen, I have heard experts put out a line of talk, and I've done it myself more than once."

"All right, smart boy," Monk said. "I bet you we find out, and don't say I didn't tell you so."

Strand looked at them anxiously when they came back out of the laboratory with their equipment. He asked, "Are you sure you can handle this? It is dangerous."

"We're as sure we can handle it as we can be," said Monk, "without knowing what it is."

"Couldn't you get more help?"

"Not right away," Monk said.

"Why can't we get hold of Doc Savage?" Strand asked. "You have not explained that."

Monk and Ham saw no reason why they should not tell him the reason.

"Doc," Monk said, "is at an uptown hospital, performing an operation."

"We can stop for him," Strand suggested. "We will telephone ahead, and they can get someone else to perform the operation. I'll pay whatever fee Savage was to get for the operation, so he won't lose anything."

"They can't get anybody else for this operation," Monk told him bluntly, "because nobody else is able to do it. And you want some advice?"

"Advice?" said Strand, puzzled.

"Don't mention money around Doc," Monk advised. "I mean, don't give him the idea you think money can buy any of Doc's services."

"That seems rather strange advice."

"Doc doesn't work for money."

"I don't believe I understand," Strand said.

Monk said nothing, but he wished he hadn't brought up the subject. Doc Savage had as good an idea of the value of money as the next man. But Doc was fortunate in having a source of wealth which he could tap at will, a secret hoard in a lost Central American jungle valley, a place presided over by descendants of an ancient Mayan civilization. The source of wealth was a result of one of their earlier adventures. It was also a secret.

"Doc doesn't do anything in which he is not interested," Monk said, and let it go at that.

Which was not exactly true. What Monk meant was that Doc could not be hired. That the bronze man was sole judge of what needed doing, and that his payment for the job was that same knowledge that it needed doing. Monk had heard Johnny Littlejohn explain it that way once, and the explanation had confused Monk until he thought about it. Johnny Littlejohn had a habit of expressing his statements in abstruse phrases, or of using words so big that no one could understand them.

Thinking of Johnny Littlejohn led Monk to mention a fact.

"There are three more members of Doc's group," he said. "There is Renny Renwick, the engineer; Long Tom Roberts, the electrical expert, and Johnny Littlejohn, the archaeologist and geologist. All three of them are down in Washington at a defense-board meeting, so they are not available to help us."

Tottingham Strand nodded. "I wish we had more help," he said.

Monk's feeling that Strand was shystering them grew stronger and stronger.

THEIR distrust of Strand was actually responsible for what happened to them, which was embarrassing. Usually, distrust kept them out of trouble. This time, it got them into it.

It happened in an involved way.

First, Strand took them into an old building on a side street in a squalid part of town. He climbed stairs. They followed, full of caution. They clambered out on the roof.

"Keep down," urged Strand in a tense voice.

He meant keep down behind the brick walls around the roof. They did so. They got roof tar on their knees, got skinned with gravel and collected dust.

Eventually, Strand indicated an old dilapidated hulk of an office building which was colored green.

"In there," he said.

"That green building?" asked Monk, surprised.

Strand nodded. "In there, somewhere. That is where the thieves took it."

"It's a big place," Monk pointed out suspiciously.

"It seems to be abandoned," Strand explained. "I think they may have rented it, or maybe they moved in without any authority to do so. Anyway, that is where they went."

"You sure they're there, now?"

"That," said Strand grimly, "I wouldn't swear to. They were there three hours ago. They may have left. We can move across this roof and get into one of the windows of the green building."

Three hours ago? This guy had said his chest had been stolen only an hour ago. Now, he said three hours. Monk glanced at Ham to see if the dapper lawyer had noticed the slip, and Ham had. They exchanged meaning looks.

"Strand," Monk said. "By the way, you said your name was Strand, didn't you?"

"Yes. Tottingham Strand."

"All right, Strand—what does this mysterious chest look like?"

"It is green," Strand said. "You'll know it when you see it. Green, and longer than a man, but not as wide. Thicker, though." He indicated the building. "Tell you what: I will crawl inside and make an investigation. If the coast is clear, I will come back and tip you fellows. If it isn't clear, use your own judgment."

He crawled away.

Monk and Ham proceeded to make their mistake. They did not have to hold a conference over it. They just looked at each other, and Ham said, "It smells to me as if he was going in there to tip his friends to be ready for us, then plans to come back and get us."

Monk was silent,

They crawled forward after Tottingham Strand. They climbed in the same window through which Strand had eased himself. Then people began shooting at them!

THERE was not much shooting. Two bullets. Both were purposefully aimed to one side.

A voice, evidently belonging to the one who had caused the bullets, said, "Stand still, you two."

Monk and Ham stood still.

The voice said, "That's fine. Now, listen. We haven't any great wish to drum up business for the undertakers. Suppose you two wandering Willies go away from here and have a forgetting spell."

Monk said, "Ham, I never heard that voice before."

"I, either," Ham said, precisely. When Ham became precise in speech, it meant he was very angry.

The voice said, "Did you come with Strand?"

Monk and Ham looked at each other.

"Who's Strand?" Monk asked.

The voice laughed grimly. "Humorists, eh? We saw you with him. Incidentally, we have him with us now."

Monk lifted his arms slowly to the level of his shoulders. Then he flexed them at the elbows and clasped his hands over his head.

"You don't need to put your hands up," the voice said. "We could shoot you dead before you could do anything."

Monk said nothing. He flexed his biceps. He made the muscle get very big, so that it pressed against a brittle container in his sleeve and broke it. When he felt it break, he winked at Ham, and began holding his breath. Ham also held his breath.

Monk lowered his arms slowly so that the gas he had released could get out of his sleeve and spread through the room.

The voice said, "Maybe you would feel better if Strand told you to go away. Boys, get Strand. Tell him to advise his two pups to go away. We don't want any more trouble than—"

The man stopped.

There was a sound like a sack, loosely filled with potatoes, being dumped on the floor.

"What the hell!" said the voice.

The voice was speaking to them through a crack in the door on the other side of the room.

"Gas!" a voice screamed. It was a new voice. "They let loose some kinda gas!"

"SOME kinda gas" might have been one description for it. Explicitly, the stuff was an odorless and colorless anaesthetic of great power and quick effect, one which became quite worthless, however, after it had mingled with atmosphere for from a minute to a minute and a half. Doc Savage and his associates used it as a regular weapon.

"Gas, gas!" the man kept bellowing.

Monk moved fast, got down, went to the right, out of range of the door. Ham also moved, dipped a hand into a pocket, brought out a small grenade, and put it hard against the door. It was the type that would explode on contact when the pin was out. It made splinters and flame out of the door.

Monk roared. He liked to roar when he was fighting. He plunged into the debris that the door had become.

He saw a man picking himself off the floor twenty feet down a corridor. The man had been tumbled that distance by the blast, but not stunned. The fellow ran. Monk got another grenade, heaved it. It did not explode. Either the grenade was defective, or Monk had not released the firing pin properly. At least, the quarry got away up a stairs.

There were two men spread out on the floor, and neither of them was Tottingham Strand. There was only the runner, the one who had escaped up the stairs. Monk chased him.

"Be careful!" Ham yelled warningly.

Care was something Monk never knew in a fight. He hit the door. Someone was trying to hold it on the other side long enough for someone else to fasten a lock. Monk yanked. There was a short struggle of muscles. Monk could straighten horse-shoes with his unaided hands. He got the door open, got a man by the neck and another man by the arm.

The stairway was narrow enough to make it a little complicated as they went around and around and over and over in a cloud of dust and profanity. Monk was entirely happy for twenty or thirty seconds, which was as long as the two foes lasted. During the fracas, Ham tried to join in, and Monk managed to put an accidental foot in Ham's face and shove. The latter incident made the brief fray a luscious success.

Monk got up and knocked dust off his hands. "Where's some more?" he asked.

Ham held his aching nose and demanded, "Was that an accident?" He added a threat, "If I thought you kicked me on purpose—"

Tottingham Strand called to them from above.

"Get help!" he shouted. "There are too many of them! And they've got that green fog coming—"

Judging from the sounds, Strand was either kicked in the throat or slugged with a blackjack.

Monk and Ham went up to see. They expected to be shot at, and to discourage that they tossed up a smoke grenade and two thin-walled containers holding the powerful anaesthetic gas.

They got their lungs full of good air, held their breaths, and climbed the stairs silently. They could hear footsteps running away, climbing higher into the green building. They came out on a floor and found another stairway and went up that into a hall like the other two, where they paused to consult each other concerning a rather strange phenomena which had come to their attention.

"Ham," Monk said.

"Yes?"

"Do things look kind of green to you?" Monk asked.

"They do," Ham admitted.

"Kind of as if there was a green fog in the air?"

"Kind of," Ham said.

Chapter III
ANOTHER WHO FELL UP

THE remarkable aspects of encountering a green fog held them there for a short time. They did not say anything immediately, but they gave the thing considerable thought.

"Gas," Monk suggested.

"I don't think so," Ham said. "I don't feel anything."

Nevertheless, both hastily dug out their gas protection, which consisted of a hood apiece, made of a material resembling cellophane in its transparency. Elastic held the hoods snugly around their necks. The things had no oxygen attachments, but they would be effective for a short time.

They went up more stairs. There was no one, nothing but the fog, and that was more green. It reminded Monk of the color of a pond frog's back.

They came to a metal door. It was locked. Ham touched Monk's arm and made signs with his fingers. This was next to the top floor, Ham signaled. He had kept track. Monk was nodding agreement when they heard Strand scream.

Strand's yelling came from above, but from outside. They ran to the windows, threw them up. Monk, always reckless, took a chance and thrust his head out and looked up.

Strand was lying across the ledge. His head, his arms, were visible. Judging from his actions, someone was holding his legs. He yelled something.

Monk wrenched off his gas hood to listen. He was badly in need of air, anyway.

Strand shouted, "Get out of the place! Get help! It's hopeless!"

Hands grasped Strand's head. They struck him. One of the hands had a gun. Strand was hauled back. A moment later the gun exploded!

The gun report had a dull, mushy quality, as if the muzzle was against the man's body when the blast came. A thin stream of red appeared, began to trickle off the ledge. The greenish fog was so thick that Monk did not see the red string until it began to spatter, blown by the breeze, over the sill of the window from which he leaned.

"They shot him!" Monk said.

Ham said, "Here, let me there. I'll fix them."

Ham had a machine pistol in his hand. The little weapon, no larger than a heavy army automatic, could discharge an enormous number of bullets per second. The bullets were very small in caliber, and of infinite variety—either "mercy" slugs which would produce unconsciousness, or explosive, or smoke pellets.

He leaned out of the window, but he did not shoot.

"Monk!" he squalled suddenly. "Look!"

Monk thrust his head out of the window. "Blazes!"

"He just fell off the ledge," Ham said.

Monk gaped unbelievingly. "But—he's falling *up!*"

The figure, hard to distinguish in the green fog, but nevertheless a figure with Strand's clothing and with the shape of a man, was falling upward and upward until it was becoming lost in the olive haze.

Monk said, "You sure that's him?"

Ham had to clear his throat before he could speak. "Positive!"

They stood there in iced astonishment until the figure was no longer visible in the sky.

The iron door blocking the stairs that led on up to the higher floor was strong. But it came to pieces under one of the small explosive grenades. They went up cautiously and found nothing.

"Blast this pea-soup fog!" Monk complained while they were looking cautiously around. "I couldn't see a rabbit twenty feet away."

"Ten feet away would be more like it," Ham said.

Their earnest and wary search disclosed no one, which was no end baffling.

"Wonder where they went," Monk muttered. "Think they could all have floated off into the sky? We didn't watch."

Ham said something violent and skeptical. "You really think we saw a man float up into the sky?"

"All I know is what I saw," Monk said. "What would you say?"

"It couldn't happen, regardless of what we saw."

"All right," Monk told him. "But you called my attention to it yourself."

Monk went to the window. There was wet redness in which he put his finger. "See?" he said. "Blood! This is where they shot Strand."

Ham pointed at the sky. "And there's where he went," he said. "Don't tell me we aren't crazy."

Monk grimaced. "I hope nothing unexpected or violent happens, like a mouse squeaking, or something. I'm in the frame of mind to jump fifty feet straight up."

They prowled around in the green fog. Monk discovered he had several small cuts on his legs. Ham found his own legs bore similar wounds. They concluded one of the men they had fought downstairs had been using a small penknife that they hadn't noticed.

Suddenly their minds were relieved.

They found a fire escape.

"That's the way the others got out of here!" Monk exploded in relief. "While we were busting down the door, they just went down the fire escape."

Ham nodded soberly.

"Fine," he said. "Now you just find the invisible strings that pulled that man up in the sky and we can go home and say we know everything."

"How about the green chest?"

"You mean the one Strand had stolen from—" Ham went silent. "Green," he muttered after a moment. "Green! This fog is green."

"Kind of significant, huh?" Monk suggested.

"I don't know what it is," Ham snapped. "Let's go downstairs and collect our prisoners."

They made the descent of stairways without relaxing caution and found that there were no prisoners. They had left at least four unconscious men behind them, and now there were none.

"Collected," Ham said.

"Yeah, the guys went down the fire escape, picked them up, then took to their heels," Monk agreed.

"You think there's any use of hunting for the green chest?"

"If there was a green chest," Monk said, "we might as well look for it."

They looked and did not find it. Later they stood on the street, disgusted.

"The fog is down here, too," Monk pointed out.

"Thicker," Ham agreed. "It seems to have covered the whole city. It is almost as green as grass."

The little man with the big hat met them on the corner. He was standing there wringing his hands.

"Gentlemen, please," he said. He put a hand on Ham's arm. "Excuse me, but have you noticed anything strange for the last half-hour?"

"Strange?" Ham prompted.

"I—er—green," said the little man.

Ham snorted. "Strange is the word for it. You mean this fog, don't you?"

"Yes, yes," said the little man eagerly. "Yes, indeed. I'm so glad you see it, too. I thought I was going slightly off."

Ham looked up at the sky. "We can understand your feelings," he said.

"I'm so glad," said the little man. "I'll run and tell my wife that we're all right after all."

Ham said, "By the way, you haven't noticed things going up, have you?"

"Up?" said the little man vacantly.

"Never mind," Ham said.

PAT SAVAGE met them at headquarters. Pat was sitting in the reception room applying adhesive tape to an extremely well-molded ankle.

"I'm sure glad to see you," she said. "What is this stuff? This green stuff?"

"Fog," Monk suggested.

"Don't be funny. Fog is gray."

"All right, you can do what I was doing—guess what it is," Monk told her.

Patricia Savage had many of the physical characteristics of her cousin Doc. She had his flake-gold eyes and his remarkably bronze hair, a little of the tanned bronze of his skin.

"Doc has been hurt," she said.

"Hurt?" Ham yelled. "Where? How badly?"

Patricia Savage operated an exclusive beauty establishment on Park Avenue and spent her odd moments trying to chisel in on the excitement that usually surrounded Doc and his associates. Pat liked excitement. The difficulty was that Doc did not appreciate the presence of Pat in his organization; it was his belief that the work was too dangerous. He had never been able to convince Pat on the point.

"Pull your eyes back in," Pat suggested. "He isn't hurt badly. Two fellows got in a street fight, and one of them had a knife. One man knocked the knife out of the other's hand and it hit Doc. Cut him a little, that's all."

"Where is he?" Monk demanded anxiously.

"He will be here before long."

Monk relaxed and eyed Pat's ankle approvingly. "What happened to your running gear?"

Pat finished applying the adhesive tape. "You know as much about it as I do. Something skinned my shin. A man on the street—clumsy oaf."

Ham went out and threw up a window, looked out. "I can't tell about this fog," he said. "It may be thicker in other parts of the city, but I can't be sure."

Pat asked, "What time did you first notice it?"

"About an hour ago, I imagine it was," Ham said.

Pat said, "I only noticed it about half an hour ago."

"Probably it took some time to spread to your part of town."

Pat stared at him. "You mean you know where it started?"

"No, I don't!" Ham snapped. "I don't know anything about it, except that it is the color of grass and danged mysterious."

"What is wrong with Ham?" Pat stared at Ham. "He doesn't look right to me."

Monk chuckled a trifle horribly. "Ham is on edge. He saw a man fall up, and it upset him."

"Up?" Pat frowned. "You mean *up?*"

Ham whirled on Monk and yelled, "You shouldn't have told that, you silly goon! Nobody will believe us!"

Pat became completely blank. "You mean to stand there in your skin and bones and tell me you saw a man fall *up?*"

"'S a fact," Monk said gloomily.

"How far up did he fall?"

"Out of sight, and no telling how much farther."

Pat contemplated them for a while in silence. "Somebody," she said, "has been dropped on his head."

Chapter IV
FAINTING SPELL

DOC SAVAGE said, "Pat, when did you first notice this green fog effect?"

"Forty-five minutes ago," Pat said.

"And you, Monk?"

"An hour and fifteen minutes ago, about."

Ham said, "Doc, that isn't all, either." He rubbed his jaw sourly. "A guy came in here with a story about a green chest that had been stolen from him. His name was Tottingham Strand, he said. You want to hear that story now? It ended when he fell up into the sky."

Doc Savage studied Ham thoughtfully. "Go ahead with the story," he said.

Ham went ahead.

Doc Savage was as big a man physically as his reputation. This was not apparent until one stood close to him, so well proportioned was his big body. There was nothing, in fact, about him that looked ordinary. His eyes were like pools of flake gold, always stirred with tiny winds, full of magnetic power. A single glance at him did not leave the slightest doubt about his muscular strength and vitality.

He looked what he was—a scientific product. Literally a product of science. Because he had been placed in the hands of physical culturists, psychologists, educators, chemists, and a raft of other scientists at childhood. He never had a normal youth. The scientists might have considered they were making it as normal as they could under the circumstances, but they were wrong most of the time.

The strange upbringing of Doc Savage had been the idea of his father, who had had a fixation of bringing up a son who would be a kind of modern knight and Sir Galahad, with test tubes and scientific gadgets for his sword and horse. The fixation of the elder Savage, long since gone beyond, was the result of some terrible thing that had happened to him; but the son had never learned exactly what it was.

Ham finished his recital.

"He fell up, as sure as I'm sitting here," he said. "I know how it sounds, and Monk knows how it sounds. But we saw what we saw."

"The green fog came up on you shortly after you had your first fight in the building?" Doc asked.

Ham nodded. "The building was green," he said. "The chest was green, Strand said. The fog is green."

Pat said, "There seems to be a green tinge to the thing."

Suddenly Doc Savage startled the others. The big bronze man made a small trilling sound, an exotic note that seemed to come from everywhere in the room rather than from a definite point. It was very low, hardly audible. Pat and the others knew it meant that Doc Savage was concerned. The sound was a small unconscious thing he made in moments of mental stress.

"Pat," he said, "suppose you get on the telephone and check with some friend in another part of the city on the fog."

Pat nodded, picked up a telephone and dialed a number. "Hello," she said. "Is Susan there? ... Oh, she isn't. Who is this, the maid? ... I see. By the way, is it foggy up there? ... It is green, eh? ... Thank you. Tell Susan I called, will you? But tell her it wasn't important."

Pat hung up. "The green fog is up in Westchester, where Susan Glaspell lives. That was her maid on the telephone."

Monk grunted, said, "I know a guy down in Jersey. I think I'll call and ask him."

He got on the telephone but did not succeed in getting his friend. He did get a friend of the friend who was at the friend's office, and who said the fog was there in Jersey, as green as peas and as thick as soup.

Monk hung up. "More than passing strange," he said.

Then Doc fainted.

SIX little devils with hammers walked around on Doc Savage's head in dignified circles, testing the ringing qualities of his skull. When Doc finally managed to awaken, he grabbed at the devils with both hands but got fistfuls of his hair.

"You all right, Doc?" demanded a voice.

The face that belonged to the voice seemed to belong to Monk.

Doc was silent until he had collected enough of himself to sit erect. He asked, "Did you fellows see what made me pass out?"

"No," said Monk's face and voice.

"How long have I been out?"

"Two or three minutes."

Doc distinguished a dapper figure that should belong to Ham. It was hard to see the lawyer's features through the thick green haze.

"The fog getting worse?" Doc asked.

"Much worse."

"Where is Pat?"

"She went out," said a voice that seemed to emanate from Ham. "She went home."

"Why?"

"We persuaded her this thing might be too dangerous for her."

Doc Savage frowned. His head seemed unusually thick. It was incredible that Pat could have been persuaded anything was too dangerous for her. "What was wrong with Pat?" he asked. "Was she ill or something?"

"I don't know," Ham said.

"Do you fellows feel all right?"

"Our heads seem kind of thick," Ham confessed. "Your voice sounds different, too, Doc. Kind of thick."

As Monk hung up the phone, Doc fainted.

The bronze man had been about to remark on the difference in the voices of Monk and Ham also. He nodded.

"Can you fellows find that green office building?" he asked.

"Sure," Monk said. "But what is the sense of going there?"

"To get on the trail of this mystery," the bronze man said. "That seems to be the only point of attack we have."

"All right," Monk said, "if you think that's the thing to do." He gave his trousers a hitch. "I'm going to get some equipment together."

He walked through a door into a library equipped with thousands of volumes which, as indicated by the titles, were all of scientific nature. He closed the door behind him. Crossing the impressive library, he entered a laboratory of vast proportions. He closed that door, too. Then he listened to be sure he was not being followed.

Having satisfied himself with these precautions, Monk said, "All right, Stinky."

Stinky was a long blade of a man who was hidden behind some chemical cases. He showed himself.

"The rest of you come out, too," Monk said.

Four other men appeared. They were not badly dressed, but they did not look like gentlemen who would put things in Christmas stockings.

Monk said, "Boys, we will have to pull it. He insists on going hunting for Strand."

Stinky grunted. He did not look happy.

"We go through the motions of a fight with you, then escape?" he asked.

"That's right."

The others looked as unhappy as Stinky. "You sure this will go off all right?" one demanded. "If this would fall through and he caught us, I don't like to think of what will happen."

Monk moved over and indicated a rope ladder hanging out of the window. "You go down this. You'll have plenty of time. What more could you want?"

"All right," the man agreed reluctantly. "Let's start dropping our eggs."

Monk then slapped the man, and the man yelled and slapped back. None of the blows that followed was hard, but all the noise was vigorous.

DOC SAVAGE wheeled around in the reception room at the first fight sounds.

"It's Monk!" Ham yelled. "He's in trouble!"

Doc hit the library door. It was locked, and it was also of metal stout enough that breaking it down barehanded was out of the question. He drew back, produced an explosive grenade.

"That door cost plenty!" Ham wailed.

Doc put the grenade against the door. It made flame and noise and changed the shape of the door. He went through. The other door, the one into the laboratory, was not locked.

Monk was walking erratic circles in the laboratory and holding his head.

"Out of the window!" he croaked.

"You hurt, Monk?"

"Not bad. One of them knocked the wits out of me for a minute."

Doc Savage went to the window. The greenish fog was an impenetrable mass so thick that, a dozen feet from his face, it was like a solid thing. He started to swing out on the rope ladder which he found there.

Monk suddenly had hold of his shoulder. "Don't, Doc!" Monk gasped. "That's just what they're figuring on."

Doc hesitated. "What do you mean?"

"I sneaked up on them and heard them talking," Monk explained. "The idea of the attack was not to damage me. It was to create a diversion to draw all of us, and you in particular, Doc, out of the building."

The bronze man was grimly silent for a moment. He made briefly the strange, low, exotic trilling which was his unconscious mannerism in moments of stress.

"You sure of that?" he asked.

"Positive!" Monk said. "For some reason they don't want us in the building."

Ham said, "That sounds silly, Monk."

"It's what they said."

"Seems kind of opposite to me," Ham grumbled. "Lots of times people have tried to get us to stay in here and not stick our noses into things. But this time they want us to leave."

Monk said, "That's why I say stay here."

Doc Savage had one leg over the windowsill. He withdrew it. "That might be wise," he said.

But five minutes later, when they were alone—Doc and Monk—in the laboratory, Doc Savage casually took hold of Monk's necktie and asked, "What was the purpose of the attack you had faked on yourself, Monk?"

Blank astonishment made creases in Monk's face for a while. "Gosh, Doc—you didn't get fooled?"

"Friends of yours, were they not?" Doc inquired quietly. It was one of the bronze man's strongest characteristics that he did not lift his voice or show excitement even under extraordinary circumstances.

"Yeah," Monk said. "Or not exactly, that is. Just some guys who were willing to make a buck and not ask too many questions. Honest guys, of course," he added hastily.

"What were you trying to do?"

Monk groaned. "Gosh, I hate getting caught like that."

"What was your idea?"

Monk gripped the bronze man's arm. "Doc, you know I have been with you a long time."

"Yes?"

"Well, I thought it entitled me to try to keep you out of danger," Monk said.

"And what was the nature of this danger?"

Monk groaned again, with earnestness.

"Ham and I saw that man fall up, and we saw the beginning of that green fog. This green fog, because it's still with us," said the homely man "We're worried. You know we don't get worried easily, Doc."

"What makes you think I will be safer here?"

Monk said evasively, "I knew that if I gave you the idea there was an enemy who wanted you to leave here, the thing you would do would be to stay."

"Why would I be safer here?"

"Look, Doc. We don't know what this is, do we?"

"Nor are we likely to find out, sitting here."

"Yes, but we better know what we're doing before we start barging around," Monk said. "I tell you, Doc—this thing is so queer it scares me."

The bronze man made no comment for at least a minute.

"Is that the way your mind works?" he asked finally.

"Uh—yes."

Doc said, "Get your equipment."

"You mean we're going to that green building?"

"That guess," Doc told him, "is much better than the idea you had."

The bronze man then closed his eyes, doubled his knees slowly until he was down on the floor, and fell forward on his side! His breathing was regular, measured, as if he slept.

Chapter V
HAM'S NECK

HAM said, "It has been about ten minutes. You fainted again, Doc."

"Where are we now?" Doc asked.

"Down in the street outside headquarters," Ham explained. He pointed. "See, there's the street sign. Can you read it through the green fog?"

Doc looked at the sign. It was readable, although barely so.

Monk said, "We thought there must be something upstairs that was making you faint. Maybe being cooped up in the place. So we came down here for air."

Doc said, "Drive to that green building."

"But listen!" Monk exploded. "Do you feel able—"

"Drive to the green building!"

Monk said nothing more. He put the car in motion and drove slowly, keeping close to the curb, blatting his horn warningly. There was not much traffic, and it moved slowly, the drivers leaning out of windows and staring.

Monk's manner was sullen, and when finally he stopped the car he said, "This isn't my idea." He got out of the machine. "Doc, I'm going back and watch headquarters."

"You think that necessary?" the bronze man inquired.

"I sure do."

Monk walked away, was speedily lost in the green void that the world had become.

Ham coughed uncomfortably. "Doc, I think he is scared."

The bronze man was silent.

"Something is sure wrong with Monk," Ham insisted. "He acted queer back there in headquarters. You know what? Could that attack on him have been fake? I sort of got the idea it was."

Doc said, "It was a fake."

Ham slapped his knee. "Then I'll bet he was responsible for you fainting!"

"You think so?"

Ham said meaningly, "You feel fine as soon as you regain consciousness, don't you? Doesn't that make you think of something?"

"Our anaesthetic gas, you mean?"

"That's it. The odorless and colorless anaesthetic gas we've been using for a long time. I'll bet Monk used some of that on you on the sly. All he would have to do would be to bust a capsule when you weren't looking, then pretend you were having some kind of queer spells. It wouldn't affect him if he held his breath for a minute, and he can do that. I've seen him hold it a lot longer."

Doc Savage's metallic features were composed, but his voice showed interest. "That might be a logical explanation."

"I bet it's as logical as cats liking milk."

"You have a theory about his motives?"

"He's scared," Ham said. "He's worried about you. He wants to scare you into not having anything to do with this mystery about a man who came to see you about a green chest, and who fell up into the sky, and a green fog that came. Doc, all Monk is trying to do is protect you. I believe his heart is in the right place."

"And you think Monk just left us because he is scared?"

"As much as I'm ashamed to say it—yes."

THE green building was tall and gaunt and empty, full of nothing but stillness and the odors of disuse. There were the sounds their feet made, of course. And there was the green fog and the air mixed with the dust their feet churned up. The temperature was low and the humidity heavy enough to be depressing.

Ham pointed to tracks in the dust, and they climbed stairways slowly, stopping often to listen.

Doc said, "You chased them all the way to the roof?"

Ham replied, "Right. Top-floor ledge was where Strand took off from."

"You searched the place?"

"After a fashion."

Doc began to hunt casually. "Where do you think Strand was seized?"

"Downstairs. First or second floor, probably. We don't know; they might have got him right after he entered the building. But whatever they did to him was done on the top floor."

"What suggests that assumption?"

"Time," said Ham. "They didn't have time to do anything to him on the lower floors. We didn't give them time. They took him to the top floor and did what they did there."

"We will go to the top floor," Doc said.

The vest was lying on a roof below. Doc Savage did not find it for half an hour, which was long after he had gone over the top floor painstakingly, making no comment except to point out that an old gunny sack had been mopped over every foot of floor space to spoil all tracks, and had been swabbed over the ledge outside.

The vest came later, after Doc had noted a freshly broken window. He had asked Ham if he or Monk had broken it, receiving the answer that they had not.

It was not a whole vest. It was half, or a little less. Actually, there was only the left side of a vest from the armhole down. Its two pockets contained four matches, a five-cent stamp, a broken cigarette, a receipt from a florist, and a cube of sugar of the paper-wrapped type with the paper wrapper bearing the name "Southern Susan," but no address or other information.

Ham said, "Southern Susan. I wonder what that is?"

Doc Savage was more interested in the receipt from the florist.

He went to a telephone and talked to the florist.

He got an address, also a name. The name was Erica Ambler-Hotts.

"I'll drive the car," Ham said. "Damn this uncanny green fog!"

He directed the car uptown, then across town in the traffic. There was more traffic than there had been, but very few of the cars were moving. Now and then one was traveling slowly. But the others were standing still. Taxicabs, trucks, passenger cars, all motionless. But the drivers and passengers were in them, just sitting there and staring, so that the effect was somewhat weird.

They stopped finally at a building which had a doorman who was togged up like a Civil War admiral.

"Miss Erica Ambler-Hotts' apartment," Doc Savage said.

The doorman acted as if he had been hit. Then he made a dash and came back with a gentleman who was wearing an afternoon suit and perspiration.

"Who are you?" demanded this gentleman. "I am the manager. I must insist that you answer me, or I assure you that I shall call the police."

Doc Savage made his identity known.

"Oh! *Oh!*" said the manager. "I have heard of you. What can I do for you?"

"Miss Ambler-Hotts," Doc said.

The manager turned the palms of his hands up sadly. "We don't know. The boy was found dead on her floor. She is not in her apartment. The door was standing open. One of the porters saw her leaving with several men, and the impression was that she was a prisoner."

"Boy?" Doc Savage said.

"The elevator operator. He was found dead in the cage on her floor. A very hideous thing. An ice pick in the back of his skull!"

"She is English?"

"Miss Ambler-Hotts? Yes, indeed. Very English. Works for one of these societies to save England, I understand, I cannot tell you the exact name of the organization."

"Did she have a visitor this afternoon?"

The manager nodded. "Yes, indeed. Gentleman."

"Description?"

"A very good one," said the manager. "Our doorman has an excellent memory, fortunately."

He described a gentleman who was not unhandsome and who had some quality about him that was arresting in a strange way. "'He was as fascinating as a razor blade,' was the way our doorman put it," the manager advised. "Our doorman is very good at descriptives."

Ham emitted an exclamation.

"The visitor," he said, "was Tottingham Strand!"

DOC SAVAGE went through the girl's apartment. Miss Amble-Hotts was, as the manager had said, very English. Particularly her clothes, her knotty-thorn walking stick, the severe pictures of herself. Judging from what written stuff they were able to find, she was an energetic, but not an important, employee of one of the British groups now working in the United States on behalf of England. A telephone call to the British group verified this. No one at the place could think of any enemies of Miss Ambler-Hotts, or any suspicious acts committed by her recently, or anything else that would lift the lid on the mystery.

There was a book with a legend in it that said:

To Erica, in appreciation of a faith as pure as the perfume of roses and as sure as gravity.
                                                    Tot Strand

"Poetic fellow," Ham remarked.

Doc Savage continued his search. Ham seemed to think the hunt had been thorough enough, and that further effort was a waste of energy. The manager of the apartment house seemed to share the conviction, because he excused himself politely and left them alone.

Ham rubbed his jaw thoughtfully, remarked, "Monk kind of worries me," he said. "We've been together a long time, Doc, haven't we?"

"A good while," the bronze man admitted.

"And Monk has worked on a lot of experiments with you," Ham continued. "He's a great chemist, Monk is. I wouldn't admit it to his face, but he is good. About the best, next to you, I imagine."

Doc made no comment.

Ham seemed lost in thought for a while. "I remember a lot of the experiments you and Monk worked on. You remember your work on that stuff called 'Compound Monk,' the chemical element combination which was so touchy and cranky that it was like Monk?"

"Monk had very little to do with developing that," Doc said. "In fact, as I recall, he took no part in the experiments."

"Gosh, I thought he did. What did you ever do about that compound? I think I remember the description you gave of it as being so sensitive to motion radiation that the absorption of such radiation by its atoms leads to the ejection of three electrons, or something like that."

Doc made no comment.

"Wasn't that what Compound Monk was?" Ham asked.

"Generally speaking."

"What did you ever do with it?"

Doc Savage seemed not to hear the query.

"Do you still have the formula for it?" Ham asked.

Without making an answer, Doc Savage went downstairs, with Ham following, and got in his car and drove four blocks to a deserted road, where he pulled to the curb and stopped the machine. He switched off the engine.

He took Ham by the throat with both hands!

"You are going to be fortunate if I do not kill you!" he told Ham.

There was something horrible in his voice which showed that he meant it.

Chapter VI
MONK VS. MONK

WHEN Monk Mayfair had left the vicinity of the green building he had proceeded to do some telephoning.

"Stinky," he said into the telephone, "it didn't work. He is smarter than we supposed. He got wise."

In an agitated voice, Stinky said, "I hope not wise enough to know who we are. If so, I am going to hurriedly see about plane reservations to South America and points beyond."

"I got out of it," Monk said. "I told him enough of the truth to satisfy him."

"How much was that?"

"Oh, that I had hired you to fake an attack on me so that he would think somebody wanted him to leave, which I told him I figured would make him stay."

"Hm-m-m!"

"Don't sound so skeptical," Monk said. "I've got a job for you."

"I don't think I'm going to like the job," said Stinky.

Monk explained the details of the plot with great explicitness, and the worst fears of Stinky seemed fulfilled.

"Why don't you just ask me to cut off my head and be done with it?" Stinky demanded.

"You going to follow orders?" Monk demanded grimly.

"Sure. What else can I do?" asked Stinky. "But I don't have to like it."

Monk hung up violently and carried a scowl out of the telephone booth. The scowl lasted until he was out on the street and in a taxicab.

He rode uptown to a hotel room, where a young man in a tweed suit gave him a wrist-popping salute.

"Washington waiting with a report, sir," said the young man.

"Get them."

Soon a man in Washington was saying, "The series of conferences ended an hour and a half ago. Colonel John Renwick, William Harper Littlejohn and Major Thomas J. Roberts went to their hotel, telephoned the new airport for their plane to be refueled, went to their rooms and began packing."

Monk snapped, "Wasn't their plane disabled? You had orders to do so."

"Sorry, sir. If you would let me finish," the man said. "They received a telephone report that their plane had been damaged. They are now on their way to the airport to investigate."

"You sure the damage was thorough?"

"Very thorough."

"Cancel the three reservations you made on the Washington-to-New York plane. Time it so they will be able to pick up the three reservations when they apply for airline tickets to New York."

"I have just done so, sir. I think the timing was right, although I have not yet had a report."

"Report at once if they leave on the plane, giving the flight number of the ship."

"Yes, sir."

Monk hung up with a satisfied expression.

He lighted a cigar and snapped his fingers and ordered a cold long drink. He sat at a window with these, enjoying the cool flow from the air-conditioning vent at his side and smirking out at the city.

He spoke only once, when he said, "Renny, Johnny and Long Tom will take that plane and fall right into my hands. I will get rid of them without a hitch."

He had spoken boastingly. After that he did nothing but smoke and rattle the ice against the sides of the glass.

Eventually the telephone rang.

The man in Washington said, "Just leaving. Flight 29."

"What is the German word for 'good'?" Monk said.

"Gut," said the man at the other end of the wire.

"That's what it is," said Monk, "in every sense of the word."

He put the telephone down and gave orders with violence and haste. The orders got him in a car, with five other men in it, in very short order. They drove to the vicinity of LaGuardia Field, but did not enter the airport. Instead, they turned off on an overpass and parked behind a large moving van. There were four more men with the van.

"One of you go to the airport," ordered Monk. "Give us the signal when Flight 29 from Washington starts to land."

The man saluted and departed.

Monk climbed into the van and made sure that the interior was lined with railroad rails carefully bolted in place. The steel rails seemed to raise some doubt.

"You sure these things will turn a .30-06 bullet?"

"They will stop a bullet from a tank gun," a man told him. "There are not likely to be any tank guns around the airport."

The truck had an additional piece of ingenious mechanism. An extra control position. Wheel and brakes, throttle and clutch, and a rod extending to the gear shift, all mounted back in the steel-protected body. The truck could be driven from that point.

"Got the dummy?" Monk asked.

A man shoved him a stuffed, manlike figure. "Fits right behind the wheel in the cab. We fixed clips to hold it there."

Monk grinned. "Probably not necessary. But it will keep anyone from getting excited over an apparently driverless truck careening through the streets. And we can't take a chance of a man sitting out front driving. He might get shot."

They settled down to consume cigarettes, look innocent, and wait. After a time they drove the truck to the big airport trucking yard and waited.

A BIG passenger plane swung in over Flushing Bay, leveled out, lowered its tail and settled on the runway.

A man stepped out of the big operations office, lighted a firecracker, a big one, and tossed it out on the gravel, where it let loose with a loud report.

"Put her in gear," Monk said.

The big engine of the armored truck began rumbling. The vehicle backed away casually and went toward the steel-wire fence. It was going rather fast when it hit the fence, and it went through the fence with about the same ease that a fist would go through a cobweb.

It went on and hit the tail of the plane, caving it in.

The men who got out of the armored truck had short automatic rifles, steel helmets, bulletproof

LONG TOM

vests, gas masks and a mad determination to do a fantastically bold job in a hurry.

The plane door was open and people were spilling out. The pilot leaned out of the control cabin with a blue revolver in his hand, and was promptly and thoroughly made dead by a bullet above his left eye.

"Get out, everybody," ordered the man who had shot the pilot. "Renny Renwick, Long Tom Roberts and Johnny Littlejohn—you three stand to one side."

A man with big fists—he was an enormous man, but his fists were still greater—came out of the plane headfirst and rushed forward until a gun muzzle practically speared him in the eye. He had a long, funeral-going face.

"Renny Renwick, I believe," said the man with the gun. "Get in the truck!"

"Holy cow!" said the big-fisted Renny.

"Get in the truck!"

He got in the truck.

Johnny Littlejohn was a man of extreme tallness and startling thinness. His clothing fitted him like a sack on a fishing pole, and a monocle dangled from his lapel by a ribbon.

He had one remark, which was, "I'll be superamalgamated!"

Long Tom Roberts was a man distinguished for nothing in particular, as far as appearances went, except his mushroom-cellar complexion, a completely unhealthy aspect.

He had nothing whatever to say, which was typical of him.

Not one of the three men really looked what he was. Renny Renwick was an engineer, one of the greatest. Johnny Littlejohn was known to scientists all over the world for his work in archaeology and geology. Long Tom Roberts was an electrical expert whose name would be in the books a hundred years hence.

They were not three men who looked, acted, or thought alike. They had one strong bond, wherein all three were associated with Doc Savage.

"Load in," said the man who had killed the pilot. "Don't try anything. Don't waste our time, either."

Renny said, "They sure caught us flat-footed." Renny's voice was a rumbling like something deep in a cave.

They climbed in the truck. It developed that there were chains and padlocks with which they were to be lashed to the truck floor.

The truck began moving.

By now there was a little desultory shooting. The dead pilot's head had leaked a plume of bright scarlet down the silver metal side of the plane, a wet red banner that had spread alarm and conviction that this was no theatrical stunt.

The truck withdrew from the mangled tail parts of the plane, wheeled slowly, and left the airport the same way it had come, by plunging headlong through the steel wire fence. Wire strands snapped like fiddle strings. The truck sideswiped a roadster, took the highway, chipping a slab off a concrete post and bending a sign double.

"You fool!" said the killer. "You aren't driving a tank!"

"I can't see too good," said the driver. "If I was out on the front seat behind the other wheel—"

"If you were out there, you would be dead," the other assured him.

Monk took charge again. He had been crouched beside the driver, watching the road. He got up and went back to the prisoners.

MONK kicked Renny Renwick in the ribs. "For a long time I've wanted to do that," Monk said.

The kick and the remark got a howl of laughter. Pleased, Monk kicked Renny again.

Renny said through his teeth, "Have you gone crazy, Monk?"

That got another bellow of mirth from the onlookers. Grinning widely, Monk proceeded to boot Long Tom in the ribs, then gave Johnny the same treatment.

"I'll be superamalgamated," said Johnny, distressed.

"He just knows that one word, eh, Stinky?" said Monk.

Long Tom said, "Who is your pal Stinky, Monk? What is this, anyway?"

Monk assumed an air of imparting a great confidence.

"Things have come up," he said, "that make it necessary to get rid of you three fellows."

"Where's Doc and Ham?" Long Tom demanded.

Monk said, "Doc himself would be surprised to know." And that also got a burst of glee.

Long Tom scowled. "What's the matter with you apes? What is so funny?"

Stinky shouted suddenly, "Hey, there's a State police car trailing us."

They fell suddenly silent, and their faces got white. Two men crawled back to the rear with long rifles fitted with telescopic sights and crouched there for a while. One of them cursed his telescopic sight loudly. The other fired. The one who had cursed released a bullet. Both of them shot again.

"They're dropping back," said one of the riflemen.

Monk said, "Slow up when we hit the first bridge. Dump three or four grenades on the bridge."

They did this, then went on. They drove for half an hour, turning off into a road that was almost nothing, and ending finally on a small bluff beside the gray-blue corduroy surface of Long Island Sound.

Monk got out and signaled to a cabin cruiser which lay offshore. The boat immediately headed in.

Renny, Long Tom and Johnny were tossed out of the truck, after being unlocked from the chains.

Renny bellowed, "What're you trying to do? What is this, anyhow?"

Monk eyed them and said, "You remember some experiments Doc was working on some time back—a compound he called 'the Monk mixture,' or something like that?"

"I don't remember," Renny said.

Long and bony Johnny said, "Say, I recall something about some such experiments."

Monk looked at Johnny as if he were very glad to hear that. "We'll go into it later, my friend." His statement had an ominous tinge, the same tone a dentist would use in saying, "My friend, we'll have to pull all your teeth."

Stinky said, "Good idea to park your revolvers and pistols in the truck and leave them. Also the two rifles you shot at the State police with. Taking chances never pays dividends."

At this point, only Monk was standing outside the truck, with Long Tom, Renny and Johnny.

The others were inside the truck, getting rid of their weapons.

This was the situation when a second Monk came around the nearest clump of bushes.

"Holy cow!" gasped Renny. "Two Monks!"

"Yes," said the second Monk. "And very strange it is, too."

THE second Monk took hold of the first Monk in the way a knife would meet butter, the second Monk being the knife.

"Start shutting off their water!" he yelled at Renny, Long Tom and Johnny.

They began taking hold of the first Monk as if they meant to denude him of arms and legs.

"Get that truck closed!" yelled Renny.

He sprang to do it himself. He got his big hands on the truck doors and forced the ponderous things shut, but not before two men had managed to pile through to the ground.

One of the two who had gotten out—it was Stinky—had a revolver. He scrambled and rolled clear, sat up and began taking a deliberate aim at the newly arrived Monk.

From the nearby bush came Ham with his sword cane. He held the blade for throwing the way a spear is thrown, let fly, and suddenly eighteen inches or so of the blade was protruding from the other side of Stinky's arm.

Stinky made strange noises and finally became still on the ground, the tip of Ham's sword cane being coated with a chemical which produced quick unconsciousness.

Monk said to Ham, "It's about time you got into action, you fashion plate!"

Ham let fly the blade of his sword cane, and suddenly eighteen inches of so of the blade was protruding from the other side of Stinky's arm.

The other man had dropped his gun and was trying to get to his feet and snatch up the weapon at the same time. Renny made a rush at the fellow and created much the effect of a locomotive hitting a cow.

Then men began to crawl out of the front of the truck with guns and plenty of rage.

Ham said, "Don't you think we'd better run?"

It was obviously the thing to do. The second Monk—the genuine one, it was by now apparent—gave the first, and fake, Monk one last punch. It was terrific! Monk took it off the ground somewhere near his heels. He made it whistle. It gave the fake Monk's jaw the shape of a wet pretzel and made teeth fly like gravel.

The five hit the brush then, traveled a few yards, changed direction, and went down the slope. Bullets began hunting them, glancing off branches and riddling foliage. Renny rumbled, "This way!" They turned again.

Johnny said, "Susurration might be perspicacious."

They ran for a while.

"I'm in no mood for those words," Monk said. "What did you say?"

Ham translated, "He said a little less noise might be wise."

Monk's eyes came out somewhat as a bullet cut a limb from in front of his face. "He's got something there," he gasped. He got down on all fours, changed his course at right angles, and crawled. The others followed the same tactics.

Back of them was shooting and shouting, running around—but not too recklessly—in the undergrowth. From the beach came angry inquiring yells. The men from the boat wanted to know what in the name of little fish was happening, as one of them expressed it in a scream.

Monk and the others sat down to see what would happen now.

RENNY punched Monk in the ribs. "How come there's two of you?"

"Search me," Monk said.

"Strange, don't you think?"

"The deeper I get into this thing," Monk said, "the less I get amazed."

"You can't explain it?" Renny asked him.

"I'm not going to try," Monk assured him.

"How did you happen to rescue us?"

"Oh, that was as simple as falling off a log," Monk explained. "I telephoned Washington and found out what plane you had taken and—"

"I was the one who telephoned Washington," Ham reminded him.

"Well, we telephoned and found what plane you were on," Monk continued, pretending not to hear the interruption. "So we came down to meet you."

"You saw what happened at the airport?"

"Yes. And we saw we couldn't stop it single-handedly."

"What did you do?"

"Got around on the other side of the plane during the uproar," Monk said, "and laid down on the front bumper. Or Ham laid on the bumper. I took the running board on the off side from the driver."

"It's a wonder they didn't see you there!" Renny exclaimed.

Long Tom was puzzled. "How come you rushed out to the airport to meet us?"

"Trouble," Monk said.

"What kind?"

"Green fog, green chests, and men falling up instead of down," Monk said. "And if that isn't enough to make you think you're crazy—Doc has disappeared."

Long Tom started to exclaim something shocked about that, but Ham hissed and grabbed his arm. Ham pointed with his sword cane, which he had recovered from the man he had speared. He indicated the beach.

"Those fellows from the boat are confused," he said. "They're rushing up the hill to help their friends. Does that give anybody an idea?"

"The boat," Long Tom said. "Let's try to take it. We might collect a prisoner, and make him talk later."

"Supermalagorgeous," Johnny agreed.

FIVE minutes later Renny clubbed down a man with a big fist, and he fell in the mud a few feet from the bow of the cabin cruiser, which had been gently beached. They gathered up the man, threw him on the deck of the cruiser, and climbed aboard themselves after shoving the boat off. Renny dashed below and started the engine.

"That," boomed the big-fisted engineer, "was what you would call almost too easy."

The cruiser—it was about forty-two feet long with a two-hundred-horsepower engine—churned backward in a quarter circle, then dug its stern down and surged forward. It took a bone in its teeth and traveled.

A few bullets began coming from shore and there was a rush to get below and behind the engine. The cabin cruiser was essentially a lightly constructed yacht and offered only slightly more obstruction to a bullet from an army rifle than a tomato can.

Monk and the others hauled the prisoner below with them as if he were precious.

Monk admired the captive.

"Nice and plump," he remarked. "Looks like

he might be a talkative fellow."

"I hope so," Ham muttered.

"So do I," Monk said. "I think I begin to put this mystery together. There's a fake Monk and a fake Ham. The two fakes are part of a scheme of some kind. There is a trap, I believe. Doc may have fallen into it. I'm even beginning to suspect that green fog."

"What do you suspect about the green fog?" Ham demanded.

"I don't know for sure," Monk said. "I'm going to make this fellow tell about that."

"Suppose he doesn't know anything?"

"That," said Monk, "isn't likely."

"What makes you so sure?"

"Intelligent face. A guy like that would be sure to know what everything was about."

While Monk was thinking of something that would fit to query the captive, the bow came off the boat! It was a case, at least, of dynamite. Or a bomb of some kind, or a box of hand grenades. The Doc Savage aides never did decide exactly what. But a rifle bullet from shore probably hit something and started the blast. The air inside the boat seemed suddenly to turn to water and smoke.

Chapter VII
PLOT LABYRINTH

DOC SAVAGE had given up choking "Ham" and had belted the man senseless with his fist. Then Doc had seized the wheel of the car and had driven away rapidly, with the horn blowing a steady moan. He traveled in that fashion until he reached the nearest police precinct station—two blocks away—where he crashed the car over the sidewalk and against the precinct steps. He got a sudden flow of cops out of the place, which was what he wanted.

"Grab anyone who looks as if he might be following me," he called loudly. "Particularly in a car!"

One of the officers recognized the bronze man and relayed the order. There was some running, two shots. Finally, the police returned.

Doc had remained in his car, by now almost blinded by the green fog.

"There was someone following me?" he asked.

"I don't understand this darned thing," one of the officers said.

"Was there?"

"Following you!" the policeman exploded. "They were all around you."

"In cars?"

"In big machines marked with red signs," the policeman explained. "The signs read: 'Danger!' They also read: 'Beware the car carrying dangerous

high explosive!" The officer came closer. "What is this, anyway?"

Doc Savage was silent for a moment.

He asked, "Did the signs on the cars also warn all traffic to stop, or go slowly, while the car they were escorting passed?"

"Sure," the cop said. "You were supposed to be the car carrying the explosive. Is there any in there?"

Doc Savage was silent again. Then he said, "That explains how they made the traffic go slowly."

"It sure went slow," said the cop. "Reports of this cavalcade have been coming in as it crossed town. It went to that old green building downtown, then went up to the apartment house district. That right?"

"And traffic stopped all the way?"

The policeman approached. "That's right."

"Why, hello, Lieutenant Evers," Doc said.

Evers dropped his jaw. "Great grief, did you just recognize me?"

"You just came close enough for me to see you."

Lieutenant Evers was concerned. "Something happened to your eyes?" He looked into the car. "What have you got there? That is your aide, Ham Brooks, isn't it?"

"An excellent imitation only," the bronze man said. He did not elaborate on the remark, although

PATRICIA SAVAGE

Evers was puzzled. "Lieutenant, will you drive me to my headquarters?"

"Why, sure," said Lieutenant Evers. He moved in behind the wheel as Doc Savage climbed into the back. "Fast or slow?" he asked.

"Fast," Doc said grimly. He had not mentioned the green fog.

"I'll have a squad car pace us," the officer said.

The pacing was somewhat, but not much, under seventy miles an hour. They took the long wide sweep of Eighth Avenue, then turned left and stopped at the stone skyscraper which housed the bronze man's establishment.

Lieutenant Evers pointed at "Ham." "You need any help getting him upstairs?"

Doc shook his head slightly. "No, thanks, Evers. But you might tell me something."

"Sure! Anything you want to know."

"Do you see anything that looks like a green fog?"

Evers swung slowly, staring everywhere.

"No. No green fog," he said. "That's a strange question."

PAT SAVAGE ran across the eighty-sixth-floor reception room to greet Doc.

"Doc, you're safe!" she gasped. Then she saw the man Doc was carrying. "Ham! What has happened to him?"

Doc carried his burden into the laboratory, placed the man on a table. He asked, "You remember that knife scar on Ham's back?" Pat nodded. Doc then stripped open the man's shirt and exhibited an expanse of unmarred skin. There was no scar.

"It isn't Ham!" Pat exclaimed.

"No," Doc Savage said grimly. "It is a very good imitation, though."

Pat said, "Doc, those fainting spells we had—they did something to us. Gas or something."

Doc nodded. "Something of the kind. They knocked all of us out, then took me away." He eyed Pat. "Did they harm you or Monk or Ham?"

"No." Pat shook her head. "We just woke up. And you were gone."

"That was when they sprang the trap," Doc said.

Puzzled, Pat said, "How do you mean?"

"Seized me," the bronze man explained, "and took me away. They had a fake Monk and Ham all ready for me, I think. At least, here is the fake Ham." The bronze man frowned. "They were unbelievably clever about it. They had an escort of cars, marked with signs that kept everyone away from my car. That was so I would think the green fog was all over the city and that no one was out driving. The signs caused motorists to pull over to the curb and stop. The signs labeled me as carrying dangerous explosives."

Doc began strapping the false Ham to a table that was narrow enough for the purpose.

"Where are Monk and Ham?" he asked.

Color went out of Pat's face in a quick rush. "They went to the airport to meet Renny, Johnny and Long Tom," she said. She waited, and, when Doc Savage made no comment, she asked, "Haven't you heard what happened at the airport?"

Doc straightened suddenly. "What?"

"A big truck and a bunch of heavily armed men smashed into the plane carrying Renny, Long Tom and Johnny," Pat said. "The pilot of the plane was shot dead when he resisted. Renny, Long Tom and Johnny were seized and carried off in the truck."

"Monk and Ham?"

"Not a word from them since," Pat said.

Doc was silent a moment. "Will you check the telephone," he said.

Pat reached for the instrument.

"Outside, I mean," Doc said. "Go to the drugstore in the lobby, or the restaurant, and telephone me here."

Pat nodded and left.

Several minutes later, she returned with a surprised expression. "Telephone operator told me the telephone was out of order," she said.

"Remember when you called your friend Susan Glaspell, to ask if the green fog was present in Westchester County?" he asked.

"Yes, of course I recall," Pat said. "I got Susan's maid."

"Notice any resemblance between this telephone operator's voice you just heard and that of Susan Glaspell's maid?"

Pat nibbled a lower lip, and a frown began crowding her eyebrows together. "Come to think of it, the voices were very much alike."

Suddenly, Pat sprang to the telephone, dialed a number at random, and said, "Give me Mr. Jonathan Doe." She listened to a voice, put the instrument down, and stamped a foot. "I was assured Mr. Doe was out of the building," she said. "That was my own telephone number I dialed, and there is certainly no Doe working for me."

Without comment, Doc returned to work on the fake Ham.

Pat snapped, "I get it! They've got our telephone line tapped, with a girl riding it and telling us that the people we want to talk to aren't there. What's the idea of that?"

"A trick."

"But why? They're pulling a fast one on us for some reason. But why?"

"The green fog."

"I don't," said Pat, "get it."

"There is no green fog!"

Pat jumped. "Wait a minute! They say, seeing is believing. I see a fog." When Doc did not answer, she demanded, "Don't *you* see one?"

He nodded slightly.

"But it does not exist," he said.

THE man who had masqueraded as Ham was wearing a woman's tight, old-fashioned corset to give himself the rather waspish midriff which was Ham's proud possession. A chemical test showed that his hair was dyed, that his skin was shaded, that he wore a metal arrangement inside his nostrils to shape them. Doc glanced at the labels in his clothes. The name was the same tailor which Ham patronized.

Pat had been thinking about the fog.

"Doesn't exist," she said. "But I see it!"

Doc said, "Step into the chemical storeroom, will you, and get No. 22800."

"That's the truth serum, isn't it?" Pat remarked. She went to the cubicle where they stored the chemicals. The storeroom was a cubicle only in relation to the general size of the rest of the laboratory. Actually, the place was larger than most living rooms.

The fake Ham opened his eyes. He had been hit very hard. The man did not say anything.

Doc said, "You did a commendable job of acting."

The man wet his lips. His first effort to speak was a croaking noise which embarrassed him.

"Thank you," he managed to say. "It should have been good. I have studied day and night for the part for over a month."

"It was very good," Doc agreed.

The man expanded. "Naturally, as I say, it was not bad. Matter of fact, I memorized everything about Ham Brooks which ten detectives were able to unearth. You should hear me spout legal terminology. I bet I could pass a bar examination."

"No doubt."

"Kept you fooled, didn't I?" said the man proudly.

"For about thirty seconds."

"You mean"—the man's eyes popped—"you got wise to us right away?"

"Almost."

"I don't believe it. Hell, we thought of everything. Every possible means of making you think we were Monk and Ham, and that there was a green fog—we used them all. We didn't overlook anything."

Doc Savage said, "You recall when you told me Pat was not there because she had gone home?"

"Yes. What was wrong with that?"

"You said she had gone because you had persuaded her there might be danger for her."

"Yes."

"That," said Doc, "was an impossibility. No one could persuade Pat anything was too dangerous."

Pat had come back in time to hear the last. "Thank you kindly," she said cheerfully. "You should know, Doc. You've tried often enough."

The bronze man slapped the fake Ham on the chest. Not hard, but with enough force to remove some air. He said, "What we want out of you is conversation."

The man's eyes became stony.

"Hell of a bit you'll get," he said.

Doc Savage contemplated the man for a while, said abruptly, "We will not waste time with you." He picked up a hypo needle and used it, and the man barked once, more in anger than pain. Then Doc stepped back.

"Watch him," he told Pat. "The stuff will take about fifteen minutes to work."

"What's that junk you gimme?" snarled the man.

Pat said ominously, "You won't care."

The chemical the bronze man had used was a type of truth serum which he had developed after considerable research. It was violent in its effect on the victim, so dangerous that Doc rarely used it except in extreme emergencies.

THE bronze man proceeded to change clothes, apply a light coloring to his face, put dark optical caps over his eyeballs to change the distinct coloration of his eyes, and pull on a coat with a built-in back deformity. He whitened his hair and took a cane.

He made a tour of the neighborhood, moving casually, stooping to conceal his extraordinary height, and wearing gloves. He did not have to pretend to be nearsighted. He was unable to see more than twenty or thirty feet because of the greenish haze in his eyes. The fog.

He studied the taxicabs at the stand on the corner. Taxicab drivers in the city frequent the same stands day after day. There was only one strange cab in the line. Doc approached the machine, opened the rear door.

"Sorry, mister," the driver said sharply. "This cab is engaged."

Doc got into the cab. "Never mind that," he said. "When do they move in on Savage?"

The driver jumped, turned his head, stared. "What you talking about, brother?"

Doc said, "Didn't you turn in the word Savage had come back here?"

The man seemed to consider the point. "Elmer send you?"

"What makes you think anybody sent me?"

The man was suspicious. "Brother, you better identify yourself."

Doc put an angry note in his voice. "You better not waste my time, fellow. The man who was playing the part of Ham is in serious trouble. Not that anybody gives a hoot about him, but Savage may have ways of making him talk."

"Oh!" The driver settled back in his seat. "So it's that way. The boys are meeting down the street. That side street on the left. Didn't they tell you?"

"No. What's the plan?"

"Straight raid. They will go into Savage's garage in the basement and take the private elevator."

"How will they manage that?" Doc was genuinely surprised. Existence of the basement garage was supposed to be more or less of a secret, and certainly no one could gain admission who did not understand the operation of a number of secret devices.

"The mechanic who worked on the place will lead the way," said the taxicab driver.

Doc made no immediate comment. A mechanic had made some repairs on the private elevator recently. The fellow had been highly recommended. But someone evidently had made a mistake.

The bronze man got out of the cab. "Keep your eyes open," he said.

HE took the fast elevator to the eighty-sixth floor, swung into the laboratory, picked up a knife and slashed the lines with which he had secured the fake Ham to the table.

"Come on," he told Pat. "They are on the verge of raiding the place."

Pat said, "Why can't we stay and fight?"

The bronze man shook his head slightly. He carried the false Ham to the elevator, went down a dozen floors and stopped at the private apartment which he had maintained in the place for some time.

Pat was surprised. "I didn't know you had this apartment."

"Keep him here." Doc put the fake Ham on a bed. The man was going under the effects of the truth serum, acting as if he was completely drunk. "If he begins to have spasmodic attacks, break some of these vials under his nostrils." He gave Pat several thin-walled, gauze-wrapped vials of the type sometimes used for smelling salts.

"Where you going?" Pat asked, concerned.

The bronze man seemed not to hear the question. He went to the door.

"If I should be delayed," he said, "you proceed with questioning the man."

Pat nodded. "Pry out of him what this green fog is, what is in the green chest and what made men fall up. That the idea?"

Doc tossed the grenade so that it blew up in the faces of the men coming in the garage door!

"We want the reason for this mystery."

"Sure. I'll get it."

Doc went to the elevator and dropped down to the garage. For convenience, he kept a store of gadgets in the garage. He selected a pair of large hand grenades and took a position near the elevator.

He watched the relays and motors which controlled the big outer door. That the foe might gain admission through the garage was surprising. They would have to operate a radio control, and the device had a combination which was changed regularly. It functioned after the fashion of relay office calls on telegraph lines. For instance, this week only a combination of dot-dot-dash-dot-dash-dash-space-dot-dot would make the device function. Next week, the combination would be changed. If they got in, they would be ingenious.

They were ingenious enough, for suddenly relays clicked and motors whined and the big door moved up.

Men started to come in. A dozen of them at the least.

Doc tossed the grenade so that it hopped across the floor and blew up in their faces. The blast was not close enough to kill anyone, but it brushed them back out of the opening as if a great hand had slapped them. The second grenade was a combination of tear gas and smoke, and he threw that one directly in their midst.

They broke and ran.

Doc wheeled, raced up a stairway, pounded across the lobby floor and dived out on the sidewalk. With great commotion and haste—still wearing his makeshift disguise—he piled into the taxicab run by the driver to whom he had talked.

"It went wrong," he said excitedly. "Clear out of here. Quick!"

The driver was not excitable. "They put out orders to get back to the meeting place in case this went wrong," he said.

Doc settled back on the seat. "The meeting place, eh? By all means."

Chapter VIII
FEAR IS A GOATHERD

THE taxi driver took him forty miles out on Long Island and turned left on a deserted road and stopped.

The man pointed. "Up there on the hill."

Doc Savage surveyed the place in the increasing darkness of early evening. It was not yet night. Red color mixed with gold splashed over the foliage as the sun rode just out of sight below the horizon. A single spike of sunlight came through a split cleft in the trees and made a long thing, like a steel broadsword blade, across the deep-blue surface of Long Island Sound.

"Deserted spot," Doc said.

"What do you want? The middle of a sidewalk?" The driver started his car again, pulled over to a wall of brush, worked his way through it, and there was suddenly a ramshackle shed with two other cars and a truck. The truck was a huge thing, marked by bullets.

Since it was undoubtedly the truck which had seized Renny, Long Tom and Johnny at the airport, Doc Savage made his small trilling noise briefly and unconsciously.

"What's that noise?" the driver grunted.

Doc silenced himself. He never knew that he was making the sound until he made it. It was something that, when the circumstances were right, was as natural as breathing.

"The wind, probably," Doc said.

"There ain't no wind to speak of."

A man came out of the shadows with a rifle. "What went wrong?"

"I guess plenty," said the taxi driver. "The attack on Savage's place to rescue that guy who was playing Ham Brooks blew up like a skyrocket."

The man looked into the back seat. "Who's your pal?"

"One of the boys."

"Which one?"

"I dunno."

The taxi driver turned around. "What's your name?" he asked Doc.

The other sniffed and said, "Mean to tell me you never even asked who he was? Hell, why not just pick up anybody and bring him out here?"

The taxi driver did not like that. He and the man seemed to have quarreled before. The driver got out.

"He knows all the answers," he said, indicating Doc. Then he reached for the other's collar. "Pal, I've told you before about getting tough with me. I don't take it, see!"

Doc Savage alighted from the cab, doing his best to look as if he was interested in nothing but the fight that was about to develop.

The man with the rifle hastily backed away from the taxi driver. "Now wait a minute, Freddy," he said. "This ain't no time to get each other skinned up."

"It looks like a good time to me," said the taxi driver, Freddy.

"Nix, nix, you sap! We've got trouble here of our own."

Freddy scowled. "Whatcha mean?"

"We got all five of Doc Savage's aides cornered," the man explained. "And it's a hell of a job grabbing them."

Freddy was incredulous. "All five? I thought only three were coming in on the plane."

The man shrugged. "Monk and Ham—the genuine ones—showed up, took their three friends away from us, got on our boat. We had a box of hand grenades in the boat. Stinky's brother put a bullet in them and the boat sank."

"What became of Savage's men?"

"They got on a pile of rocks that is exposed at low tide. There's cover for them. They're holding us off."

"If you can't get them off the rocks," Freddy said, "why not get the blazes out of here and leave them? Suppose a Coast Guard boat shows up."

"We'll get 'em." The man laughed grimly. "The tide is coming in. And fast."

There was automobile noise that approached from the direction of the highway.

Freddy said, "That will be the rest of the men who were going to raid Doc Savage's place."

The other man scowled at Doc. "Who is this bird? I still want to know."

Doc said quietly, "I can prove that." He walked over to the man and held out a sheet of paper that was blank—although this was not important—and when the man started to look at it, he hit the fellow neatly on the jaw.

Freddy was somewhat more difficult. He was quick. He went back like a skater, twisted with serpentine speed, lifting his hands as if he was surrendering, but coming out with a short, blunt black pistol that had been under his tightly fitting uniform cap. Doc got his hands on the gun, and they went to the ground, fighting to see whether the safety of the automatic would be on or off. Off it was.

Freddy croaked, "Don't hit me!" just as Doc Savage hit him on the jaw. Freddy was evidently thinking of a set of false teeth, parts of which flew out of his mouth. He rolled over on his side, spat out the rest of the teeth and was silent, motionless.

Doc left the shed. He heard four quick shots from toward the sea. He made for the Sound.

THE rock pile in the sea seemed to consist of four large boulders and enough smaller ones to make a rampart. The tide had come in until no more than two feet of the stone bulwarks projected, and waves were breaking over this.

A long, lean and fast-looking boat cruised slowly across the blade of sunlight that was fading from the water. The craft was painted as a pleasure vessel, but it was larger and slimmer, seemed charged with power. Doc Savage studied the vessel, decided it was no pleasure craft at all.

The boat nosed slowly toward the cluster of rocks. There was a report, not loud, then an enormously louder blast and a geyser of water ahead of the craft. That would be one of the super-machine pistols, the compact little weapons which Monk and Ham no doubt had brought with them. An explosive pellet. The boat was keeping out of range, for it now sheered off.

Doc Savage studied the scene as best he could, handicapped by the greenish haze in his eyes. The powerful prisms of the monocular which he carried was a help. Even with its strong magnification, he was not positive of the situation.

He moved downward through the brush, attracted by a man who was standing in view of the boat, but out of sight of the rocks. The man had two shirts tied to sticks.

Doc came close to the man with the wigwag equipment.

"All right, all right!" the man called impatiently to someone. "On the boat, they want to know what to do. What shall I tell them?"

A voice cursed the gathering night. "Give us an hour, and the tide will drown them out."

"We won't have an hour."

The other swore again. "Tell them to wait. Hold that torpedo."

Doc Savage moved away hastily, and used his strong monocular on the long slim boat again. He saw now what had made the craft look queer. A rather bulky build-up on the forward deck, giving that part of a boat a homemade appearance that did not fit the rest of the craft.

There was a housing that covered a pair of torpedo tubes, he suddenly decided. A so-called "mosquito boat," not American either, he decided.

He went back to the flagman, cautiously skirted the fellow, and found that the man who had been giving the orders had gone away for the moment.

Doc took a long chance.

He imitated the voice of the man who had been giving orders to the flagman, and said, "Tell them to lay a smoke screen around that rock."

The flagman jumped. "Are you crazy?" He scowled toward the bush where Doc was concealed. "What's the matter with your voice?"

Under other conditions Doc would have been embarrassed. He had studied voice imitation under a master. Usually, he was more successful.

He said sharply, "Signal them, you fool! The smoke screen!"

The flagman jumped at the tone, saluted. He began an expert waggling with the sticks to which the shirts were tied.

"Tell them," Doc ordered, "to lay the smoke screen, then stand by on the other side. They are to capture anyone they see. But there is to be no shooting."

"Right, sir," said the flagman.

"Be sure they wait on the other side of the smoke screen."

"Right, sir!"

DOC worked down to a point where, close inshore, the water was deep. He watched the long torpedo boat lift its nose and charge around the rock at a respectful distance, trailing a great worm of smoke that flattened.

The fact that they had smokescreen equipment aboard checked his conviction that the craft was a naval one.

The breeze drifted the smoke toward shore. As soon as it reached the beach, Doc scrambled down and entered the water.

Behind him, there was suddenly profane excitement. The flagman was assuring someone he had done nothing but follow orders.

Doc swam strongly. He would not have much time. As fully equipped as they were, they would have radio apparatus. The boat waiting on the other side of the smoke could not see the wigwag signals, but a single radio contact could tip them off that something was wrong.

Nearing the rocks, Doc called, "Monk!"

Monk's small voice squawked astonishment, and Renny rumbled, "Holy cow!"

Doc reached the stony refuge. Waves were breaking over his men. He demanded, "All of you safe?"

"I wouldn't call it safe," Long Tom said dryly. "We're all here, though."

Doc said, "Wait five minutes. Then swim out of the smoke." He pointed. "Head in that direction."

"Their boat is out there. We heard the motors."

"Your job," Doc said, "is to divert their attention while I climb aboard by the stern."

"All right," Long Tom said. "But this won't be easy. Those guys have a regular navy here. I never saw such efficiency."

Doc asked, "Is there a loose rock around here about the size of a man's head?"

"Plenty of them."

The bronze man put on one of the transparent hoods of cellophanelike material which, pulled over his head, was held tightly about his neck with elastic. Inside this, clamped between his teeth, he placed a compact breath-purifier of the artificial-lung type. It was not, of course, as efficient. But it would keep him supplied with oxygen for possibly ten minutes. He got his bearings, took the rock and went under.

LOCATING the boat was more a matter of patience than superhuman ability. The water was not deep. He merely spotted the dark hulk of the craft outlined on the water above, let go the stone, and swam up cautiously to the stern. The propellers were motionless, two big dark blades.

He ran a hand over the hull. Rough with barnacles. The boat had been in the water a long time.

With extreme care, hanging to the rudder, he got his head above the surface. No one above. He reached upward. The rail was too far away.

He unlimbered the collapsible grapple, attached to a silken cord of great strength. He always carried the thing. He tossed the grapple, hooked it over the rail, waited to see that no one had been alarmed. Then he went down into the water again and waited.

There was a shout. Sudden rush from the propellers nearly threw him out of the water. He fought the cord, managed to get hold of the rail.

They were crowded on the forward deck, except for two men who were at the wheel and controls. The last pair were amidships.

Forward, a man bellowed, "Get your hands up!"

Monk's voice answered. "Come and get us. We're surrendering! The darn tide covered those rocks."

The man who had bellowed said, "Careful, men. This smells like a trick."

Doc was on deck by that time. He went forward. The boat was traveling fast now, making a wide circle around the swimming figures of Monk and the others.

The bronze man hit the pair at the controls. He struck hard with a shoulder, sent one man overboard. The other whirled, gasped, dodged the fist Doc sent at him. He stepped backward, got out of reach.

Doc knocked the engine throttles wide open. He put the port engine into reverse, the starboard one full speed ahead. He put the wheel hard to port. The result was a hairpin turn by the boat.

Narrow beam of the craft had never been designed for such turns. It went over, not completely capsizing, but tipping fully half over, the starboard rail and half the cabin under. This happened at near forty miles an hour, and the result was like an avalanche of stone as water came over the bows. Everyone on deck was washed overboard, with the exception of one man, who got hold of a cleat. Doc picked a cover off the binnacle and hurled it at that man, and the fellow slid over the side.

It was then no trouble to go back and pick up Monk, Ham, Long Tom, Renny and Johnny. The latter immediately piled below decks to see if there was anyone left there. There was a commotion. Excited voices. Doc listened to them.

Long-bodied, big-worded Johnny put his head out of a companion and said, "A syzygy, emphatically."

Monk also came up from below. Monk's face was blank with astonishment.

"A syzygy," Monk said, "is probably the word for it."

Johnny seemed surprised that Monk should know what such a word meant. "You know what it means?" he asked suspiciously.

"Syzygy," Monk said, "is when one planet meets another, or something like that. Isn't that it?"

Johnny nodded.

Doc Savage said. "What are you two talking about?"

"A meeting of planets," Monk explained. "The way that fellow Tottingham Strand fell up into the sky, we supposed he would be floating around among the stars, by now. But he's back to Earth!"

"You mean he is on board?"

"He is tied to a bunk down below," Monk said.

Chapter IX
SYZYGY WAS NO GOOD

JOHNNY made another statement. He used small words, so he was very impressed.

"There is also a girl," he said.

"A princess," Monk corrected him. "Such a regal creature as to make your heart go flop-flop."

"Her name is Erica, she says," Johnny added. "Erica Ambler-Hotts, she says."

Doc Savage changed the subject by pointing upward. "That plane," he said, "is coming down as if it had a purpose."

The plane was a yellow craft with two flat, fish-shaped floats and a lean shark snout of a water-cooled motor. It came down in a long falling dive, not steep enough to strip off the wings. The wing slots were set, after the fashion of a dive bomber.

Monk said, "I don't like the way that thing acts."

Doc Savage—he had turned the boat back to pick up the crew members who had been dumped overboard—suddenly knocked the throttles wide open again and spun the wheel. He began to make snaky S curves over the surface.

The plane changed course two or three times, pulled out of its dive. There was a whistling, then commotion and water and smoke climbing into the air, and deep underwater noise.

"A little closer," Monk said, "and there would really have been a syzygy."

"Bombs!" Johnny muttered. "I'll be superamalgamated! A regular dive bomber."

"Navy type," Doc said.

"What navy?"

"That would be hard to tell," the bronze man said.

Johnny rubbed his jaw thoughtfully.

"Nice mixture of events, wouldn't you say?" he remarked. "A man comes, Monk tells me, about a green chest which was stolen from him. He doesn't know what is in the chest because it belonged to a friend named Montgomery, for whom he was keeping it. Then the man falls up into the sky. Then a green fog affects Doc, Monk, Ham and Pat—"

"Wait a minute!" Monk yelled. "Aren't *you* seeing the green fog?"

"Certainly not!" Johnny replied. "And now, a naval plane is dive-bombing us. It's a little mixed up, if you ask me. Some explanations would help clear part of it."

Monk collared the gaunt geologist and archaeologist. "Are you seeing any fog?"

"No!"

Monk looked blank. "That's funny. I see a fog."

Doc Savage had been watching the plane as it arched up and came back again. Machine gun bullets began boiling the water as guns on its wings—two on each wing, two through the

The boat went over, not completely capsizing, but tipping fully half over, the starboard rail and half the cabin under water.

propeller—hung out red tongues. Doc changed the course of the boat rapidly.

"Get below," he said sharply. "The decks are probably armored."

Monk and Johnny dived for the hatch. Doc yanked at a projection which proved to be what he thought it was—a steel shell which hinged up over the steersman's post, and would turn machine gun slugs and possibly the light-cannon shells with which modern planes are equipped.

Ham shouted, "Doc, you want to put out a smoke screen?"

"Good idea," the bronze man said. His voice was composed, in contrast to the gnashing rip and tear of machine gun slugs, the shotgun-loud smash of a cannon shell that suddenly tore away deck planking and exposed the silver shine of armor plate below.

The boat put out smoke, and they moved around under it.

After a while, the night was dark enough to escape. The bronze man noted that the gas tanks were well filled. He sent the boat toward the city.

MONK watched the lights of the Triborough Bridge move overhead like a great monocolored rainbow on which moved the luminous patches of automobile headlights. The boat motors were a rumble like a subway train underfoot, and two white ram horns of spray stood out from the bows and, now and then grew, longer or shorter.

Long Tom came on deck. "You want to talk to the State police on the radio, Doc?"

The bronze man asked, "Did you give them the story?"

"All but the silly parts," Long Tom said. "I didn't mention green chests, men falling up, or green fogs. I told them there were some foreign agents or something stirring up a mess."

"Were they caught?"

"Every one of them was gone by the time the police got there."

"No clues?"

"Not yet. They are checking on the plane, have the roads blocked, and the Coast Guard is starting to search all boats. Ham and Monk furnished descriptions of all those we had seen."

Monk came on deck in time to say, "The best description I gave was of that fake Monk. That sure gets me. You wouldn't believe anyone could look so much like me."

"You sure said something there," Ham told him.

"What you mean?"

"Looking like you is a feat I didn't think anyone could do."

"Look," Monk said bitterly, "I'm in no mood for that stuff you call wit."

Renny put his head out to look at the breathless spectacle which was New York seen at night from the river. They swung past the Sutton Place and Tudor City districts, high apartment houses with many lighted windows.

"They won't talk," Renny reported.

"Which one?"

"Both of them," said Renny. "The girl claims she doesn't know anything. Tottingham Strand says he can't imagine what it is all about."

Doc Savage inquired quietly, "Is he sticking to the story about a mysterious green chest which a friend gave him to keep?"

"That's his story, and he's stuck with it, if you ask me," Renny rumbled. "Personally, I don't believe it anymore than I believe storks bring little babies."

Doc turned the boat in to a pier.

Surprised, Long Tom asked, "Aren't we going around to the warehouse?"

The "warehouse" was an innocent lump of a building on the Hudson side of Manhattan Island, a structure that bore the legend "Hidalgo Trading Company." The interior had been converted into a seaplane hangar and boathouse. A pneumatic man-carrying tube of Doc's design—one gadget which would never become popular with the public; a ride in the tube was about as soothing as a trip through a forest on a skyrocket—led directly to headquarters.

"No, we shall stay away from there," Doc said. "It is probably being watched."

"Not many people know about it."

Doc was silent a moment. "These men we are fighting, whoever they are, know an incredible amount about us. They knew enough to substitute two impostors for Monk and Ham, to gain access to our headquarters at will."

Long Tom's mouth jerked open, then closed. "Doc, isn't Pat at headquarters with the fake Ham? Doesn't that mean she may be in danger?"

"Pat," the bronze man explained, "is in the same building, but on a different floor. In my apartment."

"Apartment?" Long Tom said. "I didn't know you had one there."

"Nor did anyone else," Doc said. "So Pat probably is safe."

PAT SAVAGE looked anything but safe when they walked in on her. She was ghost-pale. "Have you got smelling salts or something?" she asked.

The idea of Pat needing smelling salts was startling.

"What happened?" Monk demanded. "Did the fake Ham fall up, too?"

Pat shuddered. "He went down, if anything—the part of him that left."

"What—" Monk stared blankly.

"A button off his vest, I think it was," Pat explained. She sank in a chair. "It was awful. I thought I was tough. I was the one who ate up excitement. *Whew!*"

"Button?" Monk asked.

Pat said, "He ate it, before the truth serum got him. That is, he began to feel the effects of the serum, and he ate the button. It was a hollow shell, and there was some powder—chemical of some kind—in it. The man—the false Ham—bragged about it. He said it would keep him unconscious for days, so we could not get anything out of him. You know, like spies do, and like we have done on occasion. It's an old trick."

"Poison?" Doc Savage put in.

Pat nodded. "I don't think—I'm sure he did not know it. That was horrible, wasn't it? Whoever he was working for knew he would be in very desperate straits before he ever used that chemical-filled button. It was murder!"

Doc Savage glanced at Erica Ambler-Hotts. She was as cool as cream in a refrigerator.

"I would like you to look at the body," Doc told her.

She did not flinch. "I don't mind," she said.

She went into the other room and glanced at the body on the floor. The man had gone through motions in dying that had clawed up the rug and upset things. Erica Ambler-Hotts was not all cold stone. She lost color.

"I never saw him before," she said. She turned quickly and walked out.

Doc brought in Tottingham Strand. The man was composed, but it was the composure of a steel spring tightened to its last turn. More than ever, the man was like a tempered blade, a fine cutting instrument, impersonal, always on his feet, like a cat. He went to the body and turned the face into different positions.

"I have seen him." He straightened, looked at his hands distastefully, took out a handkerchief and wiped them. "This man tried to kill me a few days ago. He was in a car that sought to run me down."

Doc asked, "Did you go to the police about that?"

Strand shrugged. "I have explained to your associates why I did not go to the police with any of this. My friend Montgomery—he left me the green chest—requested me not to go to the police."

"You must have been willing to do a great deal for your friend Montgomery." Doc's metallic eyes were suddenly as still as hardened gold.

Strand spread his hands. "I did not know what I was getting into."

"And what *did* you get into?" Doc asked.

"That," said Strand quickly, "is something I wish you would tell me."

"What part do you want me to tell you?"

"Why men fall up," Strand said.

Doc was silent.

Strand, after smiling wryly, added, "And why Miss Ambler-Hotts was seized. They were going to kill her. But first they were going to torture her to make her tell what she knew about my actions and what I knew and what I had done."

Doc said, "You know, then, why they seized you?"

"No."

Doc Savage's face was usually expressionless, but that did not mean he could not show emotion. He displayed feeling now. The feeling was profound skepticism. It was so plain that Strand could not miss it. Strand flushed.

"My friend Montgomery got me into something," Strand said grimly. "I wish you would tell me what it is."

WHILE Doc Savage was answering Strand's last statement with silence, Monk and Ham came into the room. Monk gestured skyward with a thumb, said, "Ham and I are going up to headquarters."

"Be careful," was all Doc Savage had to say.

It was a rare occasion when Doc gave a warning, so Monk and Ham were impressed when they walked out.

Doc Savage watched Strand for a while. Doc's face was now expressionless. Then he made the low trilling which was his peculiarity. The sound was almost inaudible.

"Strand," he said, "there is a place for everything."

Strand half-closed one eye. "So I've heard."

"This is the place," Doc said, "for the truth."

The Englishman's face jerked into a mask, telling nothing except that he was on guard.

"Sorry," he said.

"You have not told the truth."

Strand wheeled stiffly. "Sorry," he said. He walked out.

A moment later, there was a rumble from the outer room. Doc went to the door. Strand was trying to leave, and Renny had his way barred, with big fists cocked. "Holy cow!" Renny told him. "You're not just walking out!"

"Get out of my way," Strand said coldly.

Renny looked at the steel expression of the man and said, "You don't make me shake in my boots, friend. Go back and sit down."

Strand did something that was hard to do. He went back and took a chair and made it seem that he had not been bluffed in the least.

Later, Renny got Doc aside. "That fellow," Renny muttered, "is not someone I would want to find in a dark alley, if he didn't like me."

Doc Savage made no comment. He went to the telephone and dialed his headquarters upstairs, using the unlisted number which would get a quick response.

Monk answered and said, "They have been in here, Doc. But they're gone. We've got the photographs from the concealed camera that takes pictures of intruders. You want us to develop the film?"

RENNY

"Bring the film and developing chemicals downstairs," Doc directed. "And there are some other chemicals you can also bring. Better get a paper and pencil and make a list."

The list of chemicals which Doc Savage named was long and complicated. He added a few pieces of equipment.

"It's a good thing you told me to write them down," Monk said.

He and Ham soon appeared, heavily burdened. Ham patted his pocket. "Here're the films. Want us to use the bathroom or the kitchen?"

"Bathroom." Doc Savage picked up the chemicals and carried them into the kitchen. He worked for some time, mixing and testing.

Monk came in with a print which he had made. "This is the best one," he said. "Look here; we've seen these guys. Some of them were in the gang that we fought out on Long Island—part of the crew that cornered us on that rock."

Doc examined the print.

Then he looked at Monk and asked, "How is the green fog, Monk?"

"Still see it," Monk said. "Renny and the others say it doesn't exist. But Pat and Ham and I sure see it. We see a fog, and it's green."

Ham had come to lean against the door. "Doc, I've noticed a queer thing about this fog."

"You mean that it seems to turn red at times?" Doc asked.

Ham stared. "How did you know?"

"Ever hear of santonin?" Doc asked.

Monk popped his palms together. "Blazes! For the love of little fishes!"

"You know what it is?" Ham demanded.

"Sure!" Monk explained. "Great grief! Doc, how did they administer it to us? Santonin. They *couldn't* have done that!"

Doc Savage said, "The fact that we saw only green indicates they used either a developed form of santonin, or a similar compound. It may have been a gas. It probably was."

"I'm going back upstairs to see how they gave it to us!" Monk yelled.

The homely chemist burst out of the room.

Ham shook his head. "I still don't know what this santonin stuff is."

"A chemical," Doc Savage explained. "It makes things appear all green or all red to its victims for several days. It is a drug."

Ham gave that deep thought. "Why," he asked, "did they do that?"

MONK came bursting back into the apartment with triumph all over his clock-stopping face. "It was easy when I knew what to look for."

"You found how they gave us that chemical?" Ham demanded.

"Did I!" Monk grinned. "How do you think?"

"Don't be cute, you lummox," Ham advised.

"You remember one of the very first things that happened to Doc when this thing began?" Monk demanded.

"The green fog—"

"No, no! Before that."

"Doc was up at a hospital performing an operation nobody else could perform—"

"Right after that," Monk said.

"Why, Doc had an accident. There was a fight. Some stranger with a knife. The knife was knocked out of the fellow's hand and struck Doc, cutting him slightly. But Doc wasn't even involved in that."

Monk grinned. "Remember what Pat was doing when we found her at headquarters?"

"Bandaging her ankle."

"Why?"

"Oh, some fellow on the street had kicked her shin or something and skinned—" Ham went silent. His eyes narrowed. "Wait a minute! That's a kind of a coincidence."

Monk said, "Remember what you and I did just before we began seeing the green fog?"

"We were in a fight."

"Exactly," Monk said. "And no doubt that was when we got jabbed with a hypodermic needle containing this advanced form of santonin."

Ham looked disgruntled. "You mean to tell me the santonin was administered with the knife that cut Doc, with a needle in the toe of somebody's shoe that skinned Pat's ankle, and to us during that fight?"

"That," Monk said, "is how we got it."

"How did you find it out?"

Monk tapped his forehead. "By using what's in here."

Ham snorted. "What's in there will never trouble Einstein."

Ham sat down in a chair, rubbed his jaw and began to realize just how puzzled he was. He scowled at Monk. He did not like to discuss serious matters with Monk, because the impulse to insult Monk was overwhelming. Rather, it was a necessary act of self-preservation, for Monk would do plenty of insulting himself if not held at bay in some fashion. Ham strained his hair with his fingers.

"Doc," he said. "Why did they give us that stuff—that santonin?"

"To make us think there was a green fog."

"For what purpose?"

The bronze man's features were inscrutable. "It was part of an astoundingly clear and elaborate plot."

Ham's eyes flew wide. When Doc referred to a thing as astounding and elaborate, it meant a great deal. One of the bronze man's habits were under-statement. Ham had heard him call an earthquake a minor tremor when the quake was strong enough to shake the hat off a man's head.

"Plot," Ham said. "Plot, eh?" He was puzzled. "They gave us santonin. That made us see a greenish film, because of what it did to our eyes. They made us think it was a fog. I remember when Monk and I were around that building—we met a fellow who asked us if there wasn't a green fog. That fellow was one of their men. He was helping to make us think there was a fog."

"But why?" Monk asked.

"To make it easier to deceive me," Doc explained, rather loudly. At least, there was per-ceptibly greater volume in his voice, although for no apparent reason.

Ham nodded. "I think I get it. They wanted to hamper your vision so you wouldn't recognize the fake Ham and the fake Monk. But they gave us the stuff, too, so that, when we were first with you, it would be common. You'd think the fog was overall."

Doc said, "Yes, and they did not want me to realize I was in a fake headquarters."

Ham stared. "There *was* a phony headquarters, then?"

"An exact duplicate."

Monk muttered, "That's a hard one to believe. I don't see how they duplicated it."

"There have been weeks of patient effort behind this," Doc Savage advised him.

THE bronze man's voice was becoming louder by degrees. The gradual increase in volume had not gone unnoticed by Monk and Ham, but they were more or less excited over the fantastic evidence that someone had gone to the enormous pains of duplicating their headquarters exactly. They were now doing as people will do when another lifts his voice—they were speaking with more volume, themselves.

Ham paused to rub his jaw reflectively.

"What," he asked, "was the idea of the fooling us with the fake headquarters?"

"A psychological trick."

Ham frowned. "I don't see the psychology in it."

"The idea," Doc explained, "was to make me think I was safe in headquarters among friends—the fake Monk and Ham were to be the friends for that occasion—and get me talking."

Monk got into the conversation with a grunt.

"I can see how it might have worked," Monk declared. "We always talk freely to each other. If Doc thought he was with me, or if I thought I was with Doc, or with Ham—in other words, if we thought we were together and nobody else around, we might let something slip. Sure, it'd work."

Ham put in a skeptical snort. "If," he said, "we knew anything to let slip."

Monk forgot himself and nodded agreement with Ham.

"That's right," he said. "We don't have anything they would want."

Doc Savage said quietly, "But we have."

They stared at him. "Huh?" Monk said.

"Compound Monk," Doc said.

Ham Brooks chuckled heartily. "Monk is a compound, all right," he said. He glanced at Monk. "A compound of a missing link and nobody could figure what else."

Then Ham stopped speaking. His jaw fell. He had remembered something.

"Say!" he exploded. "You mean that stuff—that chemical stuff—you developed a long time ago? I remember hearing somebody say some-thing about some new discovery you had named 'Compound Monk'; but nothing more was ever said about it, and it slipped my mind."

Monk said, "I remember that stuff. It was very sensitive to motion radiation. The absorption of such radiation by its atoms led to the ejection of three electrons, as against two-electron ejection by so-called photoelectric substances sensitive to light radiation."

"Greek!" Ham said.

"It's not Greek, either," Monk snapped. "It's a perfectly simple thing. You've seen light meters? Photographers use them to measure light."

"What," asked Ham, "has a light meter got to do with this affair?"

"Nothing." Monk looked exasperated. "But I can take the perfectly simple principle of the light meter and explain it to you, and use that to illustrate Compound Monk—"

Doc Savage interrupted. There was even more volume in his voice now.

"The formula for Compound Monk is in the big safe upstairs," he said. "We might get it, look it over, and see if it would explain what the mystery is about."

A moment later, Tottingham Strand appeared in the door.

"I can explain what it is all about," he said.

RENNY, Long Tom, Johnny, Pat and Erica Ambler-Hotts had evidently been listening, because they appeared behind Strand. Strand stepped aside, and they entered. Strand remained in the doorway. Noting that, and realizing there was now no one between Strand and the outer door, Monk arose and sauntered past the man, then stood where he could shut off an escape attempt.

"It was because they were fools," Strand said.

Doc made a slight negative gesture. "On the contrary, they were clever."

Strand showed his teeth with no humor. "They were trying to deceive me—and failed."

Doc said, after a moment, "You are not making yourself very clear."

"They were going to let me escape and go to you for help."

Doc Savage spoke quietly in Mayan, the tongue which he and his associates used for consultation when they did not wish to be understood by others. He spoke to Monk. He told Monk to come back out of the other room and leave the way free for Strand to take flight.

"What did you say?" Strand demanded.

Monk swallowed his surprise, though fast, and said, "All right, Doc. I'll go into the kitchen and mix more of that stuff to clear the green fog out of our eyes."

The homely chemist walked past Strand into the kitchen.

Strand was relieved. "The explanation of all that elaborate deceit was this, Mr. Savage. First, they wanted you in a fake headquarters, where you were virtually a prisoner guarded by two of their men. By two men guarding you, I, of course, mean the false Monk and Ham."

Strand stared at them.

He said, "I was permitted to escape—or so they planned. I would go to you, they knew. And they knew I would talk to you; tell you everything. The fake Monk and Ham would be present and overhear all I told you."

"Then," Doc said, "our guess at the purpose of the green fog and the fake headquarters was correct?"

"Yes. It was to get information out of you and me."

Doc asked, "They had reason for thinking you would try to reach me?"

"Excellent reason."

"What was it?"

Strand drew himself up.

"I came to America from England to see you," he said. "They knew that."

Monk's curiosity got so strong that he put his head out of the kitchen and demanded, "What did they expect to learn?"

"They wished to hear what I would tell you when I came to see you," said Tottingham Strand. "They had the fake Monk and Ham planted for that purpose. But"—his face darkened, and his hands closed—"I was too experienced for that gag. I saw through it at once. I told them so."

Monk rather derisively, said, "You're clever, huh?"

Strand smiled again, and it was like a knife blade showing its steel.

"I was not fool enough for Savage to deceive me," he said.

Monk looked as if he had been slapped. "Hey, what do you mean?"

"I mean," snapped Strand, "that I do not think Savage could have been deceived by those men even for a moment. Therefore, he was not deceived. Hence, he is working with them."

"Brother," said Monk coldly, "words like those may lose you your teeth."

"Savage has you duped," Strand said coldly. "He did not want you to know he had sold out; so he pulled that elaborate and impossible yarn about a fake headquarters to deceive you. He did not want me coming here. He wanted me away from you, but he knew I would expect to find some of his associates with him. You and Ham Brooks are the most prominent. Therefore, Savage prepared a fake Monk and a fake Ham for me."

Monk shook his head slowly.

"Man, you're as crazy as a box full of loons," he said.

Strand showed most of his teeth.

"I'll just leave you with that thought," he said.

Then Strand leaped back, slammed the door and locked it. Sound of his feet went away from the door fast.

Monk bounced forward, bellowing, "He scrammed! I knew he was fixing to!"

Erica Ambler-Hotts stood with her hands pressed to her cheeks and made an extremely coherent statement.

"Poor Tot Strand is so terrified by the magnitude of this thing," she said, "that he has made a frightful mistake."

Chapter X
THE MONK COMPOUND

THE eighty-sixth floor of the midtown building had been Doc Savage's headquarters since the beginning of his rather strange career of righting wrongs and punishing evildoers.

From time to time, he had made changes in the place, added gadgets and trick devices, until it was a remarkable labyrinth of the unexpected.

There was, for example, the wall passages by which they could move from one room to another and watch through disguised loopholes. It was possible to move from these to a lower floor, thence out of the building by the regular elevator service.

Doc Savage watched Tot Strand crouch before the big safe in the reception room and go through the contents. Doc stood in a narrow passage and looked on through the glass eye of a large stuffed fish which hung on the wall.

Strand had found the safe open. He had located a file marked: "Confidential Formulae." There were envelopes in this file, fat ones, each of which contained a notebook—a record of the experiments in developing the formula—and a package which contained samples of the formula itself, whenever the stuff was not perishable.

Strand found a package, grunted loudly.

He put his find in his pocket and fled the place. He was so nervous that he was perspiring.

Down in the lobby, he took a great deal of care to make sure no one was waiting for him.

This information was relayed to Doc Savage by Renny Renwick, who said, "He got off on the mezzanine floor. He's looking over the railing, scouting to see if the coast is clear."

Renny was sitting in the lobby barber shop, which had huge glass windows that offered a full view of the lobby. Renny had seated himself in a chair, lathered his face, and leaned back. The barber, who knew what was expected, had handed Renny a telephone when the latter gestured.

Doc said, "Tell me when he leaves and what route he takes."

"He's doing it, now," Renny said. "The south door. He is going west."

Doc directed, "Go back upstairs. Keep an eye on that girl, Erica Ambler-Hotts. She knows more about this than she has told us."

"That will be a pleasure," Renny said.

"Is Bob following Strand?" Doc asked.

"Yes."

Bob was Bob Gaston. He operated the newsstand in the south lobby of the building. Bob Gaston was also a product of the institution which Doc Savage and his associates referred to as the "college." The "college" was located in a remote section of upstate New York, and its purpose and even its existence were unknown to the general public. The purpose of the "college" was the renovating of criminals by unusual methods. When Doc caught a chronic crook, he committed the fellow to the place, where the patient underwent a delicate brain operation at the hands of specialists trained by Doc himself. As a result of the operation, all memory of the past was wiped out. The patient was then trained to hate crime and taught a trade, after which he was "graduated" as a useful citizen. Bob Gaston was such a graduate. Once a criminal, he now bore no traces of it, no more trace than he had recollection.

BOB watched Tottingham Strand enter a small apartment house in the Jackson Heights section. He calmly walked into the lobby, and entered the elevator with Strand. The place did not have a doorman, and the front door was left carelessly unlocked during the day.

Strand got out at the fifth floor. So did Bob. Strand entered Apartment 5C.

Bob went back downstairs, hurried to a drugstore, and telephoned Doc Savage. He told Doc where Strand would be found.

"Watch the place and wait for me," Doc said.

The bronze man's voice was pleased, and Bob Gaston felt very good about the matter as he left the drugstore and walked back toward the apartment house. Bob understood vaguely that, in some way, he owed a great debt to Doc Savage, although he did not know exactly what it was. Something to do with his earlier life, he suspected. His past was a blank, largely. It did not bother him, except that, once or twice, he had met men who seemed to know him, but whom he did not recognize. Such memories as he had were only very vague stirrings, nothing tangible enough to shape into an actual recollection.

Bob was perfectly satisfied. He operated the newsstand and cigar counter in the great skyscraper which contained Doc Savage's headquarters, and he made a good living. He knew that he owed his prosperity to Doc, so he was particularly anxious to please.

He now noticed a taxicab in front of the apartment house. It had been there earlier, not exactly in front of the place, but at a parking spot designated as set aside for cabs.

Hit by an idea, Bob approached the cab. "Care to rent this heap for a couple of hours, buddy?" he asked. "Let me drive it, I mean."

The taxi driver stared in astonishment. "Huh?"

"I would like to take over your cab for a while," Bob explained.

The driver had a round pumpkin of a head and small eyes as gray as pencil erasers. "G'wan somewhere else," he growled. "I got no time for stews."

"I am not drunk," Bob explained carefully. "I wish to hire your cab. I will pay you for it."

"You think I'm crazy?" countered the driver. "Hell, I don't know you. I own this cab myself. Think I'm going to turn it over to a stranger?"

This was a logical argument. Bob chuckled. "Look," he said, "would it make any difference if you knew I was working for Doc Savage?"

The taxi driver seemed to jump an inch off his seat. "Savage?"

"Doc Savage," Bob explained innocently. "I'm on a job for him, so your cab will be safe enough."

The driver had trouble getting his chin up off his chest.

"You work for Doc Savage?" he asked.

Bob Gaston nodded.

"What you doing?" asked the driver.

"I'm shadowing a man," Bob said. "I want to use your cab to keep track of him. So, driver, you can see it is perfectly all right. Here, I'll give you ten dollars for the rental of your cab the next hour."

"Ten dollars!" The cab driver sounded utterly amazed. "Sure, pal. Here, let me get out." He alighted from the cab. He removed his cap. "Here, take my cap."

Bob reached for the cap and the driver used the blackjack he had managed to slip unobserved out of his pocket; used it so hard that the leather split and small shot flew and bounced and scampered over the sidewalk long after Bob Gaston was lying motionless on his face.

With uncanny abruptness, two more men were beside the driver. "What happened, Joey?" one demanded.

"This guy followed Strand to the place," said the driver. "He came up and tried to hire my cab to trail Strand, the fool. He even told me he was working for Savage."

"Hell, if Strand left Savage, that means he's got what he came after!" exploded the other.

"We better see about that," said Joey.

There were more than the three of them. The others were concealed in the adjacent darkness. Joey made a series of gestures with his arms—semaphore signals—standing under the light in front of the apartment house.

"I told 'em to stand by for trouble," he said.

THEY went upstairs, using the stairway instead of the elevator, and climbed warily. They did not knock on Strand's door. Two of them simply hit it together, and the third stood back with a gun.

It was not a well-made apartment house, and

the door split, letting them inside. The man who had stood back was instantly inside with his gun.

Tottingham Strand dropped a suitcase. Another suitcase stood on a chair, partially packed.

Joey said, "Getting ready to leave us, Tot?"

Strand stood very stiff with hands splayed against his legs. He trembled slightly. When he spoke, it was to make low, guttural remarks that went into great detail about the debased nature of Joey's ancestry.

Joey whitened and said, "Shut up!"

Then Joey went looking around the room. He located on a table a packet and noted its markings:

Compound Monk

"You got it!" he yelled. He bounced over in front of Strand, so excited that he drooled. "You got it! You got what you came all the way from England to get!"

Strand, who had composed himself coldly, said nothing.

Joey saw the expression. He chilled. "What you looking so smug about?"

Strand indicated the package. "No good."

"What?"

"A plant. A fake. Just something Savage put in his safe for me to find."

Joey glared. "I don't believe it!"

Strand shrugged. "Oh, he sucked me in properly. I fell for an old trick—one of the oldest. He let me escape and get this, that package. He even let a clue drop to where it was."

Joey, suddenly frenzied, ripped open the package. He examined the contents, stuff which looked somewhat like quicksilver in a small glass bottle. It was heavy.

When Joey noticed how heavy the stuff was, he began getting pale. He dug a silver coin, a quarter, out of his pocket, and uncorked the bottle, put some of the contents on the coin. He rubbed. The coin got a wet silver sheen.

"Mercury!" Joey bellowed. "Ordinary mercury!"

Strand shrugged. "I told you it was just a bait."

Joey's eyebrows pulled together. "Yeah, I guess that explains why Savage's man was following you." He wheeled. "Get out of here," he told his men.

"What about me?" Strand asked.

"You go with us," Joey advised him. "And this time, we'll see if we can't do a better job of holding you."

THEY got down on the street with scared haste. Joey had rolled unfortunate Bob Gaston into the cab. He rolled him out again. Bob was still unconscious. Joey got behind the wheel. His two men and Strand climbed in the rear. Joey made semaphore signals with his arms, and they left.

They drove fast and cautiously, and in silence for a time. Then Strand spoke.

"Got some new helpers, haven't you, Joey?" he asked.

Joey only grunted. Then he demanded, "What do you mean?"

"Earlier today. The two boats. The plane. All those men going around giving each other snappy salutes."

"What about 'em?"

"Rather an augmented organization, I would say," Strand remarked grimly.

"They work for me," Joey snapped. "What of it?"

"You and Stinky and the other two didn't have money enough to hire such a collection."

"You're nuts," Joey said. "I got more money than you think."

Strand showed his teeth unpleasantly, in the strange knife-blade way he could manage. "You have an excess of brains," he added. "An impossible excess."

JOEY drove into a stretch of deserted road, and watched the rearview mirror carefully. Only one car followed. He blinked his headlights. The other car blinked its lights three times quickly, in response, and Joey breathed easily again. They were his men following.

"What's excessive about my brains?" he demanded.

You didn't have the sense, Joey, to think up that rather fantastic, but shrewd, scheme to get Doc Savage to a fake headquarters with a false Monk and Ham, so that I would escape and go to them and reveal—you hoped—to your false Monk and Ham all I knew. And Doc Savage would, in turn, reveal all he knew—you hoped."

Joey grunted disgustedly.

Strand said, "You did not think that up, Joey."

"I don't see why it didn't work," Joey said.

"You could not put a thing like that over on Doc Savage," Strand advised him.

"Hell, it was fantastic enough to have worked," Joey snapped. "They told me Savage wouldn't fall for anything ordinary, but this would be so wild he would—"

Joey then caught himself and swallowed uncomfortably.

Strand gave a laugh with an edge. "So you do have a boss, now, Joey. Someone with brains."

Joey said, "You're nuts!" unconvincingly.

Strand leaned back and sighed.

"Joey," he said, "you have no imagination. You could have sold this thing for an empire. And I actually mean an empire, a kingdom. You could have been king of any one of a dozen countries you could have named." Strand laughed. "What did you get? A hundred thousand dollars?"

"I got half a mil—" Joey began indignantly, then caught himself again.

There was genuine mirth of a cold, desperate kind in Strand's laugh.

"A kingdom, you could have gotten, Joey," he said. "You could have been king of England, perhaps. How would you like that, you miserable gutter rat?"

Joey did not say anything. He was white.

Joey went to a deserted woodland section, and got a portable radio out of a tree. He also produced a code book and began rather painfully a coded transmission that was supposed to sound like an airplane pilot attempting to contact a control airport. He got an answer, also ostensibly from an airport, and worked frantically with a pencil, paper and a flashlight. Finally, he came back to the car.

He was triumphant.

"We got a plan to get hold of Savage," he said. "This time, it will work!"

"Is Savage supposed to fall for this one because it is so fantastic?" Strand asked witheringly.

Joey snorted. "This one is so simple anybody would be taken in. We're gonna work through somebody that Savage won't suspect in a million years."

Strand said, "You do function well when you connect up with someone who has brains, don't you, Joey?"

Joey snarled, "Pop that guy if he don't close his mouth!"

One of the men slapped Strand.

Undisturbed, Strand said, "You sold too cheap, Joey. A kingdom. Think of it, you miserable dupe."

Joey got in the car and drove on, but he had become pale again.

Chapter XI
THE UNDERCOVER AGENT

DOC SAVAGE was quietly undisturbed with Bob Gaston. "It could happen to anyone, Bob," he said.

Bob Gaston was miserable over his failure. "To anyone who has no sense whatever," he declared. "Myself, for example."

"Forget it."

"It's nice of you to say that," Bob muttered. "But I made a mistake in blabbing too much to that fellow I thought was a taxi driver. I guess being a detective isn't my line of work."

"How is the newsstand going?" Doc inquired.

"Oh, fine," Bob said. "I owe you so much. That's what makes me feel particularly bad about lousing up the job you gave me."

Doc Savage left Bob Gaston at the newsstand in the lobby of the building. It was now late night, long past closing time, and the lobby was deserted except for scrubwomen and janitors. Doc rode an elevator up to his apartment.

Monk and Pat and the others, including Erica Ambler-Hotts, met him. The bronze man explained quietly that the enemy had knocked Bob Gaston senseless and had apparently made off with Tottingham Strand.

"There was nothing in Strand's apartment to shed light on the mystery," he finished, "except that Strand rented the place only two weeks ago. There were stickers on his luggage when he arrived, indicating he had come by steamship to South America, thence to New York by plane. The stickers had been steamed off his luggage, indicating he did not want anyone to know about his recent arrival. The information about the stickers came from the superintendent of the apartment house, who is a travel bug."

Big-fisted Renny spoke in Mayan, saying that he wanted to speak with Doc privately. The bronze man moved into the bedroom. Someone had covered the body of the fake Ham with a sheet.

"Strand showed us one thing," Renny said. "They are after the Compound Monk, as we call it."

"Was that what you wanted to discuss?"

"No, not exactly." Renny blocked out his big fists thoughtfully. "It's this Erica Ambler-Hotts."

"What about her?"

"I don't place her in this," Renny said. "She says she doesn't know a thing. But when Strand cleared out, she said something about his being so terrified by the magnitude of the affair that he was making a terrible mistake. I ask you this: Doesn't that sound as if she knew something?"

Doc Savage nodded slowly. "Did you question her about that?"

Renny snorted. "Yes," he said. "And you can guess about how much she told me. What the little boy shot at. Nothing."

The bronze man said, "We might hear her story again."

He returned to the outer room. He took his time opening a conversation with Erica Ambler-Hotts, as if he had no particular motive.

"By the way," he said, "how did you become acquainted with Strand?"

Erica smiled wryly. "With Tot? Oh, I've known the fellow for ages. His father was gametender on my father's estate when I was so high." She indicated something an inch or two long with thumb and forefinger. "We've plowed into each other at intervals ever since. Really nothing close between us. Just a gabbing acquaintance, you might say—"

"Can you tell us anything about Strand?" Doc asked idly.

"Nothing, I'm afraid."

"Nothing at all?"

"Nothing."

Doc Savage picked up the telephone. "I want the transatlantic operator," he said. "I am placing a call to Scotland Yard, in London."

Erica Ambler-Hotts jerked up straight. "Just a minute. You calling about Tot?"

"Yes."

"In that case," Erica said, "I had better tell you about him myself. Rather you get the information from a sympathetic source."

Doc told the telephone operator, "Never mind, cancel the call," and hung up.

Erica Ambler-Hotts took a deep breath.

"Poor Tot Strand is wanted in England for murder!" she said.

MONK dropped an apple he was peeling. Habeas Corpus, Monk's runt hog, stooped up the apple and scuttled into the kitchen, pursued by Ham's pet chimp, Chemistry.

Blank astonishment was all over Monk's homely face. He said, "That's hard to believe. Strand is a tough guy—I could see that. But it seemed to me that it was a clean kind of toughness."

Erica half nodded.

"He is also wanted for treason!" she said.

Monk muttered, "Blazes!"

"Both of those crimes," Erica announced grimly, "are punishable by the death penalty."

Monk shook his head. "I still can't see him as that kind of a man."

"Tot would like to hear you say that," Erica said.

Monk eyed her thoughtfully. "You seem to believe he is not guilty."

"That's right."

"What makes you think he isn't guilty?"

"I know Tot. That's jolly well enough for me."

Doc Savage entered the discussion again with a completely emotionless request. "Suppose you give us the details about the murder and treason charge against Tottingham Strand," he said. There was something about the flat emotionlessness of his voice that compelled an answer more than a show of agitated interest would have.

"Really, I can't give you the exact details," Erica told him. "But the way I understand it, Tot was doing a spot of service for the War Department. He was working with a man named Coxwell."

"What kind of work was Strand doing for the war ministry?" Doc asked.

Too quickly, Erica said, "I do not know. Coxwell, the man who was working with Strand, went to his superior officers and told them that he suspected Strand of selling out the English government. Coxwell had no proof. He just suspected. He was a rather sleazy sort, this Coxwell chap was, and I fancy the chaps in the War Ministry rather doubted his word."

She paused to give dramatic effect to her next statement.

"Coxwell was found killed in Strand's apartment off Kensington," she said. "Strand disappeared."

"When was that?"

"Not quite six months ago."

Doc Savage said, "Had you been in constant contact with him since?"

"Oh, certainly not. I had not seen him for months. Not until a few days ago, in fact, when he gave me a ring on the telephone."

"Any particular reason for his calling you?"

"Not that I was able to learn."

"Any reason," Doc asked, "for you to go out with a murderer?"

She tightened visibly. "Really, I don't believe you think I've told you the truth."

Doc reached for the telephone.

Into the telephone, the bronze man said, "Transatlantic operator, please."

TO the operator, Doc said, "I want to talk to Carl Morenta, of the International Game Association, Longacre Road, London, England."

He listened for a few moments.

"That is too bad," he said. "Put the call through immediately after the wire is made available."

He hung up, and explained, "The wire is being used for military matters. It will be turned back to civilian use again in half an hour. There is nothing to do but wait."

Erica Ambler-Hotts leaned back in her chair. She took out a cigarette and lighted it. They had not seen her smoke before.

"Cigarette?" she asked Pat, and Pat shook her head.

Doc Savage spoke to Monk. He used the Mayan tongue, which only his associates understood.

"Give this girl a chance to escape," Doc said. "Answer me in Mayan, as if we were holding a conversation."

"So you think she's been lying to us!" Monk said in an astonished voice, using the Mayan lingo.

"That's good," Doc told him. "Now you will receive orders to leave and perform certain duties. Ignore the orders. Instead, follow this girl if she leaves. We do not want any slips. She is our one chance to get back in contact with the mystery."

Pat Savage was not supposed to understand the Mayan lingo.

She said in Mayan, "What am I to do, Doc?"

A flicker of astonishment crossed the bronze man's usually emotionless face. "Where did you learn the language, Pat?"

"Oh, I talked Monk into teaching it to me," she said.

Monk looked embarrassed.

Doc said, "Monk, take Ham and Johnny and visit your laboratory downtown. Get together equipment that we might need. Take it to the waterfront hangar. Pat, you and Renny and Long Tom had better get out and talk to the British consular officials. I want to know whether they have any inkling about this mystery. Better talk to them personally, to get results."

Pat nodded. "If we started talking to them over the telephone about men falling up," she said, "fat lot of information we would get."

They departed, leaving Doc Savage alone with Erica Ambler-Hotts.

Doc told Erica, "I am waiting for the telephone call to England to go through. The half-hour delay will have elapsed shortly."

She nodded. "Can I do anything to help?"

"You are not scared, are you?"

"I imagine so," she said. "I have no impulse to wring my hands and moan, however."

Doc asked, "Would you be afraid to go downstairs and get something for my associates to eat when they get back? There is a delicatessen in the next block. You take the south side entrance and turn right."

The girl was expressionless, as enigmatic as the bronze man. "I would like to help," she said. "Of course I will go."

"Thank you."

Erica Ambler-Hotts arose. "By the way, Mr. Savage, why do you think Tot Strand fled the way he did? You recall he said he had come all the way from England to see you, and it sounded as if he was telling the truth."

Doc faced the young woman.

"Tottingham Strand got into our safe and seized a package marked 'Compound Monk'," the bronze man said.

Erica was shocked. She lowered her head, did things with her hands calculated to make it seem she was not concerned. She moved to the door.

"I will get the food," she said.

She went out.

Five minutes passed. And ten. An hour finally, and a bit more. Then the telephone rang. It was Renny, with his big bull-in-a-box voice.

"She's scramming," Renny said. "Holy cow, Doc! She met three very smooth-looking guys who probably live on nails and sandpaper, and they're out at a private airport on Long Island. They're warming up a plane."

Doc asked, "Have you a portable radio?"

"Yes."

"Keep in touch with me," the bronze man said. "And give me the location of the airport."

The telephone began ringing as soon as the bronze man put it down, and the operator said, "This is the transatlantic operator. I am ready with your call to London."

Chapter XII
THE FLYING MAN

ANDREW BLODGETT MONK MAYFAIR and Theodore Marley Ham Brooks had been good-natured enemies since they had known each other. The brand of good nature was hard to recognize. Strangers often yelled for the police upon hearing them engaging in what was a minor bit of persiflage, comparatively speaking.

An hour before dawn the following morning, they were crawling through brush with their two pets, Habeas Corpus and Chemistry.

They were discussing a small matter about which Monk was feeling injured.

"This Compound Monk they're talking about," Monk said grimly. "How come I didn't know the stuff was named after me?"

"I wouldn't know," Ham said. "There are probably two or three things since the beginning of creation that you don't know. Or did that ever occur to you?"

"Don't try to be nasty," Monk advised. "I'm asking you a simple question."

"'Simple' describes most of your questions."

"Why'd they name that stuff Compound Monk?"

Ham began grinning, but the grin was lost on Monk because of the darkness. However, when Ham burst into smothered laughter, Monk realized the state of the dapper lawyer's feelings.

"You shyster!" Monk sounded bitter. "There's some gag connected to them naming that chemical, or whatever it is, after me!"

"And how!" Ham chortled.

Monk thought of several bitter things he wished to say, and said none of them, because they were crawling through the runt bushes which fringed a beach. The sand was hard and gritty under their hands.

"Imitate a loon," Ham said.

"You do it," Monk snarled. "It should come more natural to you."

Ham gave a passable imitation of a loon's cry, got an answer, and they headed for the sound. Shortly they came upon the others.

Big-fisted Renny said, "We began to think you two fellows were never going to join us. All the others were here an hour ago."

"Aw, Ham had to go past his club and get the proper clothes for the occasion," Monk growled.

"Does he figure he knows what the proper occasion will be?" asked Renny.

"From the size of his suitcase, I guess he prepared for an assortment of occasions," Monk said.

Doc Savage was soundlessly beside them. He had come from the night somewhere.

Doc said, "The plane is preparing to take off. Erica Ambler-Hotts and her three companions apparently have been waiting for daylight."

Renny rumbled, "I'll wake up Pat. She could sleep through the end of the world."

He went over and tickled Pat's nose with a grass blade. She promptly slapped him, then tried to go back to sleep.

"Wake up," Renny advised. "We're about to start cutting oats around here."

"They must be pretty wild," Pat complained, "if you have to sneak up on them in the dark this way."

DOC SAVAGE'S plane was the large experimental job which he had developed in transparent plastic. Not that it was an invisible ship. Nothing of the kind. But the skin fabric was almost as transparent as glass, and some of the control cables were made of the same stuff, which was almost as tough as duralumin. The motor and the other solid parts were painted a dark color above to blend with the earth, a light color below to merge with the sky.

Riding along in the experimental craft was somewhat eerie, and did not please Monk. He picked his way through the cabin with a ghastly expression.

"If there was a hole in the floor of this thing, you couldn't see it!" he complained.

Pat watched the ground. "At least it makes sightseeing easy."

That was true. At first, they had felt no need whatever for windows. This was one of the great military values of the transparent plastic; it would enable the occupants to watch for attacking planes from any direction. But as the flight had progressed, the inevitable oil vapor from the motors had stained the plastic hull, hampering vision.

Renny pointed at the ground, rumbled, "Nice country for a giant to walk over."

"He would sure stub his toe," Pat agreed.

It was the rugged coast above Maine, a snaggle-toothed coastline that was noted for its high tides and brittle weather. The rocks were like black teeth, and, back inland, the earth had been clawed by the weather into great ravines that stretched for miles.

Long Tom Roberts lowered a telescope almost as long as his arm. He rubbed his eye. "They're about five thousand feet above us," he said. "Just went through that rift in the clouds. They seem to know where they're going."

"Ineluctable dialecticism," Johnny remarked.

"My, my," Pat said. "Two very nice words. What do they mean?"

"I think he means it's obvious," Long Tom said.

"What's obvious? Where Erica Ambler-Hotts and her three friends are going?"

"That's the idea."

"What makes it so obvious, if I may ask?"

"They've flown a straight line ever since they left Long Island," Long Tom pointed out. "That shows they know where they're going."

Monk grabbed a seat, felt of the transparent cushions to make sure they were solid, and sank on them. "Doc," he said.

"Yes?" called the bronze man. Doc was at the controls.

"You ever get that call to London through?" Monk asked.

"Yes."

"That Carl Morenta you asked for—isn't that a name you call to get hold of the head office of the British Army Intelligence service?" Monk inquired.

"Yes."

"I was just wondering," Monk continued, "why you went to such pains to let Erica Ambler-Hotts know you were calling Carl Morenta—"

Long Tom burst out in a howl of astonishment. "Down there!" he bellowed. He jabbed with his telescope. "Right north of that big ravine that runs down into the sea."

Monk stared. "What the heck is it? You've got the telescope."

"It's a man," Long Tom shouted.

Monk snorted. "What's so remarkable about a man?"

"This one," Long Tom said, "is falling up into the sky! If we keep going the way we are, we'll pass right by him. Or he'll pass by us."

Doc Savage said, "Get on your parachutes. Quick!"

There was a rippling grimness in the bronze man's tone that was like cold ice against their backs.

GETTING into a parachute is not something to be done in a hurry. There are two straps over the shoulders that snap together across the chest, and two more that snap, one around each leg. But haste makes an inexplicable snarl out of the webbing straps. Renny started it off nicely by getting the wrong 'chute. There was only one on the plane that would fit him. "Holy cow!" he rumbled.

It did not help that they all tried to watch the man falling up. By now, they could see the man falling up with their unaided eyes.

Also, they could see the plane ahead. The craft had turned suddenly, it appeared, and was coming back. It became more prominent in the morning sky.

Monk said, "Looks as if they've seen the man falling up, and are coming back to investigate."

He was wrong. How wrong, it was suddenly obvious when the other ship banked wildly.

"Gosh, looks as if they saw the man falling up, and are fleeing from him," Monk said.

Long Tom used his telescope. "The man is falling toward them," he yelled.

Ham said, "You're crazy. A man falls up. He Doesn't fall toward airplanes."

"Don't call me crazy!" Long Tom snapped. "You get in the habit of that, talking to Monk. It'll get you new skin on your nose if you aren't careful. And a man does *not* fall up!"

Ham shrugged. "Well, yonder is one falling somewhere."

Doc Savage asked, "Can you distinguish the features of the man who is falling up?"

Long Tom puckered an eye against the small end of the telescope. "Too far away," he said. "He's got his arms and legs spread out, stifflike."

The next development they could all see with naked eyes.

"I'll be superamalgamated!" said big-worded Johnny.

The occupants of the distant plane were jumping. Four figures in quick succession. Black forms that fell down through the sky.

"At least, *they* aren't falling up," Monk said.

They tumbled for a long way, almost to the earth, before the parachutes opened. As a result, they landed close together, coming down in a small clearing, the only one in miles, apparently.

The plane which they had deserted lifted its nose into a stall, fell off in a left spin and went down and down after them.

"Blazes!" Renny rumbled. He was pop-eyed. "The man who was falling up is now falling down."

The figure did not fall downward for long. It seemed to follow the spinning plane a while. Then it began dropping behind. It floated around idly. It started to fall up again. Then it changed direction.

"Holy cow!" Renny boomed. "Now, it's after *us!*"

Doc Savage spoke again, and there was more crashing concern in his voice than had been there when he had ordered them to put on the parachutes.

"Jump!" he said.

Stupefied, they watched the figure coming toward them. It was traveling, they began to realize, with surprising speed.

"Jump!" Doc Savage rapped. "Take to the parachutes. Do like the others did—fall to within a few hundred feet of the ground before you pull your ripcords."

DOC boosted open the door, began shoving the others out into space. Pat was pale when she went out. She did not care much for parachute jumping. Not that the others were enthusiastic about it, either. Monk and Ham carried their pets. Each animal had a collar, and they had snapped these inside the chest rings of their parachutes.

They fell for a long distance, closely packed, only a few score of yards between them. Then they cracked open the 'chutes, had a few moments to tug at shrouds to stop swaying and to direct their descent slightly. Then they were busy getting out of the harness, ready to free themselves the moment they hit ground, so that they would not be dragged.

Doc ran in search of the others. He found Monk first. Monk was sitting on the ground, as pale as anyone had ever seen him.

"What happened?" Doc asked.

"I aged fifty years in that jump," Monk said weakly. "My hog got to kicking around and got a leg through the ripcord ring so that I couldn't grab hold of it. I thought I was never going to crack that 'chute."

Ham came up in time to hear that and snort. "Your 'chute opened ahead of anyone else's."

Monk was too shaken to answer.

Doc Savage was watching the sky.

The others looked upward also. Suddenly, there was an explosion, a sharp blast, although not a terrific one. Distance took away some of its force.

What had happened was plain to the eye, but hard for a brain to accept. It was manifestly impossible. A man falling up was impossible, to begin with. And the fact that a man falling up could overtake a plane, plunge directly into the plane, and blow it to more or less small pieces— at least, into such a condition that it fell helplessly toward Earth—was even harder to accept rationally.

All of them watched, with breath corked tightly in their lungs, for the same thing—a glimpse of the man who had fallen up.

They did not see him.

They watched with eyes out and lips getting dry and arms and legs beginning to ache from being held stiff, until parts of the plane, heavier parts such as motor assembly, began striking the ground.

But no man!

"It was the man that blew up!" Monk breathed.

Ham's expression became strange. Suddenly, he emitted a blurt of laughter. "Blurt" was the word; the laughter came out of him without his consciously authoring it. It had a silly sound, so asinine that he caught his lips involuntarily.

Monk stared and asked, "What's the matter with you?"

Ham shook his head wordlessly. He was pale. The horrible jackass laugh he had made had given him a start. He was wondering if his mind had suddenly snapped, so that he was crazy.

Pat said, "I know how it feels. I could make a noise like that, too."

Big-fisted Renny Renwick nodded soberly. "It was the *man* blowing up. That's what does it for me."

"Does what?" Long Tom asked him.

"Makes me sure I'm crazy," Renny said.

Doc Savage said, "Do not let it worry you. There is a perfectly logical, if somewhat unusual, explanation."

Renny rumbled, "The only thing that would sound logical to me is that a man did not fall up."

A brisk twist of an emotion that probably was humor appeared in the bronze man's eyes.

"You can rest assured," he said, "that a man did not fall up."

Chapter XIII
DECEIT

ERICA AMBLER-HOTTS called: "Mr. Savage! Please don't answer me. Don't let them know where you are!" She was to the right, some distance away.

Her voice had a kind of vibrating terror.

"Get away if you can!" she added loudly. "Get plenty of help! Call on the American government. Telephone the Naval Intelligence department and tell them Morenta 72 told you to get help. Don't forget that—Morenta 72." Her tone got louder. "Repeat that name to be sure— No, no, don't! They might hear your voice and locate you. Please go!"

Monk said, "That girl sure sounds as if somebody was trying to make her eat a snake."

The bronze man made no audible comment. But he gestured emphatically, indicating that he and his men were to take cover and make no noise.

They crawled several yards. A wing fragment of their plane, the last to fall, hit the rocky ridge to the south.

Ham caught Doc's eye and used the deaf-and-dumb finger language to say, "I'm going to use Chemistry to spot them."

Doc nodded.

Ham collared his pet, and proceeded to give several hand signals. The chimp—or runt ape, for there was some scientific doubt about Chemistry's ancestry—seemed to understand.

Monk watched with no pleasure. He prided himself on the intelligence of his pet hog, Habeas Corpus. But it had not occurred to him to teach Habeas to understand hand signals which could be given silently.

Obeying Ham's gestures, Chemistry took to the trees.

"Humph!" Monk said.

They waited. The undergrowth, thick about them, was drawn tight with a kind of uneasy stillness. Not stillness, either. The sea was close by. The sound it made was a sobbing one, rising and falling, but it was always loud enough to cover small noises around them.

Finally, Chemistry dropped silently out of a tree near them. The chimp went to Ham, danced up and down, turned and took off the way he had come. He looked back with an almost human appeal for them to follow.

"Probably found a bird nest," Monk muttered. "He sucks eggs, doesn't he?"

Doc Savage asked, "Ham, will Chemistry guide me alone?"

"Probably," Ham admitted. "If you want to try it alone. But wouldn't it be safer if all of us—"

"You stay here," Doc said. "Do not move, and do not make any noise."

The bronze man moved after the chimp. He went quietly, so silently that it was uncanny. The chief of the Mok native tribe in the Amazon jungles who had taught him woodcraft would have been proud of the way he merged with the undergrowth and shadows.

Chemistry discovered that Doc alone was following, and showed a spell of indecision over the matter that would have embarrassed Ham. Doc repeated the gestures Ham had used. After he did it the second time, Chemistry surrendered and went ahead.

ERICA AMBLER-HOTTS was talking to the man called Stinky and the one who had played the part of Monk in the green-fog-and-fake-headquarters trick. There were other men. There was Freddy, the taxi driver who had been duped by Doc Savage into taking the bronze man from headquarters to the spot where Monk and the others were besieged on Long Island. Freddy wore a white bandage around his jaw, evidently part of repairs made necessary by the blow Doc Savage had struck.

Erica's three companions were there. Renny Renwick had described them as three very smooth-looking gentlemen who probably lived on sandpaper and nails. That was right. They looked exactly like that.

The three stood there, holding their hands in the air and looking like men who knew they were the same as dead.

Erica was smiling. She talked animatedly with Stinky and the fake Monk and the others.

It was clear that Erica was engaged in some kind of a double cross.

Doc Savage got the small telescope out of his clothing and began to watch the girl's lips. He was an excellent lip-reader. Her English accent, in so far as it changed her lip movements, bothered him slightly. But he was able to make out what she said.

His face got grim as he listened. One of the three smooth-looking men spoke angrily to Erica. She slapped the man. The fake Monk then knocked the fellow down. Erica showed her teeth in a kind of she-wolf smile that was utterly convincing—if one wanted to be convinced that she was a very capable thing which headed for a goal about the same as a bullet after it leaves an army rifle.

WHEN Doc Savage rejoined Monk and the others, Ham jumped and dropped his sword cane, which he had managed somehow to retain. The bronze man's reappearance was abrupt and silent. Chemistry dropped out of a tree beside the bronze man.

Ham pointed at Chemistry. "He find them for you?"

"Very efficiently," Doc replied. "How much equipment have we on hand?"

Monk and the others immediately dug into their clothing. They brought to life what was, in total, a startling assortment. It ranged from grenades—explosive, smoke, gas, flashers for producing momentary blindness—to several drums of cartridges for the supermachine pistols, gas equipment—masks, suits—and various other gadgets.

Doc selected certain items that surprised the others. Then he went away, silently as before.

IT was almost an hour later when Doc Savage appeared unexpectedly in front of Erica Ambler-Hotts.

"Oh!" exclaimed the English girl.

She was alone.

Doc asked, "Where are your companions?"

"They were captured," she said, without hesitating at all. "Why didn't you flee after I called to you?"

The bronze man shrugged. "It seemed senseless to get so close, then flee."

"You think you are close?"

He said, "This is one of the most deserted sections of the country. A very good place for a foreign power to land its agents and for them to headquarter."

She seemed startled. "You seem to know a great deal about this affair."

"It is clearing up, bit by bit." He gestured. "Suppose we join my men and Pat."

Erica nodded. Again her response was without hesitation. Doc indicated the direction they were to take. They walked through the undergrowth, using care in moving bushes, looking for the quiet places to put their feet. Monk and Renny were suddenly in front of them with machine pistols.

"Holy cow!" Renny said. "You were making so much noise we thought it must be someone else."

Erica showed surprise. "I thought we were being very quiet." She looked around. "You are all safe?"

Renny nodded.

Pat frowned at Erica. "How are you, Morenta 72?" she asked.

Erica stared at them. "You already knew I was a British agent, didn't you?"

Pat said, "Doc seemed to know it. He was going to call somebody named Morenta in England. What is Morenta? A password?"

Erica shook her head.

"Morenta isn't exactly a password," she said. "It is headquarters of a branch of English espionage service. There are various branches. The Morentas are engaged primarily in developing or securing war inventions. Each Morenta is a number rather than an individual. I happen to be Morenta 72."

Doc Savage said, "Tottingham Strand was once Morenta 7, was he not?"

Erica started. "How did you find that out?"

"I talked to Morenta 1 on the telephone after you fled," Doc explained.

"I fled because I knew you were getting too close to the truth," Erica frankly admitted. "Our orders are not to allow our identity or our missions to become known to outsiders, under any conditions. You were beginning to discover the truth. I had no choice but to clear out."

Doc said, "Morenta headquarters made that fairly clear. At least, they surmised that must be your motive."

Ham put in, "Miss Ambler-Hotts, you say Tottingham Strand used to be one of these Morenta agents?"

"Yes."

"I told you what happened," the girl said sharply. "A man named Coxwell was found murdered in Strand's apartment. And Strand disappeared."

"Who was Coxwell?"

"Another Morenta," Erica said.

Doc Savage put in, "What was behind the murder?"

"Didn't Morenta 1 tell you?"

"No."

"It's a long and bally involved story," Erica said. "We can't stay here. They are all through the woods. I think we can reach the spot where they keep their boat. I know where it is. Come on, and we'll straighten this out later."

Doc Savage said, "Good. We will travel in single file. You and I and Long Tom and Monk will lead. The others will follow."

The girl seemed dissatisfied. "How will they follow us? By keeping us in sight?"

Doc opened a small case. It contained a chemical and a pair of rather bulky goggles.

"The chemical is not noticeable to the unaided eye," he said. "But seen through these glasses, it is a brilliant yellow. We will blaze the trail with the chemical. The others will have the spectacles and can follow."*

Erica swallowed. "You fellows have the darnedest gadgets," she said.

Doc Savage, Monk, Long Tom and Erica moved forward. The girl led the way. From time to time, Doc Savage made brief marks with the swab contained in the bottle of chemical.

Erica was confident, moving straight ahead, as if her destination was definitely in mind. And it was.

THE destination was several men with rifles. One of them was the fake Monk. The cab driver called Freddy was another.

Freddy cocked his rifle, said, "One of you want to make a noise?"

Erica stamped a foot. "Quiet, you fool! His aides are following us. Be still. They will appear in a minute."

"Good," Freddy said.

They waited. Waited a long time. And no one came. Ham, Pat, Renny and Johnny did not put in their appearance.

Freddy growled, "He must have got wise."

Erica snapped. "He couldn't have. He did not speak a word to the others, except to tell them to follow. He did not even use that strange language in which they occasionally converse."

"Nevertheless," said Freddy, "something just must have come uncorked."

Doc Savage, Monk and Long Tom were led forward. There was no path, exactly. But men had gone that way before, frequently, always taking a slightly different route so that there would not be a trail.

Chapter XIV
BATTLE STATIONS SUBMERGED

THE trail led down to the sea, to a cove that was a cup in which green water churned and made sobbing noises among the rocks.

The boat in the cove was a sailing yacht, schooner rigged, not more than forty feet over all, slightly less at the waterline. A fat old woman of a hull, patched sails.

SEAGRID, NEW YORK

That was what lettering on the stern of the old boat said. But it was tied out there in the cove with lines that were too heavy.

They got into an old twelve-foot dinghy. The dinghy ferried them out to the schooner.

Freddy ordered: "Take them below."

A man shoved Monk. The homely chemist took a couple of steps, stopped, started to swing on the man who had pushed him. Then Monk became more interested in the construction of the boat. He stamped a foot.

"Doc, there's something phony about this hooker," he said. "It's made of steel."

He leaned forward suddenly to ogle the sails.

"Heck, these aren't sails!" he exploded. "They are made of steel and painted. Imitations. That's what they are!"

He got shoved again and was menaced with a rifle muzzle. They were pushed to a hatchway and started down a ladder. The ladder had wooden rungs for six feet, where there was an opening in the floor, then the rungs turned to steel, carrying them on down into the interior of the submarine.

DOC, Monk and Long Tom were locked in a steel compartment that was evidently the skipper's cabin.

Monk expressed his feelings by kicking the door.

"It looks like we're mixed up in an international incident," he complained.

"If you ask me," Long Tom said, "we fell for a woman's story."

Doc said, "Do not be too concerned about it."

They gaped at him. "Doc, you don't mean you expected this to happen?"

"Something like it," the bronze man said. He was without expression.

That was all they got out of Doc Savage, because he began to comment on the cleverness of the submarine disguise. The imitation boat which had been constructed around the conning tower. The bronze man seemed to have an extensive knowledge of the craft, because he mentioned the way it was jointed, how it was fastened to the conning tower structure so that, in an emergency, it could be jettisoned by mechanical means. The entire craft was of steel, so cleverly fashioned that they had not realized it was not a genuine yacht until after they were aboard it.

"The periscope," Doc explained, "is actually inside the mast. Presumably, it is an accessory periscope and can be cast off when the false structure is released.

"The disguise is particularly effective," he added, "because it gives the submarine a means of working along the coast and enabling it to enter almost any harbor which it would care to enter. The underwater surface of the submarine is painted so that only a close observer from an airplane would notice anything peculiar. Then, from an airplane, it would only appear that the schooner was underway, leaving a wake. The boat structure is on the forward portion of the submarine, and the after portion is painted white, mottled so that from a height it would look like a wake being trailed by the schooner."

Monk was suspicious by now.

"Doc, you seem to know a lot about this sub," he said.

Doc Savage dropped the subject of the submarine without making an answer. He selected a chair, looked over the reading matter the cabin offered, and selected a copy of the "Atlantic Pilot," the government volume of information for masters of small coastwise vessels.

WHEN Pat, Ham and Long Tom were brought aboard, not more than half an hour had gone by. The three prisoners were marched past and crowded into a steel niche that passed for a cabin across the corridor.

"How did you get caught?" Monk asked.

"Your blasted hog," Ham said. "They trailed him to us." Then, after Monk had felt the shock, Ham corrected: "They just had a piece of luck and caught us."

"Where is Johnny?"

"They're hunting him," Ham explained.

"This gets no better fast," Monk muttered.

Another forty-five minutes brought Erica Ambler-Hotts to the small steel network which ventilated the steel door. She was sobbing.

"They will not let him go," she said.

Doc asked, "Let who go?"

"Poor Tot," she said stiffly. "Tot Strand. They promised to free him if I would trick you into a trap."

From across the steel hall, Pat said, "I like that bargain, sister. I hope I get my hands on you."

Erica tightened. "Oh, it was dirty! But I thought you could take care of yourselves. And I wanted poor Tot out of it."

Pat snapped, "Why should you think they would keep their word?"

"Why not?" Erica sounded baffled. "They have all of Tot's notes, his apparatus, his working models. They even have the Compound Monk that Tot came to America to get."

Doc Savage put in, "They do not have the Compound Monk. We misled Strand into thinking he had taken it."

"Then they lied to me," Erica said miserably. "They told me they wanted merely to seize you and hold you prisoner so that you would not molest them until they got back to Europe. But that wasn't it; they wanted to force you to give up the Compound Monk."

A man came down the corridor hurriedly, a sailor in the uniform of one of the warring nations.

"Ruhig!" he yelled. "Quiet! What is this?"

Erica Ambler-Hotts whirled, said, "Get away from me, you lying pig!" She had a wrench under her arm, and she suddenly tried to lay it against the sailor's head. He dodged, clutched the girl. She crowded the sailor against the door of Doc's cell. Doc managed to get two fingers through the steel grille, and clamped them on the sailor's arm. It was not much of a grip. The sailor began to scream. More sailors came, struggled and got the sailor loose.

"Meine mutter!" he croaked. "He tore the flesh out of my arm!"

A sailor shoved a pistol through the grille and fired five times. It was for effect. The effect was impressive. The bullets moved around like hornets, splashing lead that was like driving red-hot needles.

The group spent the next fifteen minutes hunting in their hides for particles of lead.

"That looked impressive," Monk said. "What kind of an act do you suppose it was?"

"No trick," Doc said.

"Huh?"

"She told too much of the truth that time," Doc said.

Long Tom complained, "I like this less and less. These cookies are nail-eaters from way back. When they go to work on us for information, it will not be any taffy pull."

THE door of their cubicle had no inner lock, so that when sailors came for them, there was not much they could do about it. They were led to the control room below the conning tower. Another group arrived shortly with Pat, Ham and Long Tom.

The hatch was open above their heads. They could look straight up through it and see two or three stars, motionless in an inky night. The night wind was like a perfume after the oil stench.

A tall, dark, handsome man faced them. He said, "I want information, *bitte,"* with a heavy accent. "You will tell me where is the other member of your party. The one called Johnny."

Monk said, "You want in on a little secret, brother?"

The man bowed politely. "Yes, of course."

"We will tell you nothing," Monk said. "Not even the time of day."

A half inch of red appeared above the handsome man's collar. "You misunderstood us," he said. "We wish no trouble with you." His face was wooden. "Where is Johnny?"

"Mister, trouble is what I'd like to have with you," Monk told him.

The half inch of red became an inch, and the man suddenly popped his palms together, as if he was summoning a waiter.

"Bring Strand," he ordered.

He did not look irritated, but he must have been in a bad humor, from the way the sailors jumped. Four of them double-quicked out. While they were gone, no one said anything. They came back with Strand.

Tottingham Strand had not been improved by handling. One eye resembled an apple that had been in the hot sun too long. Skin was missing from his knuckles. Among other missing things was a smile, more skin, a shirt sleeve, and possibly a handful of hair, although it was hard to be positive about the latter.

Monk told him, "You look as if you and our friends here have had a conference."

Strand said five words which expressed fully his opinion of his captors. Some of the captors got red necks. Pat smiled.

"Beg pardon," Strand told Pat.

"It's all right," Pat told him. "I was trying to think of something like that to say."

Strand bowed slightly. "Thank you."

He was calm enough. His surface was ice. His eyes and his muscles were like edged steel.

Doc Savage asked in a conversational tone, "They have everything but the Compound Monk, have they not?"

Strand returned the bronze man's look with no visible emotion. "Yes," he said. "They have. But then, they have had it for weeks. I was not aware of it until two days ago."

"How did you make the discovery?" Doc asked.

The man called Freddy put in, "Shut up, you two—"

"Let them talk, please!" snapped the handsome man. His tone left no doubt about who was boss here.

"My friend Rod Bentley—the only real friend I had in the world—found it out for me," Strand told Doc Savage. "He discovered they were conducting experiments in that green building in New York City. We went there to investigate. I was cautious, and Rod was reckless. I would not go into the building. He went in instead. They caught and killed him. And when they killed him, they demonstrated that they had my invention."

Doc asked, "There was no green chest?"

Strand shook his head. "There was never one."

"You told us a man named Montgomery gave you a green chest to keep," Doc reminded.

"I told you several things that were not quite true," Strand said.

MONK put in disgustedly, "No green chest, no green fog, no sense to anything. What is this, anyway? Did a man fall up or didn't he?"

Strand showed his teeth briefly. "A man did not fall up. Not at any time."

Monk started to say something else, but caught Doc's eye. Monk went silent.

Doc asked, "Strand, you came to America to get the formula for Compound Monk?"

"Correct."

"It is essential for the operation of your device?"

"Correct again."

"How did you expect to get the Compound Monk?"

Strand's smile was steel. "By stealth or by force. Any way I could."

Doc said, "You did not think of trying a frank approach on the subject?"

Strand shrugged. "I thought that out. It was no good. To get the formula, I would have to explain things. You are too smooth to be fooled. I tried to concoct some jim-crack invention that I could use to make you think I needed the formula for some innocent purpose. It was what you Americans call 'no dice.' I knew I couldn't deceive you. So I wasn't trying."

Doc said, "But others—these fellows we are mixed up with—went ahead and tried a trick."

Strand nodded. "I guess you know what they did. They used that fake headquarters gag, and the phony Monk and Ham. They thought you could be taken in, particularly after they used the stuff that made the green fog effect in your eyes. They were after the formula, which they didn't have. They were in the same position as I myself; they had my invention, but it was useless without the key secret, which you had developed, and which no one but yourself knew. Of course, I didn't know at first that they had my invention."

"You first found out your device was in their hands when?" Doc inquired.

"Two days ago," Strand said.

"How?"

"My friend Rod Bentley told me."

"That was the first time you realized?"

"Yes."

Doc Savage was silent a moment. During the interval, he made the small trilling which was his peculiarity when disturbed. Monk and the others stared at him, puzzled.

Doc inquired, "What were you going to do with the device in the end, Strand?"

Strand became strangely white. "What do you think?"

"I do not believe," Doc told him, "that you were going to sell it."

The whiteness went slowly out of Strand's face. He smiled, and it was the first genuine smile any of them had seen on his face.

"Thank you," he said. "But you are wrong, in a way. I wanted the device to make a trade."

"Trade?"

Strand asked stiffly, "You know my record in England?"

"You mean the murder and treason charges?"

Strand displayed his eyeteeth. "I see you do know. Yes, that is it. I was going to try to trade this gadget for freedom from the charge."

"Trade it to the English government?"

Strand drew himself erect. "Exactly."

Quick and warm lights of approval appeared briefly in the bronze man's strangely flake-gold eyes.

"Did you receive offers from others?" Doc indicated their captors. "From these gentlemen, for instance?"

Strand stared at the dark handsome man, at Freddy, with contempt. "You would not believe how much they offered me," he said.

Doc Savage said nothing.

After a while, Strand lowered his eyes. "This may not matter," he said. "But if I get out of this, there will be no trade. I will give the thing to America and England jointly."

Doc said, "You mean that?"

Something in the bronze man's voice startled

the darkly handsome man. The fellow's hand made a flashing gesture, and held a gun. He held the weapon with muzzle on the floor, said, "You had better lift your hands, Mr. Savage."

Doc did not move.

"Schnell!" the man snapped. "Quickly! Your hands!"

Doc put up his arms, and his hands touched an I-beam which comprised one of the submarine ribs. Only Ham was watching the bronze man closely, and he saw what none of the others had noticed—a small globule, not larger than a pigeon egg, fastened to the side of the beam with a strip of adhesive tape. Ham saw Doc pluck the object loose.

Observing the bronze man get hold of the gadget in such a fashion, Ham understood something.

He became positive that Doc had been aboard the submarine earlier in the day.

Ham shut his eyes tightly. He knew what was coming, was prepared for it. Even then, with his eyes shut and his nerves steeled, he got a shock.

The object was a flash grenade. Tiny as the thing was, it gave off a completely blinding light. Actually, what it emanated was more than light. The chemical contents burned in such a fashion that they emitted rays of a wavelength extremely shocking to the optic nerves. The effect was something like looking at an arc welding flame for a period of time, except that it was created in a fraction of a minute.

Following the flash, a man screamed and a pistol exploded. Feet pounded up the steel companionway. They got the hatch closed.

"Crash dive!" shouted the dark, good-looking man. He repeated the order in his native tongue.

There was fighting. Monk was one of the battlers. Monk's warfare was always noisy. A pair of fists were making big noises, which was probably Renny. The place began to fill with sailors who were not blinded.

The submarine began sinking under their feet, rumbling a little, water displacing air in the tanks.

Doc said loudly, "Monk, Renny—stop fighting! We have no chance of breaking out of here!"

"Holy cow!" Renny complained.

But they stopped.

Chapter XV
THE WARSHIP

THE bronze man's next statement made Renny feel better.

Doc said, "Commander, you will surrender to us immediately."

The dark man jumped. He said several things which were not complimentary and which expressed his personal feelings thoroughly.

Doc said, "Very well."

"Was nun?" the man snapped. "What do you mean—very well?"

"You might," Doc said, "put a man on your underwater sonic apparatus."

The dark man swore and yelled at a sailor. The underwater sonic equipment was part of all warship equipment. In the present modern form, it was a most efficient device for locating a ship by the sound of its engines and propellers.

The sailor made an excited report. "A vessel," he said. "Very near, sir."

"What type?"

The listener-operator seemed puzzled.

An expert trained for the job could identify craft—tell destroyer from cruiser, freighter from battleship—by the difference in sound.

"Rather difficult to identify, sir," he reported.

"What is it?" yelled the commander.

Suddenly nervous, the listener said, "It is a strange type of vessel, sir."

Doc Savage spoke again. His voice had volume enough to cut through the excitement and a calm power that was convincing.

"Tune your radio to the Navy band," he directed.

The commander stared, whirled and gave an order to that effect. The radio room, for convenience, adjoined the control compartment. The operator cut in a loudspeaker, from which a brisk voice came, saying, "Crew 7, how are you coming with those mines across the cove entrance?"

The radio clicked off, came on again, and another voice, very muffled, said, "We are on the fourth row, lieutenant. A fish could hardly get out of that cove now, much less a submarine."

"Good," said the first voice. "Send one of the light boats into the cove and put down a small depth charge."

There was a short wait. Then the listener reported, "A boat seems to be coming closer, sir. I do not identify its motor. It has a strange sound."

He hardly finished when there was a thumping jar. The submarine rolled violently, tumbling people off their feet. Monk took occasion to land a hard blow on a sailor's square jaw. Another sailor instantly menaced the homely chemist with a pistol.

Ham, suddenly pale, warned, "They'll shoot you, Monk!"

The radio said, "Hello, the submarine. *Wie geht es Ihnen?* How are you?"

There was deathly stillness. Somewhere, a thin stream of water was snarling through a sprung seam.

"Hello, the submarine," said the radio voice.

"You better answer us if you know what is good for you."

There was another silence, and it was pretty bad.

Doc Savage said, "I suggest you answer. At this close range, your radio will function."

The commander swore. He sounded as if something had hold of his throat.

The radio said, "Light boat, put down another small depth charge."

They were prepared for the blast that came, but it was bad anyway. The submarine rolled, jarred. The backrush of water into the vacuum created by the blast made a suction that lifted the conning tower hatch, and a sheet of spray knifed in and drenched them. It shut off in an instant, but everyone dodged wildly.

The radio said remorselessly, "Hello, submarine!"

More silence. And a sailor made the sounds of a small duck as he breathed.

From the radio: "All right. We won't fool with them anymore. Boats 5 and 9. Get in there with heavy depth charges. Blow all the water out of that cove."

With a face completely drained of everything including expression, the submarine commander stepped to the radio room door.

"Tell them we surrender," he said.

The radio operator relayed the information, having difficulty with his English.

The radio, in great relief, said, "I'll be superamalgamated!"

DOC SAVAGE hit the control panel as Renny got a sailor by the neck and bellowed, "Holy cow! He gave it away!" Monk, for once, was a little slow getting into a fight. The homely chemist had known it was Johnny up there somewhere, but he had not expected Johnny in his excitement to use a big word and give away the deception. He was caught by surprise. Johnny usually did not make mistakes in a crisis.

The others—Ham and Long Tom and Pat—joined the fight. Renny slammed his victim against a bulkhead. He went on in a rush for the engine room. Distances were short inside the submarine. He got to the engine room. Being an engineer, Renny knew the intricacies of a submarine. He knew that, if they could blow the air supply out of the tanks, the submarine would not dare submerge again. Because, without compressed air, it could not expel water from the tanks to rise again. He worked valves, at the same time shouting at astonished engineers that they were prisoners.

JOHNNY

At the control room valves and levers, Doc Savage did the same thing Renny was attempting—blew the tanks and brought the submarine to the surface like a cork.

They could hear the rush and roar as the sub broke surface.

"It is a trick!" screamed the commander. "Down again! Quickly!"

But there was no trick about the sudden rending blast from the bow section. Nothing false about the stream of water that flooded through a gaping aperture.

Johnny had put a high explosive grenade against the bow of the submarine as soon as it came out of the water.

Doc said loudly, "Get overboard. The boat is going to sink." He repeated it in the language the sailors spoke, for effect.

The fighting broke up in an anxious rush for the conning tower hatch. Monk and Doc fought side by side, with fists.

"Strand, can you swim?" Doc demanded.

"Excellently," Strand said. He was cool again. "So can Miss Ambler-Hotts."

"The north shore of the inlet," Doc said.

"Right-o." Strand took Erica's arm, started her up the companion stairs. He followed.

There was no actual fighting now, only struggle to get out. Water coming in the rent bow was like roaring thunder. Doc Savage backed his men to the ladder. They climbed, Pat first, then Ham and Renny and Monk and Long Tom. Doc followed them, kicking off clutching hands.

"The north shore," he said.

As they swam away they could hear the commander bellowing to his men to head for the south shore.

Johnny was standing in the shallow water, holding a long paddle affair and a notched stick with which he had been imitating the underwater sound of a boat.

Monk scrambled out beside him and said, "Those big words of yours danged near upset the cart."

"I'll be superamalgamated!" Johnny gasped. "What happened? What went wrong? I imitated boats, used the radio and threw hand grenades into the water near the submarine, just as Doc had planned. What went wrong?"

Monk said, "A word."

"Eh?"

"That 'superamalgamated.'"

"I do not," said Johnny, "comprehend."

"You were imitating a navy in first-class style," Monk told him. "In fact, you were a regular warship all by yourself. Then you got excited and used that word."

"I—" Johnny groaned. "I did, didn't I? It slipped out. I'll be superamalgamated!"

"The word," Monk assured him, "expresses what danged near happened to us."

Someone took a shot at them with a sidearm. They crawled away. Rocks shoved up around them, heavy cover. They took shelter.

Doc asked, "Did you contact the Coast Guard by radio, Johnny?"

Johnny was gloomy. "Yes, they will be here shortly."

Erica Ambler-Hotts put a hand on Doc's arm. "It looks as if you pulled a trick of your own."

Ham told her, "Doc saw you getting the ultimatum to turn him in to save Strand's life. He can read lips. He knew you agreed. So he hatched a scheme."

Erica was silent a moment. "The submarine was mentioned in that conversation. The fact that the supposed sailing craft in the cove was really the sub."

"Right," Monk told her. "So Doc went aboard."

Erica gasped. "I do not see how he could do that," She turned to Doc. "How did you manage?"

Doc said, "It was luck, largely. The guard on the forward deck mistook my voice for that of the man they called Freddy. I went below and made a tour of the vessel, managing to plant various gadgets."

"You put the flash grenade—I guess you call it that—on the control room ceiling, then?"

"Yes," Doc admitted. "However, there were other gadgets concealed at various vantage points. We had the submarine well prepared for a fight when we permitted ourselves to be seized and taken aboard."

Ham added something else. "The submarine couldn't have left the cove, anyway."

Astonished, Erica demanded, "Why not?"

"Doc jammed the steering mechanism when he was aboard."

The beam of a searchlight appeared like a white needle out of the sea, and Ham said, "That must be the Coast Guard."

Which was a good guess.

Chapter XVI
THE FRIEND

SUNLIGHT slanted against the panes of Doc Savage's skyscraper laboratory and was cut into thin bright sheets by the Venetian blinds. Rooftops were a forest below the windows, and out beyond, the vista was lost in a blue haze of incipient fog.

Doc Savage watched Tottingham Strand without emotion. "You are sure, Strand, that you wish to give this thing to the American and British governments jointly."

"Right," Strand said. Much of the steel was gone from Strand's manner, as if something bitter had been taken out of his existence.

"You understand this is no trade. It will not affect the murder and treason charges which are against you."

Strand nodded. "I understand that fully."

Pat came into the room. She was looking pleased with herself and, in the frock she was wearing, she was something to make men walk into lampposts.

Pat indicated the roof. "Those generals and other officers are ready for the demonstration," she said.

Doc Savage nodded.

Erica Ambler-Hotts jumped to her feet. She took Strand's hand. "Tot, I'm glad you did this," she said.

Strand's eyes fell. "I'm not proud," he muttered. "I should have done it in the first place. It makes me no happier, because I know exactly why I didn't. I was looking out for myself. I wanted to trade the thing for my freedom."

Erica said, "You were always an efficient fellow, Tot."

"Sure," Strand agreed wryly. "And see what it got me?"

Erica smiled. "It is getting America and England an amazing war weapon. You are giving it to them voluntarily, Tot. Nothing can take that from you. You have not only a great inventive mind, Tot. You have a heart."

She kissed Strand then, and nobody was surprised. Her tone had said that was exactly what she was going to do.

Strand's reaction was a little more surprising. He seemed to tighten from head to toes, then give way. His arms went about Erica, and he buried his face against her hair. They saw that there were tears in his eyes.

Ham looked on, utterly disgusted. He knew love when he saw it. What disgusted him was the fact that he had been giving Erica some admiring attention himself.

Monk shoved open the reception room door without knocking, looked at the embraced couple, grimaced, said, "Anybody want to look at what the Coast Guard caught?"

Strand and Erica came apart, wheeled.

Monk said, "I only brought one. The Coast Guard caught most of them. But this was the really interesting specimen."

Monk shoved a man into the room, a man who somehow resembled a whipped bull pup.

"Rod Bentley!" gasped Strand.

Rod Bentley said nothing. There seemed to be nothing he could say. The handcuffs on his wrists were explanation enough of his present status.

Strand said finally, "I looked on you as the best friend I ever had." He laughed. It was not pleasant. "You made a fool of me in the greatest way."

Rod Bentley stared at space.

Strand said, "Rod, you were an enemy agent?"

Bentley curled his lips slightly. "I am not English. I am proud of it."

Monk said, "Bentley was kind enough to explain why he disappeared so that you would think he was dead. He had the idea Miss Ambler-Hotts had gotten wise to the fact that he was not what he secmed."

"I did suspect," Erica said. "I never told Tot, because no one could have made him believe. That, incidentally, is why I was seized by the agents here in the city after Tot called on me."

Strand seemed beyond words.

Doc Savage produced a packet of papers bound with a rubber band. "This seems to be an appropriate time for these." He tossed the packet on the table. "Your pardon, Strand."

Strand nodded slowly. "Pardon?"

Doc nodded at the documents. "The orders Rod Bentley received over a period of two years. He kept them. They were on the submarine. I found them when I went over the craft before we faked the capture and were brought aboard."

Strand looked at the papers as if they were gold. "What do you mean by the word 'Pardon'?"

Doc said, "Rod Bentley rigged the murder of which you are accused. His orders there will show that. He planted the suspicion of Coxwell, the man you killed. He planted suspicion of you also. Then he told Coxwell you were framing him, and egged Coxwell into attacking you. He warned you, and you killed Coxwell when he came."

Strand shut his eyes tightly. "So that is how it happened."

Doc added, "They wanted you to be an outlaw. It would give them a chance to buy your contraption."

Strand's nod was slow. "Yes, I can see, now,"

Pat said, "They're about ready on the roof."

THE thing was about seven feet high and fatter than a man because it was full of gas. It looked somewhat like a man, too, because there were four distended limbs that somewhat resembled arms and legs. On the ends of these projections were the devices that made the thing so uncanny.

The assembled Army officers, United States and British, watched with interest.

Tottingham Strand told them, "The device really has two vital parts. First is the gas, which is lighter than air and highly explosive. Thus, I get both lift and explosive violence in one operation."

"What," asked an officer, "makes it go fast enough to overtake a plane?"

"The rocket principle," Strand said.

"A thing as light as that could not carry enough rocket fuel to push it around over the sky until it found a plane," said the officer.

Strand nodded agreement. "The rocket fuel will drive it only a mile or two. As a matter of fact, it cannot overtake a fast plane. But it can *meet* one."

He stepped over and slashed a cord which held the unusual manlike gadget to the roof. The thing immediately began rising.

"A man falling up," Renny rumbled. "Holy cow!"

Strand said, "Watch. It will rise slowly to five thousand feet, when the built-in altimeter will automatically arm the detonator device. The thing thereafter will be explosive upon contact. Somewhat like an ordinary mine."

The Army man said, "It hits a plane and explodes. We understand that."

"Right-o." Strand smiled. "The altimeter keeps it from being effective below five thousand feet. Your own planes can fly under it with perfect safety."

"Won't it chase them?"

"No. The pursuit device cuts in at the same time the detonators are armed."

"Then this altimeter arrangement will keep it from rushing at objects on Earth?"

"Yes," Strand said.

"But it will chase any moving thing in the sky?"

"Not *any* moving thing," Strand corrected. "Only very hot objects, such as airplane motors giving off heat and movement."

The Army man grunted. "Will you explain that fully?"

Strand hesitated, then turned to Doc Savage. "Mr. Savage, would you attempt that? I am afraid I cannot go into the details without becoming too technical."

Doc Savage nodded quietly. "You gentlemen," he told the Army men, "are familiar with the ordinary photoelectric cell which is in light meters."

"I've got one for my camera," admitted an officer. "It registers light. That's all I know about it."

Doc nodded again. "The device in Mr. Strand's apparatus is similar in principle," he said. "The photoelectric cell is composed of a compound which, upon the absorption of motion, ejects two electrons. This compound differs in that the absorption of motion and heat by its atoms leads to the ejection of three electrons."

The officer pondered. "I take it that one of the arms which is nearest a plane motor picks up this radiation, and that sets off the rocket affair so as to drive the thing in that direction. That it?"

"That," Doc said, "is exactly it."

"What is this compound?"

"It is called Compound Monk."

Ham pointed upward. "The thing is after a plane now," he said.

Strand watched placidly. "There is no need for alarm," he said. "The pilot of the plane understands that the gas will not explode because the detonators have been removed."

They watched the device strike the army plane in the sky. The pilot shut off his motors before the collision occurred, so that no harm was done. The plane began to spiral slowly toward Floyd Bennett Airport. They saw the crew reach out with hooks attached to poles and gather the device into the ship.

"Holy cow!" Renny muttered.

LATER, Monk got Doc aside. Monk was perturbed.

"Who named that stuff Compound Monk?" he demanded. "How come I never knew about this?"

The bronze man smiled slightly. A display of emotion was rare with him. "It seemed a good idea at the time," he said.

"I don't get it," Monk growled.

Pat overheard and laughed. "I thought it was a perfect name," she said. "This compound is very sensitive to the presence of movement and warmth. It chases movement and warmth. Everyone knows that you chase after any pretty girl who happens along. Both you and Compound Monk chase hot numbers. Get it?"

Monk didn't like getting it.

"I can see that was one of Ham's ideas," he growled. "Where is that shyster? I'll make a compound out of him."

DOC Savage sat at a dinner in a restaurant with Monk and a friend.

The girl appeared and walked directly to their table. She was very pretty. She was a stranger. She seemed to know what she was doing.

She carried a small soft purse and she jammed this against Doc Savage's left side below the shoulder blade and squeezed.

Then she opened the purse, took out the hypo needle which she had just emptied into Doc Savage's back and placed it on the table in front of them.

"You naturally know what that is," she said. "However, it might be interesting if you also knew it was—*was*, mind you—filled with germs."

Doc Savage contemplated the girl.

"What," he asked, "do I do now?"

"You help me," the girl said. "I need your help. I had to have it; so I used those germs on you. You've now got to do something about those germs, and you can't do anything about them without helping me. Get the idea?"

"This seems a little strange," Doc said.

"You haven't seen anything yet," the girl said. "Wait until you find out about the three wild men."

THE END

INTER ISSION by Will urray

Two imaginative novels from 1942 comprise this volume of Doc Savage adventures. Although written months apart, *The Man Who Fell Up* and *The Three Wild Men* were published in consecutive issues during the thick of World War II.

During the war years, Lester Dent was living comfortably in La Plata, Missouri, going into New York several times a year to confer with his editor, John L. Nanovic, over future plots. When this was not possible, Nanovic would mail Dent story springboards from which to work. Both of our selections commenced from these plot premises.

The Man Who Fell Up was written in July of 1941, from a two-page Nanovic premise. It ran:

> Doc Savage is in his office, 85th [*sic*] story. The day is heavy with fog; all you can see looking out the window is fog. Monk comes in. Then, all of a sudden, Doc seems to lose his senses. It seems to him he gets dizzy and slumps down in his seat. But it is only momentary. He snaps out of it. False Monk is there, asking him whether he feels okay. Doc does. False Ham comes in. Doc looks around. Same office. Same fog outside. But, though Monk and Ham look real, Doc knows they're not.
>
> What has happened [is] that Doc has been cleverly kidnapped. The villain has set up another office, just like Doc's, <u>including</u> most of the gadgets which are supposedly known only to Doc and his men. The villain waits for a foggy day, when he pulls his trap on Doc, and transports Doc, while knocked out by queer gas, to the fake office, where he maintains foggy atmosphere artificially.

REASON:

> Battle over new radio-beam idea that would be worth a fortune commercially, for transport planes, etc., or worth a great deal for enemy power as equipment for bombing planes. The two-fold purpose of the invention can be used to put more suspense in story as to what real purpose is.
>
> The villain wants Doc to be away from his office for just about a day, because that is the time the inventor of this new device is coming to Doc to offer it to him for final polishing and adjustment. So villain, taking Doc away, substitutes himself for Doc. His purpose is to prove to inventor gadget is no good, at the same time taking finished idea for his own purpose. He expects the inventor will not believe him, but he had that fixed; he will change an adjustment in the mechanism so that when inventor uses it, it means destruction.
>
> His plans go all right until Doc gets back, transported to his place exactly the same way he was taken away. Villain had gotten onto all of Doc's gadgets except one, which records everything that takes place in his office, and projects it on special sheet (similar to the radio newscasts which print paper in subscribers' homes) which is

in Doc's Hudson River hangar. Doc, knowing this, purposely allows kidnapping to go through as planned, and then starts on trail. First, he gets to inventor's gadget and corrects it, so that the plane crash does not happen. That brings villain out stronger, and Doc begins his work.

> Result: Doc had, by his aid, saved the inventor's gadget, and even improved it. It remains American property, good for commercial flying, and not for war purposes. Villain is caught and punished. Villain's intention was to hold up passenger companies for vast sums for his gadget, as well as offer it to warring nations willing to pay biggest price.

Attached to the premise was a clipping from the New York *Times*, dated April 27, 1941, describing a new radio-beam invention, which allowed pilots to tune in on ordinary commercial radio broadcasts emanating from both their departure and destination cities, and remain on course without the need for reliance on the old-style radio-beam, which can be lost and hard to recover. By this method, a transatlantic pilot could fly a true course between New York and London simply by tuning into radio stations in both cities. The article also mentioned the new beam system's value for military bombing runs. This latter wrinkle inspired the plot.

From this springboard, Dent presumably produced a typical Doc Savage outline, a chapter-by-chapter description of the action. It does not survive, however. For unknown reasons, Lester threw out the radio-beam invention, substituting a more imaginative creation of his own. Once John Nanovic approved this, Dent was off and writing. Nanovic does not seem to have complained about the substitution.

One element in the story—which was never seen again—was Doc's new transparent aircraft. It was not an original concept. Such a plane was showcased in an early issue of *The Avenger*. In one 1940 editorial, Nanovic talked about this idea, and others:

> In our *Doc Savage Magazine*, we have Doc Savage use all kinds of modern scientific instruments and apparatus, and we can check each year and prove that the 'far-fetched' device, such as a flashlight without batteries; a portable receiver and transmitting set ; infrared lanterns; aerial torpedoes, and others that we used have become practical. For example, we used an airplane made of plastic glass in one of our stories; six months later, such an airplane was announced as practical.

Some have pointed to both of these aircraft as sources for Wonder Woman's famous Invisible Plane, but it seems to have been inspired by a real-life prototype. Besides, it debuted late in 1941,

Lester Dent

before *The Man Who Fell Up* was published.

When Lester turned in the finished manuscript, Nanovic complained that it was unusually short. He also asked Lester not to reference the war in Europe going forward, writing, "First, don't put a war flavor in either of the two you have. We don't want to get too much war stuff or even comment on war, in them. In this one, we can't get out of it, so we'll let it go."

No doubt that was the main reason Nanovic put that story aside for a full year. *Doc Savage* sales had slumped in the summer of 1940—a problem plaguing other pulp magazines that year. Perhaps it was held back until overall sales picked up.

Nanovic also asked for significant revisions on this story, something that was rare with Dent's fiction:

> It looks as if you are overdoing the mystery part of it—the part that keeps the reader in the dark as to what all this is going on for. Although it pays to keep the reader wondering, I think you've got to give him a bite or two, occasionally, to keep his curiosity aroused, and to keep him from figuring that the thing is a little too deep for him. You've done that well, as a rule, explaining a little of the mystery from time to time. But keeping the payoff until the end. In this one, you haven't; it keeps mysterious right along, and tends to get a little confusing as a result.
>
> For example, (unless I missed these things in reading) you make no real explanation of the green mist. You say what it is, how administered, but don't exactly say what purpose intended for. In addition to the point that the crooks don't want Doc to recognize the fake office, it would slow Doc up, etc. And how about explaining where the fake office was? How did Doc get in it, etc.?
>
> This also holds true, here and there, for spot explanation of what the characters are doing.
>
> Since the British guy came over here to get Compound Monk, how did he know what it was, and where to get it? Were Doc's experiments made public, or how? And, presumably, the device he had worked out, had worked, therefore he had to have something like Compound Monk already—so why did he have to go to all this trouble to get Compound Monk? If he didn't have the stuff to make it work, how did he know that Compound Monk would be the thing to make it work, etc? This is pretty much up in the air in my mind. Perhaps, in reading over your copy, you might see all the answers.
>
> Even so, they should be pointed up somewhat. I usually read the manuscript fast in a first reading—but that's how readers probably read it. If I miss stuff, they might miss it, too, so it's best to play safe.
>
> Finally, in the end, I think a few more explanations as to the benefit of the weapon in preventing bomb attacks, on open cities, etc., are in order. The ending doesn't show the weapon emphatic enough to make all the trouble worthwhile.
>
> Of course, as I said, these are all questions after a swift reading. Maybe a careful reading will find the answers—but we've got to make them a little more clear than that. See what you think about it after going through your copy, and then we can figure out what to do. There's no particular hurry on it, as I have scheduled it for a later issue.

During the long period this story lay dormant, America's entry into the war no doubt occasioned additional editorial tinkering, too. Doc's men are now involved in Defense Board work, something that would not have been the case prior to Pearl Harbor. And the villains are obviously German Nazis.

When *The Man Who Fell Up* did come into rotation, it happened to fall on the month when the American Magazine Association called for its publishers to display an American flag on their July, 1942 covers in solidarity with a nation at war. We were approximately six months into the war at that point. An estimated 500 magazines—including comic books—participated.

Street & Smith decided to commission artist Charles De Feo to paint a single flag image, and run it on almost every cover for that month. Every S&S pulp, from *Astounding Science Fiction* to *Wild West Weekly*, ran that same image. A few slick exceptions, such as *Charm*, opted for their own upscale version. This probably didn't help sales any, but it sure saved S&S on their art budget that month!

The year of 1942 was a tough one for pulp magazine publishers and S&S was not immune from the austerity measures that war was imposing on everyone. Paper rationing was already underway, and it became increasingly clear that the longer the war dragged on, the more mid-range magazines would have to be sacrificed to be able to print the best-selling titles. Wartime demand for reading material was ferocious. Returns were miniscule. Even weak titles were selling out of their print runs! So difficult choices would have to be made.

Doc Savage magazine, which had been tottering on the edge of a major retrenching in the latter months of 1941, and would probably have been demoted to bimonthly frequency, slowly slid back into the black. And there it would remain all through the austere war years.

The Three Wild Men was written in January of 1942—a month in which the magnitude of the Japanese attack on Pearl Harbor and its repercussions were still sinking in. America was at war. How Doc Savage fit into the new reality would be a problem discussed intensively in the troubled months to come. But for this story, it was business as usual.

The springboard for *The Three Wild Men* also survives and it shows how much Lester Dent could deviate from the editorial guidance he received. Since it does reflect the finished story's core idea, not reading it until you've finished the novel is recommended. Many Doc readers are rereading this tale, and they may be safe to proceed.

Doc Savage plot

Recent article in *Satur. Eve. Post* showed how doctors have proven that certain portions of the brain control not only certain actions, but certain thoughts, and that changes or removal in these parts is reflected in the resultant action. Villain, who has done much experimenting along this line illegally, had found that he can turn this to great advantage, and thus purposely gets hold of innocent people, and operates on them.

His purpose in the operations is to make each of these individuals react in certain ways to certain things. By picking out certain key individuals, he does not change any one individual enough to make an alarming change in that person, but just enough to have *some* of his action differ, yet, when the actions of all of the ones he's operating on take place, the result will be a tremendous amount of influence, or wealth, placed at the beck of this scientist.

Doc's lead to scheme of this sort may come from fact that, unknowingly, the villain picks on one of the "graduates" of Doc Savage's school, and makes him do something which is contrary to what that man should have done as a result of Doc's operation. Because Doc keeps close check of these "graduates," he learns of it immediately, and rushes out to find out where his own operation might not succeed. Villain gets worried and thinks Doc suspects, and thus starts action.

(By using actual detail on this operation idea, the story would not be too fantastic. The operation is delicate, but painless and very simple to the expert.)

For reasons of his own, Lester killed the crime college angle and played up the bizarre behavioral possibilities in the tale. Hence, *The Three Wild Men*—an idea not present in Nanovic's premise. Not long after this, Dent wrote *The Talking Devil*, which revisited the theme of Doc's secret crime college. We reprinted this recently. Regardless, Dent included new information about the college's graduates, and their role in wartime.

Here's how John Nanovic described the mayhem:

> We don't expect to have most of our readers get excited about the novel in this issue—the novel which deals with three wild men on the loose in New York. The first remark we heard in the office on this was that it was a gross understatement: that there are not only three, but probably three thousand wild men running around New York City all the time, if you were to judge by any subway rush hour crowd. (Well, for that matter, we might add that there are plenty of wild women, for the gentler sex takes no back seat— nor any seat!—when it comes to rushing wildly to or from the subway cars!)
>
> Anyway, all those blasé New Yorkers who seem to be rushing around so wildly all the time, either getting places, or just rushing around because there isn't much else to do, aren't the kind of wild men we give you in "The Three Wild Men." These wild men Kenneth Robeson writes about are really wild guys; they wear bearskins and top hats, chase subway trains because they think they're snakes, and do other whacky things like that. And a few other things they do aren't quite so whacky, as you'll find out if you read the novel. For behind this wildness is a scheme that is fantastically clever; that is diabolic to say the least. And who is behind the scheme; how it is expected to work out; and how Doc Savage and his gang fight it, is something exceptional in the way of stories, even when considered in the light of the many exceptional stories which have featured Doc Savage's adventures in the past. This is a yarn you will like to the very end.

After this story, the authorities remain suspicious of Doc Savage, an unresolved problem that would complicate subsequent stories, such as *The Fiery Menace* and *The Laugh of Death*.

And now, *The Three Wild Men*... •

John Nanovic

THE THREE WILD MEN

by Kenneth Robeson

A Complete Book-length Novel

Throughout the world, each major city had three such figures, all famous men. And Doc Savage was wanted by the F. B. I. for maliciously deranging their minds.

Chapter I
HONEY FOR BAIT

THE bright-eyed girl left the Fifth Avenue bus at Thirtieth Street and walked north one block and west one block. By that time three gentlemen, and

they were really gentlemen, were trailing her hopefully, not because she looked like a girl who could be picked up, but because she really was such a wonderful-looking thing.

She sat at a table in a restaurant which served a three-dollar luncheon.

Eventually, the head waiter approached and asked her, "Miss Cushing?"

She nodded.

"A call for you," said the head waiter. He carried a telephone which he plugged in at her table. Having done that, he bowed with the extra flourish that he reserved for customers like this one and departed.

"Yes," the girl said into the telephone.

"Boy, oh, boy!" said a brash male voice in the receiver. "Cut off my tail and call me beautiful! Where did they dig up a gorgeous butterfly like you?"

The girl asked coolly, "Who is this, please?"

"This? Oh, this is poor, downtrodden Mr. Adam."

"Adam looking for his Eve, I presume."

"This Adam," said the brash voice dryly, "happens to be looking for three wild men."

The girl tightened noticeably. "Oh!" she said. Then: "You were to meet me here."

"Sure. I'm meeting you now. This is it."

The girl's eyebrows drew together slightly. "You mean that you are not going to join me?"

"Butterfly, joining you is what I'd like nothing better to do. But it might not be smart under the circumstances."

"Are you sitting where you can see me?"

"Sure."

The girl put the telephone down and casually lighted a cigarette. She turned slightly to the right to shake out the match and turned a little to the left to blow out smoke. She removed a fleck of tobacco from her lip with a fingernail, then picked up the receiver.

"Nice job of looking around," said the brash man's voice. "But you didn't see me, did you? So now let's get down to business."

The girl was slightly irritated. "First," she said, "let's have an understanding."

"With you, butterfly, I would like nothing better."

"That," the girl interrupted, "is exactly the point. I do not like you. I have not seen you, and I have no desire to do so, and I am sure I dislike you. I have no doubt, in view of what you are doing now, that you are a completely contemptible individual with no moral, social or other virtues."

"Ouch!" said the voice.

"I, on the other hand, endeavor to be a lady," the girl continued dryly. "Suppose we put it on that basis."

The man's voice became a little ugly.

"Sure, I'm the stableboy. You're the queen," he said. "But today, you take orders from me. You got that through your pretty noggin?"

"If I did not have it in my pretty noggin," the girl snapped, "would I be here?"

"All right, all right. Have you ever met this guy you are to hornswoggle?"

"Doc Savage?"

"Yeah. Clark Savage, Jr., or Doc Savage, the Man of Bronze, whatever you wanta call him. Ever met him?"

"No."

"You got your work cut out for you, butterfly. You sure have."

SUDDENLY, the brash male voice stopped being brash and was coldly emotionless, dictating details and instructions like a machine. The switch in manner of the man revealed something of his character. He had some qualities besides being a hand with the ladies. His impudent approach to the girl, for example, had some of the qualities of an animal playing with a mouse, as a cat would give a mouse a bat or two with its paw before getting down to serious business.

He said, "Savage is in town. My part of this job was to find that out. All right, he's here. If you've heard anything much about him, you know he has five men who are friends and assistants. I think the five are in town, too. You hearing me?"

"I'm hearing you," the girl said.

"Doc Savage and one of the assistants, named Monk Mayfair, are having lunch in the Restaurant Manor, two doors west of here. They are lunching with a Turk named Mustaphet Kemel. Mustaphet is supposed to sell Turkish tobacco to American manufacturers, and he has occasion to travel around over the world a lot, selling tobacco, of course. But Mustaphet is also a secret agent of the Turkish government—the Turkish government thinks. The Russians also think Mustaphet is their agent. So do the French. So do some others. Only Mustaphet isn't the pup of any of them. He's Doc Savage's pup, and nobody else's."

The brash man chuckled.

"That has no bearing on our day's work," he added. "It just goes to show you that Savage is not a minnow. He has lots of pups like Mustaphet. How many, nobody knows. Incidentally, he is no spy and no international schemer."

"I know what Doc Savage is," the girl snapped.

"All right, all right. I've told you where he is in the restaurant two doors from here. Go in and take him. He's a big bronze man, very handsome, who doesn't look so big until you get close—"

"I know what he looks like."

"Hm-m-m! I presume you also know what you are to do?"

"Yes."

"Good."

The girl's face got suddenly white.

"It isn't good," she said. "Are they going to kill him?"

The brash voice laughed, and there was something so fierce in the mirth that it sounded a little unbalanced. "Three wild men," he said. "It's all very remarkable, wouldn't you say?" And he laughed again like a skeleton rattling.

MUSTAPHET KEMEL was an innocent-looking piece of chocolate, as innocent in appearance as was, probably, the boy in the fable who rubbed the lamp and caused the jinni to pop out of nowhere. He was eating peas with his knife like a cowboy.

Lieutenant Colonel Andrew Blodgett Monk Mayfair was the fellow in the red shirt. Monk was a remarkable fellow who was half a man high and two men wide, with rusty-red hair that made his wrists look as if they had been sprinkled with shingle nails. His forehead did not appear high enough to contain one of the most complete assortments of knowledge about chemicals in the world. He was eating his third steak, to the horror of the waiter.

Doc Savage had not spoken a dozen words the past hour and had done it in a way that dominated the conversation entirely. He had, although he was not trying to exercise it, that power. It was a carefully developed power. He was a man, a giant bronze man, about whom almost everything was carefully developed. He was younger than either Monk Mayfair or Mustaphet.

The restaurant was a little like Doc Savage, very famous but making no show about it. It was on a street of notable and subdued restaurants.

Paul Wock was the head waiter. He was a good head waiter and had a knack of attracting large tips.

Still and all, fifty dollars was a large tip, even for Paul.

Fifty dollars was what the girl handed him. Five tens, crisply new.

She said, "Look, Paul, this is for not seeing me. I want to run to Mr. Savage's table. You are not to notice me in time to stop me. It is a joke. You understand, Paul. A gag. I am to throw my arms around Mr. Savage and kiss him. Embarrass him, you see."

Paul tried to recall having seen her before. "I see," he said, not seeing anything but the fifty. "Oh, yes, a gag, I'm sure. Yes, indeed, I'm sure."

"You understand. All you have to do is not stop me until I kiss him," the girl said.

The fifty was hypnotizing Paul. "I'm sure," he said. "Yes, indeed, to be sure."

"Then it's O.K.?"

Paul made the bills disappear with a neatness that only head waiters seem to master. "To be sure, Miss … Miss—"

"Smythe," the girl said. "Johanna Smythe, to be sure."

"To be sure," Paul agreed.

So the very pretty girl whose name was not Johanna Smythe, or Joan Smith either, went to Doc Savage's table without being molested. She walked to the table quickly but not rapidly enough to draw the attention of Doc Savage and his party, who were engrossed in conversation.

Only she did not kiss Doc Savage.

She jabbed him with a hypodermic needle! She had carried the needle completely concealed in a small, flexible purse, and she simply jammed the purse against Doc Savage and squeezed. The jamming was done against his back, on the left side below the shoulder blade.

Doc Savage gave a normal start and looked up. His flake-gold eyes—one of his unusual features, his eyes were like pools of loose flake gold, always stirred by tiny winds—were rather wide.

The girl calmly opened her purse, removed the emptied hypo needle and placed it on the table in front of Doc Savage.

"You would naturally know what that is," she said. "However, it might make it a trifle more interesting if I told you that the needle was just filled with germs."

Chapter II
THE SECOND FIDDLE

IT was dramatic. Probably, "melodramatic" was the word, and enough to be on the silly side. It made Mustaphet Kemel laugh. He threw back his head and smacked his knees and sounded like one of the donkeys the tourists used to ride out to see the Pyramids.

"You must be an Oriental," he told the girl. "The women of the Orient are like that. Dramatic. Bizarre. Even a trifle ridiculous."

She did not like that. She did not like Mustaphet.

She examined Mustaphet's ears. "If they were a little longer, you would *look* like a jackass, too," she advised him.

Mustaphet's grin hung on his face like a dead duck.

Doc Savage had been contemplating the hypodermic needle with, considering the circumstances, a noteworthy lack of excitement. However, he was looking a little like a machine—if a man could look like one—which was the way he looked when he had gotten into trouble.

He also did another thing—a thing which only

Monk Mayfair, who knew Doc better than Mustaphet, knew that Doc had done. It was a trilling sound. A low, exotic note, hardly noticeable, with an eerie quality of seeming to come from everywhere rather than from any particular spot. It was a thing that Doc Savage did absentmindedly when under mental stress, so Monk knew that Doc was not quite as unconcerned as he looked.

"Germs?" Doc Savage remarked.

"That's right," the girl said.

Doc considered her statement. "What is right about it?"

"Eh?"

It was evident that she had expected more of a reaction out of this. His unconcern was getting her rattled.

"Germs," she snapped, "are what make people ill. Or did you know?" She told Doc Savage, "The germs in that hypodermic needle were a very special germ. They are now in your body. By now they are circulating all through your body, so it is too late to do anything about that part of it."

"Then I am to assume," said Doc Savage, "that there is another part of it?"

"Right as rain," said the girl.

"What is the other part?"

"The part," she told him, "where you find out how to kill the germs."

"Why kill them?"

"Because it's a case of kill or cure. You want to cure yourself, don't you?"

Monk whistled. "Brothers, this rates a brass medal or something. She shot a bunch of germs into Doc so he will have to find the cure to save himself."

Doc Savage contemplated the girl, who was extremely easy contemplating.

"Is that the general idea?" he asked.

She nodded. "It's the specific idea. It's the nail hit right on the head. Your assumption is correct."

"What," he asked, "do I do about it?"

"You get busy finding the cure," she advised, "if you know what is good for you. In about three days you will be very ill. In about another three days there will be slow music and flowers which you will not smell—unless you get busy."

Doc Savage looked faintly pensive. "Three days is not much time to work on a thing like this. Finding cures is something doctors spend years doing."

She compressed her lips.

"You better do it in three days," she advised.

Doc Savage shook his head. "I might prefer the preventative," he said.

"Preventative?" She frowned. "You mean a vaccine? There isn't any." She shook her head.

"Anyway, you couldn't vaccinate yourself because you've already got the germs."

She took a deep breath and a step forward.

"I'll tell you what I'll do," she added. "I'll take you to a place where you can see more of the germs. Maybe that will help."

"Take me where?"

"I'll show you."

"Is it near, this place where we can see the germs?"

"I'll show you," she said.

Doc Savage shook his head again. "No, thanks. I prefer the preventative."

"Preventative?"

Doc Savage unbuttoned coat, vest, shirt, and showed her what was underneath—a bulletproof vest with a mesh fine enough that the needle could not have penetrated.

"A nice preventative, wouldn't you say?" he suggested.

The girl then turned and ran.

MONK MAYFAIR popped his eyes at the girl.

Mustaphet Kemel, on the other hand, popped his eyes at the bulletproof vest. They had been discussing the subject of such vests when the girl interrupted them. Mustaphet was reporting to Doc Savage that a certain extremely competent and unscrupulous scientist in a Baltic country had developed a bulletproof fabric. Mustaphet had wanted to ascertain if Doc would be interested if he, Mustaphet, should produce, say in a convenient interval of two months or so, a sample of the new alloy fabric and the formula for its production. Mustaphet's business was supplying such items; it was his real business, that is. But it was not a question of money for Mustaphet when he was dealing with Doc Savage. Mustaphet owed Doc Savage a great many things, including his life, which he would repay if necessity required. Also, he owed to Doc the life of his small son, which was the greater debt by far of the two. Mustaphet felt that even a lifetime of little services—such as this one about the Baltic scientist's bulletproof vest—would be but a small down payment.

Mustaphet had not known that Doc Savage had already developed such a bulletproof fabric.

Monk Mayfair stood up. Monk did not have bulletproof vests on his mind. He was thinking about a pretty girl.

"You going to let her run off like that?" he asked Doc.

"With pleasure," Doc Savage admitted.

"There's no pleasure in that for me," Monk announced. "Anybody object to my catching up with her and sort of broadening our acquaintance?"

"You'll be sorry," Mustaphet predicted.

"A girl as pretty as that one. Sorry?" Monk snorted.

"No objections," Doc Savage said.

Monk was off. He was full of enthusiasm.

Mustaphet watched Monk depart, and sighed. "Shake a skirt in front of Monk, and he is off."

"A pretty skirt," Doc corrected.

Mustaphet chuckled. "And if the skirt contains danger, it is further to Monk's liking." He laughed. "What a combination, that Monk. As homely as a mud fence around an African cannibal village; yet women are fascinated by his ugliness. A forehead that does not look as if it could contain a spoonful of brains; yet great chemists all over the world consider him a genius. A paradox, that fellow. And when he has his pet pig with him, he becomes something of a circus side show. Monk and his pig named Habeas Corpus. What a pair!"

Doc Savage made no comment.

Mustaphet changed the subject, asked, "What about that bulletproof vest I mentioned? The one that Baltic fellow has developed?" Mustaphet leaned forward. "You want a sample of the mesh and the formula?"

Doc Savage nodded slightly. "Get it."

"It might *not* be superior to your own," Mustaphet pointed out.

"True. But again it might, and that would be unfortunate. The Baltic fellow, as you call him, happens to be a genius of an ilk, and he is tied up with a war-mongering clique. If he has something definitely superior, it will do no one any good."

Mustaphet nodded. "And if he does have something, you will then take measures to see that the secret does not reach the wrong hands?" he hazarded.

"Right."

Mustaphet leaned back. He studied Doc Savage, then shook his head slowly, approvingly. "They call you the world's troubleshooter, the man who rights wrongs and punishes evildoers in the far corners of the world. That is, those who know you well call you that. But they are somewhat wrong. You prevent a great many unpleasant things before they happen. I doubt if you get proper credit for that."

"Credit," Doc Savage said quietly, "is not important. I do not run an advertising agency."

"Just what it is that you do run," muttered Mustaphet, "is a thing that puzzles a lot of people." He beckoned the waiter and called for the check. "In six weeks, not more than two months, you will see me again, and I will have visited the Baltic fellow," he said.

"I would *not* like it," Doc Savage said slowly, "if you should accidentally happen to kill the fellow."

Mustaphet smiled slightly. "Do not worry. I know your rules against such things."

MONK MAYFAIR caught the girl as she was walking south on Fifth Avenue. Monk overhauled her and touched her arm. She whirled nervously, her lips parted slightly and she seemed undecided whether to run or scream.

"With your mouth open like that," Monk told her with all the gallantry of Sir Galahad on a Sunday, "you are the most beautiful of all."

From rage and fright the girl began to look as if she wanted to screech with mirth. This was one of Monk's secrets in his way with women.

Monk affected them the way finding a toad in their slipper would affect them. First impulse was a howl of fright; second one was mirth. The next stage was amused and interested toleration, like keeping a toad around to study such a homely thing. From this stage, Monk had others which he developed, the success of which invariably amazed the beholders.

"You're not angry?" the girl asked incredulously.

"Me? Why should I be?" Monk chuckled expansively. "This is a great day for my tribe. It's the day I met you, in case I'm too subtle for you."

"You didn't come to take me back to Doc Savage?" the girl demanded.

"Of course not," said Monk gallantly.

"Then," said the girl, "why did you follow me?"

Monk looked as if she was very obtuse, indeed. "Haven't you been followed before?"

She studied him, trying to decide just where to peg him. "Not," she said, "by one of the world's leading chemists."

"Ah, you've heard of me." Monk was pleased.

"Yes, and I've heard you have quite a touch for female hearts," she informed him.

"It's a lie!" said Monk. "It sounds like that low-life, Ham Brooks, the lawyer. You don't, by chance, know him?"

"No."

"Good," said Monk. "Not knowing him, you rank that much higher in my estimation. Were there really germs in that hypodermic needle?"

"Germs?" For a moment the girl did not seem to know what he was talking about. "Oh, germs. To be sure, the germs."

"Were there?"

"Were there what?"

"In the hypo needle. Germs. Like you said."

She looked confused.

"No, there were no germs," she admitted. "That was just a lie. A trick."

Monk gazed at her approvingly. "That is just

what I would have told Doc," he said, "if there had been time."

LATER they were in a shooting gallery, shooting at little white ducks, and the girl seemed puzzled as to just how she had gotten there. Puzzled, but more at ease. That was Monk's technique. Put them at ease.

Monk said, examining a rifle, "I knew the minute I saw you, and heard you say, 'That needle is filled with germs,' or whatever it was you said—I knew right then that you were all right. I knew the wolf wasn't a wolf at all."

"How did you know that?"

Monk aimed at a duck. "You see that little white duck? It is moving, and it is one of a chain of little white ducks. As sure as you see that little duck, you know another one will pop up. And just as sure as you see a girl like you, you know she is all right."

The girl touched Monk's arm. "Thank you," she said.

"She may be as unexpected as fleas," Monk added, "and she may blow your hat off. But she will be all right."

The girl picked up one of the small-caliber rifles. She aimed casually and knocked over a duck. She shifted to a smaller duck, and knocked that one over. Monk's eyes got round. She was a good shot.

She asked, "What do you know about Doc Savage?"

Monk shrugged. "As much as anyone, I guess. He is a man you think you know well; yet you never do know him."

"How do you explain that?"

"The way he was developed, I guess. You know his dad put him in the hands of scientists about the time he outgrew his three-cornered underwear. From then on, the best scientific minds did their best to make him a prodigy."

"From what I hear, they succeeded," the girl suggested.

"Yeah. He's human enough, though."

The girl shot some more small ducks. There was only one smaller target, and that was a row of matches. The girl fired three times with measured precision, and three matches burst alight.

"Annie Oakley!" Monk exclaimed admiringly.

"Just Dead-eye Dick's daughter," she corrected. "Look, I wanted help."

"Help?"

"When I pulled that thing about the germs. It was silly, wasn't it? Melodramatic."

"You made it convincing enough for me. My hair is still on end," Monk told her gallantly. "What kind of help?"

"Some people are in trouble. Very serious trouble."

"Doc's your man."

"Oh, but I couldn't go back to him after that trick I pulled."

Monk brightened noticeably.

"Why not," he offered hopefully, "let me offer my assistance?"

"You wouldn't mind playing second fiddle?"

"Second fiddle," Monk said, "is the instrument I play loudest."

THE girl was very slick in the next thing she did. It was executed casually and simply. Monk did not notice the part of it where she rubbed her fingers on the ejector mechanism of the rifle and got grease on her fingers.

She turned to Monk and showed him her hand. "Oh, the darned gun had grease on it!" she said. "I had better go wash my hands. I don't want to ruin my gloves. I just bought them today."

"Sure," Monk said. "Then you can tell me what all this mystery is about, and what kind of help it is you need."

"Of course," she said quickly.

This was a large shooting gallery, an emporium somewhat more elaborate than the usual run. There were other items of amusement other than the shooting gallery, and there were telephones in the ladies' washrooms. The girl used one of these. She dialed a number.

She recognized the voice which answered and said, "It went wrong."

A man was on the other end of the wire. He demanded, "How could that happen?"

"Doc Savage was wearing a bulletproof vest. The tip of the needle did not go through it. I was so flabbergasted that I ran away."

The man swore a rather genteel oath. "I cannot say I blame you."

"I balled the thing up."

"Not," said the man, "providing you did not mention anything about three wild men. Did you?"

"Not a word."

"Even a hint that would tip him off that this matter concerns three wild men would upset the apple cart."

"I didn't give a hint," the girl insisted. "But I've got something else to tell you."

"Something else?"

"There is a Doc Savage assistant named Monk Mayfair."

"To be sure. Monk Mayfair. The man who has a pet pig named Habeas Corpus."

The girl laughed without any humor at all. "Right now he is minus his pig. He is following me around."

"Following you around!"

"Monk Mayfair," she said, "is in my hair, with love in his eye."

The man's voice at the other end of the telephone wire became excited. "Oh, oh! Maybe it isn't so bad then. Can you lead this Monk into the same trap we intended for Doc Savage?"

"You want that?"

"We'll try it. We're desperate. As a last resort, we've got to try everything."

"All right," the girl said. "I'll do that."

"Good."

As an afterthought, she said, "Wait. One thing isn't good. That Mr. Adam you employed to locate Doc Savage."

"What about him?"

"I didn't like him. He kept calling me his butterfly."

The man laughed. "Didn't mean a thing. He even calls me his butterfly."

"I didn't," said the girl, "like our Mr. Adam."

Chapter III
TUNE ON THE FIDDLE

THE girl with the bright eyes and Monk Mayfair rode uptown in a taxicab driven by a thin Negro who had only grunted at them.

Monk said, "Really, you lovely thing, I don't want to argue with you. But I fail to see why you can't tell me the whole story, whatever it is, here and now."

"Wait until we get uptown," the girl said.

"I don't want to wait until we get uptown," Monk explained. "Patience is the thing I have the least of. My good friend Ham Brooks, whose neck it is my ambition some day to wring, says I was born without any."

The girl was somewhat thoughtful for a moment. "Perhaps we could stop by and pick up your friend Ham Brooks. He is also a Doc Savage assistant, is he not?"

Monk snorted and shook his head violently.

"Not on your life. He thinks he is a lady killer. You'd find him as interesting as a bucket of mud."

"Mr. Brooks is rather handsome, isn't he?"

"As ugly," Monk lied, "as a crow without feathers."

"I was just thinking that Mr. Brooks might be willing to help me also."

"Not on your life," Monk insisted. "You think this is a two-man job?"

"Yes.

"If it is a two-man job, I can still handle it. A ten-man job, too. You should see me in action."

"I soon will, I trust," the girl said, a shade strangely.

Monk had a faint inkling that there was something strange in her voice, and he fell silent, trying to figure it out. He was wordless and contemplated the back of their dark driver's scrawny neck during the rest of the ride.

They got out—to Monk's approval and surprise—on the part of Park Avenue where the extremely wealthy lived. Monk gazed about. He had often reflected that people living in this neighborhood had more money than sense. Ham Brooks lived not far away. They charged you fifty cents for a coke in some of the restaurants around here.

They entered one of the finest buildings. The doorman bowed like a jackknife and said a crisp, "Good afternoon, Miss Cushing."

The elevator was as large and ornate as a bedroom in a harem, Monk reflected.

"So your name is Cushing," Monk whispered.

"Abba Cushing," she explained.

Twenty floors up, they went like a breath of spring, then out into a hall that should have been in a palace.

"Yi, yi," Monk said.

A door was opened for them by a butler in knee stockings and a cutaway coat. At least, Monk presumed the functionary was a butler because Monk had never seen that kind of trappings on a servant before. He made a mental note to hire one of those after he made his next million dollars. One would probably be a handy gadget to have around.

"My father," said Abba Cushing.

The man who was coming toward them was Monk's idea of what, say, a senator should be. Tall and capable, with regularly formed, confidence-inspiring features, and just enough gray hair to make him distinguished. The man was discreetly and impeccably dressed; there was nothing about his attire to suggest the conscious effort to reach sartorial perfection. The man looked as comfortable as a very good shoe. A fine old gentleman, was Monk's instant thought.

The fine old gentleman put out his hand to Monk.

Unexpectedly, there was a gun in his hand, a dark-blue gun that was capable of ejecting a bullet the diameter of Monk's little finger, which was not small. And the weapon was held as if the holder knew how it functioned.

"Welcome, Mr. Mayfair," he said in a deep, melodious, pleasant, calmly undisturbed voice. "In case you also are wearing one of those bulletproof vests, I assure you that I can shoot you in the head!"

MONK finally got his mouth closed and the lump swallowed out of his throat. He gave the girl

**The fine old gentleman put out his hand to Monk.
Unexpectedly, there was a gun in his hand.**

the accusing look of an abused sheep. "Nice going," he muttered. "Very nice. Do you eat your brothers and sisters, too?"

The fine old gentleman with the gun laughed. "You misjudge us," he said. "I am Raymond E. Cushing. This is my daughter, Abba, whom you were fortunate enough to meet."

Monk eyed the gun. "I don't see what is so fortunate about it."

"Oh, come, come! You are jumping at conclusions." Mr. Raymond E. Cushing gestured slightly with the weapon. "Won't you step into our parlor?"

"And meet more flies?" Monk inquired sourly.

"Possibly. I trust not."

Monk accompanied the man—Cushing kept behind him—into the parlor, which proved a room that seemed large enough at first glance to berth a yacht.

It contained a round half dozen old gentlemen who probably owned yachts—also steamships, railroads, factories and political empires. Some of the gentlemen were not so old. Monk examined them and out came his eyes again. He recognized two of them. Andrew Casteel, the rubber baron, and C. C. Gross, who was someone fabulous in international finance. Both had more money, thought Monk, than Heinz has pickles. The other gentlemen also looked filthy with money.

There was enough combined gold in the room, it occurred to Monk, to sink a battleship.

Somewhat impressed, he said, "You platinum-plated old ducks have bit off more than you can chew. You'll regret this, and I'm the boy who'll make you."

Raymond E. Cushing smiled grimly.

"Can't we keep this on a gentleman's plane?" he suggested. "Threats and angry words belong in the gutter."

"In the gutter is where you'll wind up, with me standing on your necks," Monk advised.

Cushing shook his head quickly. "Hold on. Hold your horse, Mr. Mayfair. We want your help."

"Help?"

"Yes."

"You picked a fine ring-tailed way of starting out to get it."

Cushing put away the gun. "Do you feel better with the weapon out of sight?"

"Not a bit," Monk growled.

Cushing drew the gun again, held it in his hand. "In that case, we will abolish the pleasantries and get down to business. The business being—we want something done about the three wild men."

Monk, suspecting his ears had not done him right, demanded, "The *what?*"

"The three wild men," said Cushing.

Having given that thirty seconds of the deepest and the blankest kind of thinking, Monk blurted, "I don't believe I understand. I don't savvy. Three wild men. What the hell!"

Cushing turned slowly to the other old gentlemen. "My friends, it seems he is going to act dumb."

They nodded.

"Shall we," inquired Cushing, "proceed according to plan?"

They nodded again, immediately.

"Plan?" Monk demanded.

"We are going to give you to the three wild men," Raymond E. Cushing informed him. "Now what do you think of that?"

Just what he should think of a matter of three wild men did not occur to Monk, although he gave the thing the best efforts of his brain. They went down from the palatial apartment in a freight elevator and got into a limousine so long that Monk doubted if it could turn the corner. During the trip to the limousine, the other fine old gentlemen all produced guns. There were guns everywhere, all good ones. Some of the possessors did not seem fully skilled in their use, though this was not encouraging.

"This is great stuff," Monk muttered. "Three wild men! Boy, somebody's crazy!"

No one commented. The fine old gentlemen loaded into the limousine and the overflow got into another. The girl, Abba Cushing, drove the car Monk was in.

It was not a long trip. Only to the millionaire's yacht basin on the nearby East River frontage.

THE most puzzling things began to happen.

First, it suddenly developed that all the fine old gentlemen were scared. They had not looked or acted frightened, which was probably natural for them. To get as much money as they probably had, each one of them needed to be a gambler with a deadpan face.

However, they each were as scared as a mouse in a cage of famished cats. This became evident when they had an argument about who was to get in a power tender and accompany Monk out into the river. There were no loud voices in the argument, but they were not men who had to raise their voices.

The argument ended as was to be expected when such iron-willed men get together. Nobody would go. Then they took a fresh start and reached a compromise.

They would wait until darkness. Then they would draw lots to see who took Monk out into the river.

Monk gathered that their destination was to be a yacht anchored in the slack water along the opposite shore. It was, as far as Monk could tell from that distance, a not very large yacht that seemed to be substantial and comfortable. Comfortable in a seagoing way, that was, for the distance was too great to tell anything about the luxury of her furnishings.

So they spent the late afternoon and the early hours of the darkness aboard another yacht which was tied to the dock. During the wait, Monk learned absolutely nothing about three wild men or anything else pertaining to the affair. He did get the thorough conviction that his captives thought he was lying to them when he disclaimed any knowledge of three wild men.

There was one interesting point, however. What they were going to do to him was what they had planned to do to Doc Savage. Whatever that was.

After it became very dark, with thunder gobbling and thumping its chest in the great distance, Raymond E. Cushing approached Monk Mayfair and presented a smile and a substantial glass of champagne, which Monk considered the next thing to drinking vinegar.

"We will sally forth now," Cushing said. "We have drawn lots. Myself and my daughter and Mr. C. C. Gross were the abashed possessors of the short straws when it was over."

"You take me on the boat ride?"

"Right."

"That's right, don't tell me a thing," Monk muttered. "Leave me in suspense."

"Don't you care for it?" Abba Cushing asked.

"Sure. Pretty soon, my suspenders will snap." Monk scowled. "You know, you are not nearly as pretty as I thought you were."

The girl laughed grimly. "Come on, second fiddle," she ordered. "We'll see how loud a tune you can play."

As they walked out past the other rich men, Monk noted how white their faces were. It gave him an unpleasant sensation. It would take a lot to scare fellows like these. True, they were elderly gentlemen with soft hands and pink skins; but their minds were not soft, and fear is a thing of the mind. Monk began to feel his hair want to stand on end.

THEY got in a power tender, the ritzy name for a motorboat. Instead of heading straight for the yacht, Cushing made note of the direction of the tide flow here and headed upstream. He stopped the motor when the boat was in such a position that the outgoing tide would carry it down to the yacht. There was a brisk tide at this point in the river, and it tossed them about merrily. Except for the ripple of water, and the occasional hungry sucking sound made by a whirlpool in the tide rush, there was a complete and depressing silence.

"Yo-ho, and a bottle of rum!" Monk said hopefully. "How about a note of song to cheer us on our way?"

They were as silent as undertakers.

"You have nerve of a sort," Cushing said finally in a low, grim voice. "I hope there is more to it than words."

"I am a foolhardy man, not a brave one," Monk advised him. "So it would make no difference. I love your daughter. Or at least I did. I'm not so sure, now, that she's the sugar on my oatmeal."

No one commented, and that made Monk feel uncomfortable, wondering if they thought he was crazy. If they did, they had nothing on *him*. He thought *they* were nuts!

He said, "Three wild men! Hah!"

"I wouldn't be too loud," Cushing said. He sounded like a man in a dark jungle, approaching a man-eating tiger.

"Huh?"

"The boat," Cushing whispered, "is just ahead."

Their ominous manner, their deathly seriousness, silenced the usually irrepressible Monk. He peered ahead through the sultry night. The yacht was there. He could distinguish it first as a thicker place in the night, then its clean lines began to take on shape.

C. C. Gross, the fabulous international financier, was steering with practiced skill. He sent the tender along the starboard side of the yacht.

It developed that a landing stage was hanging over the rail. The boat drew alongside this, and the Cushings caught hold and held on.

"Get aboard," Cushing ordered Monk.

With the utmost interest, Monk asked, "What happens after I do that?"

Cushing gave him a totally unsatisfactory answer.

"You'll find out," Cushing said, and prodded him onto the landing stage with a pistol.

MONK stood there and listened to the boat depart. They were not afraid of noise, now. They started the motor and gave it the gun, and the boat departed with about as much stealth as a dive bomber. Somehow, that was very disquieting. They *had* been afraid. There was nothing to be heard, seen or felt to be afraid of. But that was worse. The most terrible fears are the intangible ones. Eventually, the boat faded into the sulking distance, and there was nothing left but the gurgle of tide water, like blood coming out of a body, past the yacht. Monk shuddered. He did not shudder easily, as a rule.

Presumably, this was what they meant by giving him to the three wild men. This and whatever the future held, and Monk was anticipating the future with, somehow, no pleasure at all. Giving him to the three wild men. That was the way they had put it. It meant nothing. At least, it didn't make sense.

"So what the hell happens next?" Monk said.

He sat down to wait. He had decided to stay near the water because, in case he did not like what was to come, he could dive overboard. He was a good swimmer. When scared he was an excellent swimmer.

He contemplated the Manhattan shore line which, with its myriad lighted windows showing through the darkness, was like a compressed night heavens.

Twenty minutes of that palled. "Blazes!" Monk muttered. He got to his feet, listened, then shook the ladder hopefully. Nothing happened. He was not pleased. The silence on the boat, the utter and complete silence that could have been in a tomb, was not reassuring. Something was supposed to happen, and it wasn't happening. It was too much like a bomb with the fuse lighted.

He began to climb the steps of the landing-stage ladder, one step at a time. It took more effort than he had expected, more mental effort. He was scared himself, he began to realize, without knowing what there was to inspire fear.

The ladder made no noise whatever. It should have squeaked. The lashings which held it should have groaned. They made no sound. Monk became so preoccupied with the ghostly quiet of the ladder that he forgot to notice when he should reach the deck and, reaching it, all but fell on his face. He did stumble and make considerable noise, then found himself standing there as stiffly as a fawn caught in the glare of a flashlight.

He heard nothing to alarm him, however. And not hearing anything, he was the greater alarmed.

It was about then that he was taken by the coat lapel. The fact that he was first seized by the coat lapel was only incidental; almost instantly the grip was transferred to his neck.

He was thrown to the deck. Not silently, but like a ton of loose bricks. He was pounced upon. He tried to fight back. Monk was strong, stronger even than he looked, and he resembled a bull ape. He could take a pony-sized horseshoe in his two hands and change its shape. But he was licked in this fight before he even got going. He was spread out on the deck and held helpless.

Monk was thrown to the deck like a ton of bricks.

An explanation of how he could be so manhandled occurred to Monk.

"Doc!" he gasped. "Doc Savage!"

Doc Savage said, "We should wear perfume, or something, so that we could recognize each other in the dark."

Chapter IV
THE WILD MEN

MONK moved about slowly to locate his various bruises. "We should at that," he admitted. "It wouldn't be a bad idea. How did you get here?"

"By trailing you," Doc Savage told him.

Monk was in thought for a moment. Then he snorted. "Hey, did I get sucked in! And I don't mean by that girl, either. You let her get away this afternoon after she used the hypo needle on you so you could follow her."

Monk stopped to make noises of self-disgust.

He added, "And that taxi the girl and I took—the driver! Now, I remember he looked familiar. He was a Negro, only he wasn't! Great blazes and little oceans! The driver was Ham Brooks in disguise!"

"Ham thought you recognized him and took his cab deliberately," Doc remarked. "Didn't you?"

Monk groaned. "No, but don't ever tell Ham the difference. If he thought I was dumb enough to not recognize him just because he had blacked his face, he'd run me ragged with his ribbing. Keep it quiet, will you?"

Doc Savage changed the subject.

"What is this about?"

"You know as much as I do," Monk said grimly, "providing you don't know a thing that makes sense."

"What did they do to you?"

"Put me on this boat. They called that giving me to 'the three wild men.'"

Doc said, rather strangely, "Three wild men?"

"Sure! Sounds crazy as a pet coon, doesn't it? Maybe it is." Monk paused to listen. There was no trace of life in the adjacent night. "You been over this boat, yet?"

"I just came aboard," Doc Savage explained. "I waited until certain they were going to put you aboard the yacht, then came aboard by the anchor line. I had a canoe. It is tied to the anchor cable."

Monk was thoughtful for a moment. A few minutes ago he had been scared and had admitted it to himself. Now, he should be feeling better, for two reasons. First, there had been a climax—when Doc Savage seized him—and following a climax there logically should be a letdown and a more rational viewpoint. Second, he had been joined by Doc Savage, and Doc for a companion was about equivalent—when one knew the full capability of Doc Savage—to the protection of the Army.

Strangely, Monk did not feel at all easy. That was disquieting. It was not a natural result at all. It was alarming.

"Doc," Monk said.

"Yes?"

"Is there something about this boat that gets you?"

"What do you mean?"

"I can't exactly make words out of it," Monk admitted. "Maybe it is the result of the way those people acted. There were several men besides the girl, and all of them were important, capable people." Monk digressed to name the men he had recognized and give a rough idea of their importance. "They were scared," he explained. "Of what, I don't know. But they were afraid, no two ways about it. I'm sure that when they put me on this boat they were certain something drastic was going to happen to me."

Doc Savage asked, "You have no slightest idea of their object in putting you on the boat?"

"Without ideas, that's me."

"What would you say," Doc suggested, "to our searching the boat?"

"Let's go."

AS if to express an ugly cast over the decision to search the yacht, the sky gave a whoop and a grumble of thunder, after which lightning popped down out of the sky with great light but no sound. Lightning should precede thunder, but this was reversed, and somehow it made Monk's hair want to stand on end. The river looked wide and slick with the wave corrugations on it like the crawling devices on a snake's belly.

Feeling their way, for it was intensely dark on deck, they located a door. The moment he was inside, Monk explored for a light switch, found it, snapped it on. And nothing happened.

He took a step into the cabin then felt something that felt like soft flesh underfoot, and gave a great jump with his heart between his teeth, only to discover that it was nothing more formidable than a very rich and deep carpet.

"Maybe it's *me* there is something wrong with," Monk muttered sheepishly. "Not the boat."

He was trying to talk himself out of the way he was feeling, which was somewhat as if he was crawling into a grave that might be occupied by a corpse. The corpse part of the sensation gave him slimy chills. It was not a feeling of danger at all. Danger he would have welcomed. Danger was something you could recognize. This was something else.

Monk made a respectable try at jumping out of his hide when Doc Savage turned on a flashlight. The beam stood out in the darkness like a white rod and roved. They saw, now, that it was an ordinary yacht, perhaps with a little more than the average quota of mahogany and teak work.

"Nice piece of flotsam," Monk suggested.

Doc Savage asked, "Monk, did they search you before you were put aboard?"

"Yes. Sure!"

"Did they leave you matches or a flashlight?"

"No, come to think of it, they didn't. You think that would have any bearing?"

"Hard to say. The thing does not exactly make sense, yet." The bronze man did not offer any further comment, and Monk was too oppressed with the sensation of evil, or of depression—there was some distinct sensation—that pervaded the boat. It was uncanny. Now that they were inside, the feeling was infinitely greater.

Because he preferred to have company, Monk followed Doc Savage, who headed for the yacht's bridge. The bridge was an enclosed affair, more of a pilothouse. Doc began yanking open drawers and soon found what he wanted. Monk peered over his shoulder and saw that it was the log book.

The boat, according to information on the log fly leaf, belonged to a man named Root Too Hooten.

"Hah-hah," Monk said. "That name is the first funny thing that has happened."

There was nothing mirthful on Doc Savage's face. He asked, "The name is not familiar?"

Something in Doc's tone sobered Monk. "Should it be?"

"Hooten," Doc Savage said, "is a Dutchman who went to Borneo when he was fourteen years old, without a penny. He became one of the most wealthy men in the Dutch Indies, and one of the most influential. He has done more to shape the political destinies of that part of the world than any other white man."

Light came to Monk. "Sure, I'll take it back; I've heard of him. One of those men who is a power behind the throne in Oriental affairs. I read an article somewhere."

"The article," said Doc Savage, "happens to be the only one ever published about him. Hooten permitted that one only because his nephew was a young man endeavoring to be a writer."

Monk looked sharply at Doc Savage. This evidently was not idle conversation about Hooten. Doc did not do things like that.

"What are you getting around to?" Monk asked.

Doc Savage thumbed through the log book then returned it to the drawer where he had found it. "This boat," he said, "has been lying at anchor here in the river for nearly a year. The only people aboard during that time have been the captain and two sailors, who have been keeping the boat in condition."

Monk was more puzzled. "Which leads up to what?"

"For slightly more than three weeks," Doc Savage said, "Root Too Hooten has been missing. The man is very important in Dutch Indian financial circles. Doubly important, considering the present condition of the international situation. So a frenzied search has been made for him. Two of the largest detective agencies in the United States have every operative looking for him. Other agencies in Europe and the Orient are at work trying to find him."

"Doc, have you been asked to help locate him?"

"No. We are not a detective agency. Furthermore, we do not do jobs for pay."

Monk rubbed his jaw. "I thought maybe you had taken on the job of trying to find Hooten. If you had, that might explain why we were roped into this thing, whatever it is."

"It would, if we had been called in," Doc agreed. "Only we were not."

Monk rubbed his jaw again, then his forehead. "I sure feel queer. Kind of shaky and scared."

Doc Savage looked at him. The bronze man's metallic features had a strange expression.

"I have the same feeling," Doc said.

THEY had left the pilothouse and were continuing the search of the boat before the significance of what Doc Savage had just said dawned on Monk. He started to say, "Well, it's funny that such a flashy boat would give a man the creeps—" He brought up short. "Wait a minute! You mean that?"

"The queer, depressed, shaky sensation?" Doc asked.

"That's it, exactly!" Monk exploded. "Do *you* feel that way, too?"

"Yes."

"Wait now!" Monk exclaimed. "This is no hunch I'm talking about. This is definite. It's a real feeling. It's nothing vague, like a hunch. It's a big sensation."

Doc Savage said grimly, "My sensation is the same. Large."

"It's like I'm having hell scared out of me," Monk explained. "Only there's nothing here to scare a man."

"Exactly, in part."

Monk was dumfounded. "I got it the minute I began to climb on the boat. I thought it was caused by my noticing how scared those other people were. But *you* wouldn't get the sensation because of that. You didn't see how scared they were."

Doc Savage made no comment.

Monk had small, twinkling eyes. He batted them rapidly. "You said *in part.* What'd you mean by that?"

"That," Doc said, "is how much you might be wrong."

"Partly wrong about what?"

"About there being nothing on the boat to scare a man."

Monk gave that some thought. "Say, what're you feeding me? We have seen nothing, heard nothing and found nothing."

"We found fear."

"Huh? Does that make sense?"

Doc Savage made no comment.

"I'm sorry," Monk said. "I didn't intend to get sassy about it."

That was another thing that showed how Monk was feeling. Under normal circumstances, an apology was the last thing to be expected from him, even to the bronze man, for whom he had more respect than he probably had for any other individual.

They did not search any farther. Instead, Doc Savage gripped Monk's arm, said, "Out on deck!"

Not understanding, but not asking any questions either, Monk raced after the bronze man. They reached the deck. Doc went immediately toward the bow. Monk expected Doc to go down the anchor cable to the canoe in which he had arrived.

Doc began working with the anchor cable. He got the winch loosened, and the cable went out with a great roaring. It was chain cable, and sparks flew out of the guide chocks as the force of the tide pushed the boat back. When the end of the cable was reached, the boat stopped with a yank that almost unfooted them.

Doc began working with a cotter pin on the last link of the chain.

"You going to turn the boat adrift?" Monk asked blankly.

"Without delay," Doc agreed in a grim voice.

WHAT Doc Savage did next was no more explicable than turning the boat loose. He ran back and hauled down the kerosene anchor light, which Monk realized was lighted and burning as the law prescribed. The lighted anchor marker was an eerie touch on the otherwise blacked-out vessel.

"You light that?" Monk called.

"No."

Monk was positive it had not been lighted when he was put aboard the yacht. And yet there had been no noise and no movement.

Doc Savage took off his coat. He tied it to the forestay with many turns of the line which had held the anchor light aloft. Then he ripped open the fuel container of the anchor light and poured its contents over his coat. He set the coat afire. The blaze crawled up like a magically growing red animal.

"Gosh!" Monk gasped. He found himself seized by Doc and bundled toward the low brass rail. "Overboard," the bronze man said. "And wait in the canoe."

Monk hesitated, then took a header into the water. It was cold in contrast to the sultry evening.

A moment later, Doc Savage landed in the water beside Monk. The bronze man came in cleanly and seemed to barely wet his back before he was swimming beside the canoe.

Overhead, the blaze from the kerosene-soaked coat shot upward with cardinal glee, casting a ruby glow over the river's surface.

There is a trick to getting from the water into a canoe, and Doc Savage managed it. He strained water out of his hair with his fingers.

"Follow the drifting boat," he told Monk, who had the paddle.

Monk, not understanding the situation at all, but convinced there was a great deal more in it than met the eye, dug the spruce paddle into the river water. It was not difficult to keep pace with the yacht, the tide taking care of that.

The yacht drifted. The coat blazed with surprising prominence. The blaze was no small beacon in the dark night.

Then Doc Savage lifted his voice to its loudest.

"Help!" he yelled. "Get the Coast Guard! Get the Harbor Police. Help! The boat is afire!"

Doc Savage's voice at its loudest was something not ordinary. In the course of scientific training which the bronze man had received throughout his childhood, his vocal abilities had not been neglected. Apartment dwellers in Tudor City, half a mile away, opened the windows and put their heads out.

Monk's pride was hurt. He said, "What do we need with help? We were just on that boat. Why'd we leave it? I, personally, can lick as much as the Coast Guard."

Doc Savage did not argue the point. He said, "Keep your eyes open."

The advice was a little unnecessary, it developed. Keeping the eyes open was certainly no requisite to witness what happened. A blind man, if he could not have seen the flash, could have heard the explosion. And an elephant would have been jarred by the blast. The flower of flame which

The flower of flame which came out of the yacht reached straight up at least two hundred feet.

came out of the yacht reached straight up at least two hundred feet.

The explosive had been in the hold of the yacht, deep enough under the waterline to create a great commotion. A miniature tidal wave came boiling toward the canoe. Monk grabbed the gunwales, hung on. The little craft climbed up on the wave like a hog tackling a snowdrift, went askew at the top, then promptly capsized, dumping them into the river.

ONCE in the water, Monk realized the force of the tide. Not that he was in any danger. But it was not a place for an unskilled swimmer. He saw, outlined against the flames that were now bundled over the wreckage of the yacht, what of it was still afloat, the shadow of the canoe, already right and with Doc Savage in the little craft. Monk swam over, reached the stern and boarded the canoe rather ungracefully.

After he was in the canoe, Monk sat there in complete silence for a while.

"Since when," he asked, "did you become a fortuneteller?"

"Fortuneteller?"

"You knew the boat was going to blow up."

Doc Savage's voice was quiet, but noncommittal, as he said, "There was no certainty that it would blow up. But it was reasonable to suppose that something would happen to it if we got off and did something to attract attention to it."

"Hey," Monk said. "You mean it blew up because we got off?"

"Partly."

"What was the other part?"

"We attracted attention to the craft with the burning coat," Doc Savage said. "And there was my shouting. That probably helped."

"I don't get it," Monk said frankly.

"They did not want attention drawn to the yacht. They did not want it boarded."

"Why not?"

"The fear."

"You mean," said Monk, "the fear that we were feeling. That sensation we were talking about?"

"Yes."

Monk gave the matter some thought.

"What," he asked, "about the three wild men?"

Doc Savage, suddenly alert, asked, "Did you see any sign of them?"

"Heck, no! Of course not!" Monk leaned forward. "Wait a minute. Are you kidding? Do you suppose there were really three wild men on the yacht?"

"Possibly," Doc Savage said.

Monk growled, "There's going to be another wild man around here if this thing doesn't begin to make sense before long. It'll be me."

Doc Savage, with nothing to show that he had noticed anything unusual in the surrounding night, said, "Perhaps a diversion might help preserve your balance. There appears to be one swimming ahead of us."

Chapter V
GENUINELY WILD

MONK was startled into silence until he had crouched forward in the canoe and listened until he was sure there was a swimmer in the river. Then he muttered that he wanted Doc Savage's flashlight, which was waterproof and, furthermore, was operated by a spring generator gadget which was dependable. He gripped the flashlight, located the sound of the swimmer, and pointed the beam at the sound.

"It's the Cushing girl! What do you know?" he exploded.

The canoe was a small one which Doc Savage had hurriedly rented that afternoon. While it would carry three people, it certainly would not haul more than that. They got Abba Cushing aboard, along with some roiled river water.

As Monk lowered the girl into the bottom of the canoe, he felt her shaking uncontrollably. He turned his light on her again. She was, he saw, fully clad. No bathing suit. And she was infinitely more scared than she had been that afternoon.

It developed that she did not know who had rescued her.

"Who … who are you?" she asked tensely.

Monk turned the light on himself. The girl promptly screamed and slumped over in the canoe. Dumfounded, Monk examined her. "You better look at her, Doc," he muttered.

Doc Savage's inspection was brief.

"Fainted," he said.

Monk let that soak in, then tried a laugh that was not a success. "Heh, heh! Do you suppose a look at me had that effect on her? I'd hate for Ham Brooks to have seen that."

Doc Savage made no comment. He sat silent in the canoe for a few minutes, then dug the paddle in and sent the small craft toward the spot where the yacht had blown up. Very few fragments of the yacht remained afloat. There were life preservers, one of which had a flare light attached, the type which ignited when wet; and this had blazed up to shed an awesome red glow over the scene. Doc kept out of the light and circled the spot.

They found no one else floating or swimming in the vicinity.

Then, from the Manhattan shore of the river, came a series of sounds that did not belong in a well-ordered night. There was feminine screaming. Two women. There was sound like a dog barking; yet it was not a dog. Following this in a few seconds, a crash which was partly glass breaking. The dog barking that was not a dog barking came again.

Doc pointed the canoe toward shore and dug the paddle in. The lightning crawled and jerked across the sky, and this time there was following thunder, as there should have been.

Monk explored in the bottom of the canoe to see if there was another paddle wedged there, but there was none, so he held the girl's wrist. Her pulse was strong.

Then, abruptly, there was a dock above them— a ponderous thing—and the canoe jarred against a landing float. Monk lifted the girl ashore, while Doc steadied the canoe.

Doc ran along the dock, vanished in the darkness. He seemed to have something on his mind. A moment later, Monk heard him call out in Mayan. Mayan was the forgotten language of the ancient civilization of Sun Worshipers of Central America. Doc and his aides used it for communication with each other at times. As far as they knew, they were the only individuals in the so-called civilized world with a speaking knowledge of the language.

Doc was calling out in the darkness for Ham

Brooks. Apparently, he was having no luck.

He came back shortly.

"Ham was posted here," he said. "He is gone."

Monk, genuinely anxious, muttered, "I hope nothing has happened to Ham. I hope he never finds out I was concerned about his safety, though. The overdressed shyster lawyer!"

Doc said, "Monk, you stay here with the girl." He wheeled and went away into the night.

Monk noted that the bronze man headed in the direction of the weird noises they had heard when out on the river. The thing that stuck in Monk's mind about the sounds was the laugh, one like a dog barking. He shuddered, then scowled at his own uneasiness.

NOT more than five minutes later, a man hurried out on the dock from shore. Monk crouched beside the girl and kept carefully silent until he saw the newcomer silhouetted against the momentary flash of a distant automobile headlight. He saw that the newcomer carried a cane.

"Ham!" Monk called.

Ham Brooks rushed to Monk. He was still in the blackface makeup which he had used to drive the taxicab early in the day. He was breathless.

"Where's Doc?" Ham demanded.

"Went off a few minutes ago," Monk explained. "I think he went to investigate a bunch of funny noises we heard on shore."

"What happened to the yacht?"

"Blooey!"

"What do you mean?"

"Just blooey," Monk explained. "Hell, we haven't the least idea of what is going on. At least, I haven't. I'm in complete ignorance."

Ham said, "Complete ignorance is your natural condition. Were you hurt?"

"Naw, just wet. The explosion overturned the canoe. We just got off in time, though. Boy, did she go up! There must have been a barrel of nitroglycerin in the hold."

Ham discovered the form at Monk's feet. "Who's this?"

"Abba Cushing."

Ham said, "I'll take care of her. You go hunt Doc."

"You'll take over nothing," Monk informed him, "except maybe a boot in the britches. I know what you're trying to pull. She *is* darned pretty, and I saw her first. I'm the caretaker, my fine-feathered friend."

"That face of yours is probably what is keeping her unconscious."

"Be that as it may, brother, my face is by her side to stay." Monk became more belligerent. "Since you feel that way, you better take a walk.

Go on, scram! Vamoose, hombre, before I dump you in the drink."

Ham said rather hastily—Monk was an impulsive fellow who sometimes did what he promised—and in a firm tone, "Doc told me to come help you guard the girl."

Monk was startled. "Oh, so you saw Doc!"

"Yes," Ham admitted, "I did,"

"Where was he going?"

"To have a look at the three wild men who swam ashore after the yacht blew up," Ham explained.

DOC SAVAGE found an excited policeman standing beside a call box and talking to his sergeant on the telephone. The officer spoke earnestly with some profanity, with gestures of his hand which was not holding the receiver.

He finally reached the end of his patience and said, "All right, don't believe it and be damned! Just sit there and don't send any radio cars down here. See what the newspapers have to say about it tomorrow!" He banged the receiver back on the hook.

Doc Savage said to the officer, "Could you tell me what is going on? What is this talk about three wild men?"

The policeman happened to be one who did not know Doc Savage, but who believed in being patient with citizens.

Said the officer, "What is the world coming to, Johnny? Here I'm walking my beat with nothing on my mind, except that maybe it's gonna rain before morning. And what happens?"

"What did happen?" Doc supplied.

"A naked man pops up."

"Naked?"

"Well, not the way he came into the world, entirely. But naked enough. He had on a leopard skin thing. A sarong, you might call it."

The officer stopped to throw his arms into the air to show how he felt about the whole thing.

He continued, "This sarong guy runs up to me and snatches my necktie. He runs and ties the necktie on a horse that's pulling a cart by us at the time. This scares the horse and he runs off. There is a fat man on the cart, and the horse scatters the fat man and a wagon load of tomatoes over the street. Then this sarong guy makes a run at a fat lady. He lets out the awfulest laugh that ever came out of a radio, and scares the fat dame into an even louder scream. He seems partial to fat people. I'm fat, you notice. And about that time I come to life and chase him. And he knocks down another fat man as he runs away."

The policeman got out a handkerchief and mopped his forehead.

"I'm chasing the sarong guy, see. He laughs at every jump. Laughs like them wild men they used to have in phony circus side shows when I was a kid. Sounds like a dog barking. A laugh every jump. Me right after him. Up a tree he goes."

The officer threw both arms in the air in desperation.

"Up a tree I chase him. A crowd gathers. I climb the tree. He's gone. Thin air. If this is a gag somebody is pulling, they'll land on their pants in the jailhouse. That they will."

The tree up which the representative of the law had pursued the wild man was not hard to find. It would have been difficult not to notice the tree, because there were approximately a hundred people gathered around it, with more arriving.

The tree was one in a park which faced an array of the better apartment buildings of the neighborhood.

"That the tree?" Doc Savage asked the policeman.

"That's the tree."

Doc Savage sauntered casually toward the tree, went around it, using his eyes. Several citizens were gathered about the trunk, and at least two were up among the branches with flashlights, exploring the mystery of what had become of the wild man.

Doc Savage went back to the policeman and remarked, "There must have been a number of witnesses to your chase of the wild man."

"Johnny, we made more noise than a circus parade," the officer said. "Why shouldn't there have been witnesses?"

Doc said, "Your wild man got out of the tree."

"Sure."

"He must have used the telephone cable, which passes near the large branch of the tree. He could swing from the tree to the cable, go hand-over-hand along the cable to that apartment fire escape, and from there to almost anywhere."

"Sure," said the cop. "I figured it out like you did—too late to do any good."

"Your wild man must have been very agile."

"He wasn't *my* wild man, Johnny. And 'agile' was the word for him, like you say. Listen, that bird was as strong as a bald eagle who had just lost his feathers."

At this point another pair of policemen arrived. They looked a little embarrassed, until they heard the onlookers talking about the wild man who had gone up the tree and supposedly vanished.

"You mean you had another one here?" one of the newcomer officers asked the fat policeman.

"Another? You mean there was more'n one?"

"We had two over on the next street."

"Wild men?"

"No other word would suit 'em," said one of

the policemen. "Little one had on a leopard skin and a plug hat. Big one had a leopard skin and the cuffs of a shirt on his wrists, and neither of them had anything else."

"They chased three perfectly respectable businessmen for two blocks," supplied the other officer.

"Howling that they were going to catch them and cook them and feed them to their saber-tooth tiger," said the first.

"Saber-tooth tiger's name was Clarence," added the other. "Or so they said."

The officer who had merely chased his wild man up a tree sighed with relief. "I'm glad somebody saw one besides me. I was beginning to think those pancakes the old lady feeds me every morning had done something to me, like I've been telling her they would."

"What happened to the one you treed?"

"Got away."

"So did ours," advised one of the two policemen. "Got clean away. Like rabbits, they were."

"Rabbits never made that much noise."

His companion laughed. "You know something, McGorrick?"

McGorrick seemed to be the officer who had talked to Doc Savage. He asked, "What?"

"Ned here thinks he recognized one of the wild men. You remember a poster out for some Dutchman with a lot of money? Ned says he thinks this wild man was him. The big wild man, Ned means."

McGorrick said, "You mean that Dutch millionaire named Root Too Hooten? I noticed that poster. Offering a big reward to anybody who locates him, his family is."

"Not his family, one of his companies. Ned says the big wild man was Hooten. You reckon Ned could be right?"

Doc Savage eased back from the policemen, merged with the crowd and spent the next half-hour prowling the neighborhood. It was an intensive and alert half-hour, but he turned up no further sign of three wild men.

Chapter VI
HELP FOR FRIENDS

MONK MAYFAIR and Ham Brooks were not being friendly when Doc Savage joined them. Ham Brooks—he was Brigadier General Theodore Marley Brooks, a noted lawyer, as well as one of the nation's best-dressed men—was gripping his cane and threatening Monk. The cane was a sword cane; its tip was kept coated with a chemical mixture that would make a victim unconscious rather quickly.

Ham complained, "Doc, this polecat Monk told Miss Cushing that I'm his Negro chauffeur. I have nothing against chauffeurs, black or green, but I detest a liar."

Doc Savage said, "So she has regained consciousness."

The girl answered for herself. "Yes, sometime ago. I've been hoping you would come back. Did you find them?"

"The three wild men?" Doc asked.

"Yes."

"No. No trace."

"That," said Miss Cushing in a stricken voice, "is terrible."

"Is it?"

"I was hoping that you would find them," she explained.

"Why?"

"So you could help them," Abba Cushing explained. "I am going to tell you something now that I wish you would believe. I came to you this afternoon to get you to help those three men."

"You used," Doc Savage pointed out, "rather strange methods." He turned his flashlight on the girl. There was color back in her face. She was undeniably easy to look at.

"I know I did," she admitted. "Foolish methods, too. But we thought it would work."

"What would have happened if it had worked?" Doc Savage asked curiously.

Abba Cushing made an embarrassed gesture. "That wasn't germs I tried to shoot into you. It was water. We figured out that business with the hypodermic needle because we had heard that you were a very unusual man who was interested only in the unusual. We thought that would be unusual enough even for you. We figured it would appeal to your liking for adventure and your interest in danger."

"It was spectacular and dramatic enough," Doc admitted.

"Also nutty, I can see now. But we thought at the time that it would work. By work I mean get you interested. After you were interested I would tell you that the germs had come from a certain place, and take you there. I was to take you to my father's apartment. That was where we took Mr. Mayfair. I presume Mr. Mayfair has told you what happened to him. The same thing was to be done to you, had we succeeded in decoying you there."

Monk put in, "What happened to me didn't make sense."

"It will when you know the rest."

"I hope it does," Monk told her. "I am beginning to feel very dumb about the whole thing."

"A more or less permanent condition, I hope," Ham put in sourly.

Monk ignored him.

Doc Savage said nothing.

The girl said, "You see, we are sure that you made the wild men wild!"

DOC SAVAGE was astonished enough that he made, for a moment, the low, exotic trilling sound which was his unconscious habit in moments of surprise. Ham dropped his sword cane, and Monk was knocked wordless for several minutes to come.

"I?" Doc Savage said. "I made the wild men wild?"

"Of course."

"This," said Ham, "is making less and less sense fast."

Out on the river, a police boat siren hooted briefly twice, which was evidently some kind of signal to other police boats which had been prowling around the spot where the yacht had blown up. The signal got a response, and the boats slowly quitted the vicinity, apparently giving up the search.

Abba Cushing said, "The three wild men have names."

"I'm glad of that," Ham said.

"Their names," she said, "are Irving Eenie, Miner Thomas and R. T. Hooten."

Ham whistled. "The first and last ones—Irving Eenie and Hooten—have a few more dollars than the Sahara Desert has grains of sand. But Miner Thomas—who is he?"

"His name," said Abba Cushing, "is not Miner Thomas. That is his nom de plume. His real name is Mehastan Ghan."

Ham's whistle was louder. "The little man, half Englishman and half Tibetan, who is the religious leader of millions of Orientals?"

"Yes."

"Those," Ham asked incredulously, "are the three wild men?"

"Yes."

Doc Savage put in, "Miss Cushing, you might go ahead and put together some kind of story that makes sense."

"Meaning," she said, "that you probably won't believe me. O. K. Here it is. And it's the truth. Those three men—the three wild men, if you insist on calling them that—are friends of my father and of my father's friends."

Monk came to life to ask, "By your father and his friends, you mean that gang of gold-plated old gentlemen who put me on the yacht."

"Correct," Abba Cushing told him. "And they are, in turn, very close friends of the three wild men. So, when something happened to the three wild men—when they became wild—we naturally began doing what we could to help them."

"What made them wild?" Doc Savage asked.

"You should know. You did it."

"You sincerely believe that?"

"Yes."

"Why?"

"Because," said Abba Cushing, "of the proof. It was conclusive. Oh, you did it all right. My father hired a famous doctor to do what he could for the three men. The doctor gave them some kind of drug that helped them slightly. The drug brought them back near enough to rationality that one of them was able to scrawl an accusation against you. He wrote, 'Doc Savage is behind this.' He wrote some more, but it was not readable."

"Who," asked Doc Savage with interest, "was present when this accusation was made?"

"My father. And the accusation was genuine enough. It wasn't any trick. Mehastan Ghan wrote it in Hindustani. My father does not read or write Hindustani—in case you're trying to say he faked something."

"Was that the only time I was accused?" Doc asked.

"You sound interested."

"Naturally."

"And you sound innocent. You are not innocent, of course. You are a good actor."

"Was there another accusation?"

"Yes," said Abba Cushing, "there was. You were seen prowling in the vicinity."

"Did your father see me that time?"

"No," the girl snapped. "My father was very reluctant to believe you guilty. It was a man named Junior Waddell who saw you. He pursued you, but you escaped."

"This Junior Waddell," Doc Savage remarked, "must be a remarkable fellow."

"He is. He is as large as you are, and very strong. He was a football star at Harvard."

Ham muttered, "I'm going to disown my alma mater."

"Now," said Abba Cushing to Doc Savage, "what are you going to do about all this?"

The bronze man straightened. He extinguished his flashlight and put it in a pocket. "Find the three wild men and help them," he said. "That is what you wanted, is it not?"

WHEN Doc Savage did not do what he had told the girl he would do, Monk and Ham were surprised. They had taken it for granted he would live up to his word, because the bronze man never said he would do a thing, either in fun or in earnest, without doing it. In that respect, he never joked. At the best, he was not a man who was inclined to pull a joke. When he did, it was to exhibit a subtle kind of humor that missed fire for most people, or did not dawn on them until several days later. A little humor of the slapstick kind, Monk and Ham often thought, would do Doc some good. He was not exactly a sober-sides, but it seemed to them that he passed up a lot of fun.

Doc Savage double-crossed the girl after the police department got in touch with him. The police and Doc worked together sometimes, and the bronze man held a high honorary commission on the force.

Contact with the police was by telephone, a sergeant reporting, "Mr. Savage, we found one of the wild men."

"Where and how?"

"We pulled him out from under a subway train. The wild man got a hatchet somewhere, and he took out chasing the subway train, yelling that it was a big worm and that he was going to kill it. Unfortunately, he caught the train."

Doc Savage, Monk Mayfair, Ham Brooks and Abba Cushing went down to the police station. The girl was manifestly surprised when they took her along. She had been considering herself a prisoner, and she announced her intention of telling the police that she was being held a captive against her will. However, when they reached the police station, she did not say anything, except to identify the dead wild man.

"It's Mr. Hooten!" she said, and pressed her fingers to her cheeks.

There was nothing much to the trip to the police station except that. It was not actually the police station, but the morgue, which happened to be in close conjunction. Doc Savage examined the leopard hide, saronglike garment, which the wild man had been wearing.

The leopard skin was a piece cut from what was evidently a quite new leopard skin rug of the type sold in department stores. It bore a price tag, having cost eighty-three dollars and ninety-eight cents. The hatchet was an ordinary hatchet, source unknown.

Doc Savage and his party left the morgue. Abba Cushing went with them, not explaining why she did so. She looked as if she didn't know herself.

Monk said, "I thought you were going to tell the cops on us."

"It wouldn't do any good!" she snapped. "You have too much of a pull with them." Then she shuddered. "I don't know what to think. You do not act guilty: This thing is so fantastic I'm afraid it's getting me so I can't think clearly."

Doc Savage then informed Abba Cushing that he was going to double-cross her.

"We are not going to hunt the wild men," he informed her. "Instead, we are going to resurrect one of them."

"Resurrect?" said the puzzled girl.

DOC SAVAGE went to the police officer in charge of the precinct where the wild man had chased and caught the subway train. "Have the newspapers been informed of this?" Doc asked.

"Not yet," said the officer. "One has called up about it. They got a report about something of the sort and wanted a statement. I told them there was no statement yet."

"Here is what I want you to do," Doc Savage told the officer. "First, have you a bottle of red ink? Two or three bottles would be better."

"Sure."

"I am going to dress in the leopard skin," Doc Savage said. "And you will wrap me up in bandages. Spill some of the red ink on the bandages to look as if I was hurt badly. Then we will call an ambulance from a hospital where I am acquainted, and they will take me there. You will give out word to the newspapers that I am the wild man and that I am badly injured."

The policeman said, "I don't get this."

"I want to pretend to be Hooten and be taken to a hospital."

"Sure, I understand the details," the officer said. "But darned if I see why."

"You will tell the newspapers I am the wild man."

"I heard you the first time."

"You will say nothing about the wild man being dead."

"You're not explaining this."

Doc Savage continued, "You will also tell the newspapers that the wild man was suffering from a mental condition, and that the shock of being hit by the subway train has straightened him out. Such things sometimes happen."

The officer rubbed his jaw dubiously. "This needs an explanation before I will go along with you."

Doc said, without resentment, "Suppose you call your superior officer and see if you need an explanation."

"Don't think I won't." The police officer went away, used the telephone, and came back with a sheepish expression. "I don't need an explanation from you, the boss says."

Doc Savage nodded. "Good. You will go ahead with it, then?"

The other nodded. "But exactly what will I tell the newspapers about that shock business? They'll probably want to know how I know the shock of getting hit by the train straightened out your mental condition."

"That part is very important," Doc told him. "Tell them that I was able to give my name as Root Too Hooten. Tell them that I said I was on the yacht in the Hudson River, the yacht which blew up tonight."

"Holy smoke! So that's where the three wild men came from! Did they blow up the yacht?"

Doc pretended not to hear the question, and added, "Tell the newspapers that I requested that my friend, Raymond E. Cushing, be brought to see me. On second thought, make the word 'demanded.' Make it sound strong. Say that I was very excited and insistent about seeing Cushing."

The officer nodded.

Abba Cushing had been listening, and she now looked indignant. "What are you doing?" she demanded. "Trying to get my father into trouble?"

Doc pretended not to hear her, also. "Let us get going on this."

The police sergeant punched a button and told the officer who responded, "Go out and get some bandages, Phil. Get plenty of bandages. Better get another bottle of red ink."

ONE of the policemen bandaged Doc to resemble a man who might have been hit by a subway train.

While the bandages were being applied, Doc Savage turned to Monk and Ham and Abba Cushing.

"Go to headquarters," he directed, "and get on the transatlantic and transpacific telephones, contacting our agents. Ask them to begin an investigation to see if there are any reports of wild men."

Monk, startled, said, "Blazes! You mean call Europe and places like that?"

"Exactly."

Monk nodded dumbly, too surprised to ask any more questions about that angle.

Ham Brooks inquired, "What do we do then? Stick around headquarters and wait for reports on that?"

"The one of you who guards Miss Cushing can do that," Doc said. "The other one had better come to the hospital where I will be taken, and be ready for developments."

"Which one of us," asked Ham with much interest, "takes care of Miss Cushing?"

"You had better decide that for yourselves," Doc said.

A police patrolman came in and reported, "The ambulance is here to take Mr. Savage—the wild man—to the hospital."

DOC SAVAGE was halfway to the hospital in the ambulance when he changed his mind. The fact that he did change his mind was totally unexpected. He did not often do such things.

"Go to headquarters instead," he said.

At headquarters, he spent two hours in the laboratory which was a part of the establishment. He was working, Monk and Ham saw, with the chemical section. He was making something.

What he was making proved to be several buttons. They were ordinary buttons, dark ones which would match almost anything in color.

He gave two of the buttons to Monk, two to Ham, and kept two himself.

"Sew these on your shirts," he said. "Sew them on the shirts rather than the coats, and sew them close to the neck, but not too close, so that you can reach them with your teeth should you be bound hand and foot."

"Buttons?" Monk said. "Teeth? I don't get it."

"At the right time," Doc said, "you had better eat them."

"Eat them?" Monk eyed the buttons.

"Yes."

Ham said, "You mean they're pills?"

"Eat them," Doc instructed, "if it should at any time appear that you are in imminent danger of becoming wild men."

"Great glee!" Monk said.

Doc Savage then put back on the bandages and

**One of the policemen bandaged Doc to resemble
a man who might have been hit by a subway.**

the other paraphernalia which was to make him look somewhat like the wild man named Hooten. "Tell the ambulance to come and pick me up," he said.

Chapter VII
THE EPIDEMIC

MONK and Ham liked to put Doc Savage's worldwide organization to work. It gave them a thrill. Doc Savage had developed the organization of late months; and considering the efficiency which the thing had already shown, Monk and the other members of Doc's group of associates were surprised that he did not make more use of it.

The organization was a direct outgrowth of the rather fantastic method Doc used of disposing of such crooks and malefactors as he caught. The bronze man maintained a secret hospital in upstate New York—he and his associates referred to it as the "college"—to which criminals were sent. There, they received a complicated brain operation, the technique of which Doc had developed. The operation wiped out all memory of their past, and following this, the "students" received a course of training which filled them with a hatred of wrongdoers and equipped them with a trade or profession by which they could earn good and useful livelihoods.

Doc Savage had, of late, taken to scattering these students in the far corners of the Earth. He got them jobs—often in business firms in which the bronze man had a substantial interest, but not always—and fettered them with no other obligation than that they should perform service in the gathering of information from time to time, as called upon.

It was these men whom Monk and Ham began contacting after they went to Doc's headquarters on the eighty-sixth floor of one of the most imposing skyscrapers in the midtown area. They used a system. They called some of the agents and gave them the names of other agents whom they could call, relaying the information that Doc Savage wanted to know about any reports of wild men.

The silly angle of what they were doing got the best of Ham. He burst into laughter.

"You'd think the population of Borneo had been turned loose," he said.

"There are no wild men in Borneo anymore," Monk advised him.

Abba Cushing had been watching them. She was not impressed as much as they had hoped she would be by the worldwide telephoning, probably because she was the daughter of a man who no doubt did a lot of it himself.

"We'll get results for you," Monk told her.

She tapped a toe on the rug with ill temper.

"You are acting," she informed them, "like a pack of wild men yourselves. Or idiots, I should say. What on Earth makes you think there are more than three wild men?"

"What makes you think there aren't more than three?" Monk countered.

"That isn't an answer that makes sense," she snapped. Then she added: "However, it is about what I would expect."

While they were waiting for action from overseas, and for the young woman's temper to cool, Monk and Ham produced their pets. Monk had a pet pig that was a runt. Ham had a pet chimpanzee—or possibly some species of ape—that was also a runt.

"Habeas Corpus," Monk introduced the pig.

"And Chemistry," Ham said of his chimp. "Don't be alarmed if he seems to resemble Monk. The resemblance was purely an accident. Both their ancestors hung by their tails from trees, that's all."

The two animals had a bad effect on the girl. She gazed at them as if the last of her confidence were gone. "You two fellows are just a couples of goons," she said grimly. "And here I have been hearing that Doc Savage and his associates were one of the most remarkable groups of men. I heard you were capable of doing anything. Somebody has lied. You're a bunch of clowns."

Ham smiled. "Monk may be a clown."

"You're a bigger one," Abba Cushing advised. "You and that scrub ape, or whatever it is! And you're supposed to be a lawyer. A Harvard man! What a laugh!"

Monk laughed, and Ham's neck got red.

"Clowns or not," Ham snapped, "there is something going on here that we do not understand, and we're going to get at the bottom of it. You can bet your bottom dollar on that."

"Then why aren't you out trying to find the other two wild men, Irving Eenie and Miner Thomas? They're the ones who need help. Or don't you want to find them?"

"Of course, we want to find them," Ham said indignantly.

"I'll bet," she snapped, "that you don't. I'll bet you are at the bottom of this yourselves." She leaned forward, her face pale with emotion. "Yes, sir, I'll bet you are back of it. You are just eccentric enough to start something as insane as this affair of the wild men is. It is the kind of a thing you would concoct. It would take minds like yours to do it."

Monk looked at Ham and said, "I don't think she likes us."

"It's pretty obvious," Ham muttered.

"I believe," offered Monk generously, "that I'll let you take over the guarding of her. Doc said one of us should do it. You can have the job, Ham."

"The heck I can have. It's yours." Ham scowled.

Monk told the girl, "And just for the way you've treated us two fine fellows, we're going to see what we can dig up on your father."

THE record of Raymond E. Cushing, man of finance and, at times, of somewhat eccentric ideas, was easily traced. There was nothing secret about his career. It was in "Who's Who" and on the tongue of anyone in Wall Street.

Born poor, Cushing had done what many Americans had done, amassed wealth—tremendous wealth in his case—at an early age. There was nothing shady in his amassing of wealth, at least nothing more shady than in the amassing of any man's wealth.

There had been a period of Cushing's life, shortly after he amassed his first half dozen million or so, when he had made a considerable splurge as a philanthropist, donating ungodly sums to various things. There was nothing reprehensible about this, unless it was that the man might have used better judgment in his donations. The money had not done the good which Cushing had intended. There had been maladministration in many cases, and apparently Cushing had quit philanthropy in disgust. As far as anyone knew, he had not devoted a dime to charity since.

There was one other item. The revolution which Cushing's sugar company had foisted on a Central American republic. There were many revolutions brewed by American business concerns about this time, but this one had a little different cast in that Cushing had apparently owned a genuine desire to reform the country. He had reformed it, putting in some fine old gentlemen, natives, with a great reputation for honesty. These fine gentlemen had turned out to be as big, or bigger, crooks than anyone before or since.

Cushing, then, was a violent philanthropist who was invariably beset by poor judgment and bad luck.

Renny Renwick phoned then. Renny was Colonel John Renwick, one of Doc's associates, an engineer, at present in South Africa for the British government.

Monk talked to him. Monk had a goblin-pestered look when he hung up. "Yes," he told Renny at the last, "by all means look into it."

Monk hung up. He wheeled, to confront Ham.

"That was Renny in South Africa," he said. "He called us up to report that there are three wild men down there."

"Huh?" Ham's mouth hung open. "Three?"

"Three," Monk agreed. "There was three of them here. There are three of them down there. Quite a coincidence, wouldn't you say?"

DOC SAVAGE occupied a wing in the hospital that was quiet, facing the river. The river was the same one in which the yacht had sunk the night before, and the spot was not far from the one where the boat had gone down. The point of the sinking was visible from the window, but this was a coincidence.

Doc had not asked for this particular room, although he was spending his time sitting up in bed and gazing out over the river. There was a police launch anchored where the yacht had sunk, and a tugboat of some size. Divers were working from the tug, evidently searching the shattered remains of the sunken yacht in search of clues or bodies. Neither of these had been found, as far as Doc Savage was able to tell from that distance.

In the hall outside the bronze man's room stood a burly guard. He was there to keep away the newspaper reporters, who were nagging the hospital for an interview with the wild man.

The fact that the wild man was reported to be R. T. Hooten, the noted Dutchman, had stirred up the newsmen no end. Some of the leading special news writers had been assigned to the story. There were headlines in most of the morning sheets about the affair.

Doc turned his head as there was a knock on the door. It was the guard. He said, "That Chinaman is here again. The big, ugly one. He got shirtee, he says. Last time it was coatee."

"Let him in," Doc said.

The Chinaman was Monk Mayfair. He asked, "You likee mo' laundly, chop-chop?" Monk looked exactly like a Chinaman, provided a Chinaman could be found who had descended from an ape, which was very doubtful. However, it was a very effective disguise.

"Chop-chop," Doc Savage agreed.

"There's three more wild men in London, England," Monk said. "Isn't that something to hang on the fence? I don't get it at all."

"Three in South Africa, and three in England?" Doc asked.

"That's right. Three in each place."

"Who reported the London trio?"

"One of our agents. Bill Lee, the guy who used to be a professional thug. After Bill told me that the three wild men in London were all mighty prominent, I got in touch with Renny again and asked him about it. Sure enough, the three in South Africa are prominent men. At least two of them are. The third has not been identified for sure, but I'll bet he is prominent, too."

Doc Savage was thoughtful for a moment. Then he asked, "Did you find out anything about the three wild men in each place?"

"Sure. What you want to know?"

"What kind of men are they?"

"Well, in South Africa, there's a noted mining man, one of the leading political bosses and a professional reformer who has a great following both among the natives and the English."

"What kind of men," asked Doc, "are they in London?"

"A fellow who owns a flock of factories, another man who has been mentioned frequently as probably the future government leader in England, and another famous reformer— Wait a minute!"

Monk's face got a blankly quizzical expression, and he sank into a chair. He sat there turning things over in his mind.

"A reformer in England, a reformer in South Africa, and a reformer in New York. You *would* call this fellow Miner Thomas, alias Mehastan Ghan, a reformer, wouldn't you?"

Doc Savage said, "A financier in South Africa, a financier in England and a financier here in America."

Monk nodded vaguely. "Yeah, that just dawned on me. And a man of great economic influence in South Africa, one in England and one here."

"Exactly."

"It takes on a pattern, doesn't it?" Monk muttered. "But darned if I see what kind of a garment the pattern could make. Darned if I do."

Doc Savage made no comment. He lay quiescent, completely wrapped in bandages so that he resembled a mummy. Only his nostrils, one eye, his mouth and his right hand were not wrapped with bandages. After he had been silent for a while, there came gently into the room the low, trilling sound which was the bronze man's absent-minded trait. It had a puzzled quality for a moment, then sank back into nothingness.

Monk said, "This wild man thing is an epidemic."

DOC SAVAGE seemed to reach a decision. The strange life in his eyes, like flake gold in movement, became more alert.

He asked, "Have you and Ham been talking with Miss Cushing?"

"She's been talking to us," Monk said gloomily. "You know, for such a pretty girl, she sure has a tongue like a witch."

"Have you," inquired Doc, "asked her why the yacht was blown up in an attempt to kill us?"

"Sure!" Monk nodded. "She's got an answer to that one."

"Does she admit her father and her friends blew it up?"

"Not her. She says we did it ourselves."

"Why should we do it, does she think?"

"In an effort to kill the three wild men who were on the yacht. The three wild men were being kept there by Cushing and his friends, receiving treatment from doctors which was not doing them any good. She says we probably wanted to get rid of the three wild men, once we saw that we were suspected. So what simpler method would we take than to blow up the yacht? Isn't that a sweet line of reasoning for you?"

"Has she explained what she was doing out on the river?"

"She said that she had a weak moment. She began to wonder if I was really guilty. She had come out in a rowboat to get aboard the yacht and have another talk with me. She was close to the boat when we blew it up, she says." Monk scowled. "She even accuses us of trying to kill her!"

"Does she account for our not continuing the attempts?"

"Sure. She says the police and everybody knows she is with us, so we wouldn't dare attempt to kill her again."

"She has a more or less logical explanation, or line of reasoning, for everything."

Monk groaned, "Oh, brother, has she! You know what she says we are doing? She says we are practicing up for something by testing out some kind of devilish experiment. She says you are using human guinea pigs for some experimental work. She says that is what it is."

"So I am experimenting on the wild men, eh?" Doc Savage said grimly.

Monk glanced sharply at Doc Savage. He saw that the bronze man was extremely disturbed. There was hardly a noticeable change in Doc's voice, and his features were hidden under the bandages, but Monk knew him well enough to be sure that Doc was agitated. Understanding Doc's emotions was more a matter of sensing them than actually witnessing any change.

"That's her nutty idea," Monk admitted. "She says it's her father's idea, too."

"The fact that wild men have cropped up in South Africa and England should change her mind about its being my work," Doc said.

Monk snorted.

"On the contrary, Doc. She knows Renny is in South Africa. She says he's your agent there, seeing how the experiments will work in different climates."

Monk stopped and ran a finger around his collar.

"You know what else she claims? She says

you've got five associates. Two more besides Ham and Renny and me. She claims one of the others, either Long Tom Roberts or Johnny Littlejohn, is in England."

Doc Savage's flake-gold eyes were absolutely rigid for a moment.

He said, "Johnny Littlejohn is in London, now."

"Yeah. I didn't tell her that."

"Monk," Doc Savage said, "someone seems to have done a very subtle and complete job of involving us in this thing."

Monk nodded. "Yeah, and they knew where Renny and Johnny were. That means they know a lot about us. Renny didn't advertise the fact that he was going to South Africa, and Johnny didn't advertise that he was going to England. They are on war work, so it is a secret. Or was supposed to be. It means that whoever we're up against not only has an organization, but brains as well."

Doc Savage was silent for a while. "There is just one other thing," he said finally. "Has the girl mentioned the strange fear we felt when we boarded the yacht?"

"The fear? No, she hasn't said a thing about that."

Chapter VIII
ONE TOO MANY SHIRTEE

WHEN Monk Mayfair left Doc Savage's hospital room he took his departure with specific instructions which he had received from Doc. The instructions baffled Monk; he did not understand them at all.

"Post yourself near the hospital," Doc Savage instructed him. "Have a fast car and a fast boat handy, and have Ham Brooks bring one of our planes around to the riverfront several blocks below here."

"In other words, get ready to follow somebody in a hurry," said Monk, understanding that much of it.

"Exactly."

"Who will I follow?" Monk asked. "Don't tell me you are going to produce a wild man. If you are, just say so. This thing has gotten screwy enough that nothing would surprise me."

"This man," Doc Savage told him, "may be acting wild, but it will only be because he is excited. You will actually recognize him because he is smoking."

"Smoking!" Monk swallowed twice. "What you mean?"

"I mean smoking," Doc Savage said. "Probably you had better be on your way now, so you can get set. The news of my presence here, or the presence supposedly of Hooten, has been in the newspapers

long enough to begin to get results."

Those were the instructions with which Monk left the hospital, and he did not understand them.

There was one comfort. It was not the first time he had not understood Doc Savage's instructions. On other occasions, the improbable-sounding instructions issued by the bronze man had turned out very foxy indeed. That was one thing that made life interesting when you were associated with Doc Savage. Not only did the most fantastic adventures seem to happen along, but the bronze man's system of attacking the trouble was frequently more fantastic than the trouble itself.

It was Doc Savage's unorthodox methods, the surprising gadgets he concocted and had the imagination to use, which accounted for his remarkable record, Monk suspected.

Having left the hospital, Monk visited a nearby drugstore and telephoned Ham Brooks about bringing around the airplane. "I'm supposed to follow a smoking man, now," he said.

Ham laughed. "This will round out Miss Cushing's opinion of us," Ham commented.

"Look here!" Monk said ominously. "You're not making friends with that girl?"

"Why not?" Ham demanded. "When we drew lots to see who would stay, you handed me the short straw. Don't think I didn't notice you cheating. So whatever I do, it's no hide off your back."

Disgruntled, Monk slammed up the receiver in Ham's ear. He turned and left the drugstore, stopped on the sidewalk, and stood there wondering what he should do about watching the hospital, where would be the best spot.

A man's voice asked him casually, "Got a match, buddy?"

Monk started feeling absently in his pockets for a match.

The voice said, "You gottee shirtee, fliend?" in a fake pidgin English.

Monk started violently and looked down at the stocky blue gun which the stranger had produced and was holding against his stomach, just above the belt buckle.

"You catchee hole in shirtee, you movee," said the man. "And, brother, don't think I don't mean it, either."

WHEN the burly guard in the hospital next knocked on Doc Savage's door, it was to report, "There's another Chinaman out here. This one says he wants to talk to you about shirtee."

"The same Chinaman?" Doc Savage asked.

"Not unless he's shrunk a lot, this one ain't."

Doc Savage lay back on the bed and inspected the gadget which he had rigged on the ceiling of the room. This consisted of several small paper sacks stuck to the ceiling with suction cups, and connected with a string. The string, not at all conspicuous because it was made of a rayon fabric and was very thin, led to Doc Savage's bed. He took hold of the end of the string and set himself.

"Send him in," he said.

When the guard immediately got slugged in the hall it did not surprise Doc Savage. Monk and Ham, in visiting Doc here at the hospital, had been instructed to use a kind of laundry code to identify themselves and give the word that nothing was wrong. First trip was to be to see Doc about a coat, the second about a shirt, the third about a necktie, and so on. Here was a second shirt. There was to be no second shirt. Therefore, something was wrong.

So Doc set himself. When the door popped open he was ready.

The man who came in was not large, but he made up in dynamic purpose, and armament, what he otherwise lacked. He was man hunting, and he was what would be called completely equipped. He had a gun in his left hand, while his right hand tried to contain both a gun and a hand grenade. There was suspicious bulk under his coat that might be a bulletproof vest. Hooked over one of his arms was an industrial-type gas mask which was as effective as anything against tear gas and other types likely to be used by the police or, the man probably hoped, Doc Savage.

After the man came into the room, Doc Savage pulled the cord. He pulled it slowly, moving not much more than his fingers, so that the man would not be alarmed.

The cord broke the sacks, and the sacks showered their contents down on the man. It was a powder. It looked innocent enough at first glance. The man cursed.

After he had cursed, he stopped. Then he yelled. There was pain, astonishment and horror in the bellow. He did a kind of Indian war dance, moving his feet up and down, but not traveling around the room. He did some slapping at himself as if he had mosquitoes. In the course of this he lost the grenade he was holding in one hand.

The grenade bounced off the wall and hopped across the floor like a hard egg. That scared the man. He wheeled and all but crashed the door off its hinges getting out of the room. He went down the corridor with the best speed he could manage.

Doc Savage came out of the bed, rising almost straight up. He was scared. The grenade had scared him. He had not figured on that.

The bandages he had split previously, and had been lying on the splits so that they would not be noticed. The bandages came off with no more difficulty than a covering of dry leaves.

He got the grenade. Ten seconds was the average time one of the things took to make up its mind. He was all convulsed to give it a mad pitch out of the window; then he relaxed and looked sheepish. He put the grenade on the table. Then he decided someone might pick it up and get hurt, so he pocketed it.

The pin in the thing had not been drawn.

DOC SAVAGE went into the hospital corridor. The guard was squirming on the floor and did not look badly hurt. There were no nurses in the hall, despite the commotion. Doc had specifically requested that the floor be vacated, so that no one would get hurt if there were trouble.

The bronze man went down the stairway, which was obviously the route taken by the fleeing man. He traveled fast, and reached a service door which opened upon the same street as the front entrance of the institution.

His gadget—the powder he had taken such pains to get on the man—was working. The stuff, upon exposure to the air, reacted violently, giving off a certain amount of heat, not enough to kill a man but enough to make him extremely uncomfortable, and also produced quantities of dark vapor resembling smoke.

The stuff was a result of some experiments Doc had been making in an effort to develop a chemical mixture which would create artificial heat in the garments used by ski troopers and other soldiers in cold-country fighting. This material was worthless for the purpose because of the smoky vapor. But it had occurred to the bronze man that it would be ideal for a purpose such as the present one, and he had had a supply of the stuff on hand.*

The man who had tried to raid the room had taken the middle of the street and was moving fast. He was smoking, literally. The chemical on his clothing had reacted with the air, so that he seemed to be afire.

There was no sign of Monk Mayfair.

Doc Savage moved with casual efficiency. Against an emergency, he had a car parked in the

---

*As the readers have noticed who have followed Doc Savage in previous adventures, it is the policy of the publishers and author to omit all exact chemical formulae, in order that such information may not fall in the wrong hands. There are two reasons for such omissions: First, tinkering with these chemicals by inexperienced persons might easily result in explosions or burns. Second, the primary purpose of the stories is the conveying of entertainment, and the deleting of such information as might be dangerous in the wrong hands does not, we hope, detract from this entertainment value.—The Editor.

neighborhood. It was a small machine with few distinguishing features. He entered it, then drove after the running man. The latter stopped a taxi-cab, but the driver took one look at him and drove on hurriedly.

The man who had been doused with the chemical went in search of another cab. The stuff on his clothing had about completed its reaction. There was now very little smoke.

The man found another cab, got in, and the machine took him away. Doc followed.

If Doc Savage had any feeling that anything unusual had just happened, he did not show it in his manner. This stoicism with which he usually accepted a thing of this sort was a source of amazement, sometimes hilarious glee, to Monk and Ham and his other associates. Doc, however, had a different viewpoint. Many of the things he did—this smoking chemical was an example—were ridiculously fantastic. But he did them for a definite purpose, and the results, not the oddness of the method, interested him.

He was fully aware that the un-conforming methods he used made him look eccentric. He did not mind. His methods were productive of results in a high percentage of cases, and they had an awe-creating effect on enemies. So it was the result and not the method that counted.

He followed the cab ahead with care, leaving nothing to chance, taking nothing for granted.

And when the man with the armament left the cab while it was caught in a traffic jam, and ducked into a subway entrance, Doc saw him. The bronze man left his car in a loading zone and descended the subway steps, on the opposite side of the street. Subways are the most difficult places to trail people. But this station had the advantage of being one that was not heavily patronized.

It was a typical New York subway station—a pair of tracks, one for uptown trains and the other for downtown, and on each side of them a long platform for the passengers. Entrance to the downtown platform on the west side of the street, entrance to the uptown platform on the east side. The quarry had taken the east entrance. Doc took the west.

Looking across the tracks, through the array of supporting pillars that held the street overhead, Doc located the man. The fellow had gotten rid of his coat, which had been discolored, no doubt, by the chemical. He was in his shirt sleeves. He stood at a newsstand, pretending to read a paper he had purchased, but actually standing so that he could see anyone who came down the street stairs to that platform. It had not occurred to him to watch the opposite side.

A subway train soon came rumbling in and stopped at the platform on which the man stood.

Doc Savage promptly dropped to the tracks, took care to keep clear of the electrified rail, leaped across the tracks and climbed up between two of the cars.

The cars were connected by a kind of bellows, and an arrangement of metal bars and a protective grille to keep passengers on the platform from being crowded down between the cars. It was a difficult spot to hitch a ride, but possible if a man was strong.

At the next station, Doc Savage climbed over to the platform and boarded a car in the conventional manner. His quarry was in the car forward. Doc located him through the open door between the cars and remained where he was.

AT the third stop, the man left the train. He walked casually down the street and entered a large chain drugstore. The business establishment had a side door, and Doc entered by that route. There was a group of telephone booths in the back, racks containing bargain books, the usual array of bargain counters and drug counters. A soda fountain, cigar stand and news rack were in the front.

The man was standing at the news rack, holding a magazine and again watching to see if he were followed.

Surmising the man's object in entering the drugstore, no doubt, was either to use the telephone or to get something in the line of an unguent for his burns, Doc sidled into one of the phone booths.

Doc took down a receiver, dialed the operator, asked for the wire chief, and said, "This is U-93, Department K. I am talking from"—he glanced at the number on the telephone—"Circle 0-7000. It is one of a battery of booths. Hook me up so I can eavesdrop on any conversation from any one of the other booths. Quick."

"Yes, sir," said the wire chief. "Just a moment."

There was an interval of silence.

The man put down his magazine and sauntered back toward the telephone booths.

The wire chief came back on the wire. "Sorry, sir, but did you say you were U-93, Department K?"

"Yes."

"Your credentials have been canceled," said the wire chief. "Sorry, we cannot do anything for you."

Doc Savage stared at the mouthpiece in blank astonishment. U-93, Department K, was his identification number with the Department of Justice. He had expected it to get its usual magical results. Canceled? Evidently, there was a mistake.

Mistake or not, there was no time to argue

**The man was moving fast. The chemical on his clothes
was reacting with the air, so that he seemed to be afire.**

about it. The man was entering a booth. He was
cautious and picked the farthest booth.

There was nothing to do but take a chance. Doc
Savage took the booth adjoining the man, pulled
the door shut, and decided that the other man,
alarmed, was not making his call. Doc dialed at
random, held the receiver down, said, "Let me
speak to Alice … Hello, Alice, this is Joe. How
about tonight?"

He went on with the kind of conversation a
young man might have with his girl.

Eventually, the man in the adjoining booth, his
alarm gone, dialed his number.

Doc did not get the number from the dial
clicks. He had performed this feat a number of
times; it was not too difficult if one developed an
ear for telegraphic clicks. But this time someone
in the drugstore burst into loud laughter at the
wrong time, and he lost out.

The man's voice was audible, however, by
snatches. He made a fairly complete report on
what had happened to him. He explained that the
man in the hospital room had not been Hooten,
but Doc Savage. He described, profanely, the
business of the smoke. He was emphatic about his
flight being cautious. No one had followed him,
he insisted.

The man said, "Did the boys bring in that
Monk Mayfair?"

Evidently the answer was in the affirmative,
because the man said, "That's fine." He laughed.
"He should make an interesting wild man."

Doc Savage's metallic features lost color. It was
the first he had heard that Monk was in trouble.

The man in the adjoining booth said, "I tell you
it's safe enough. I could come in right now.
Nobody is following me."

He evidently got a skeptical answer from
whomever he was talking to, because he tried to
argue and got shouted down. Doc Savage could
hear the angry rasp of the receiver through the
telephone booth partition. It was a man's voice at
the other end, or a very raucous-voiced woman.
Probably a man.

"Oh, all right," said the man in the booth
hastily. "I'll go to my hotel. You say you want me
to wait there?"

Evidently, that was the plan.

"O.K.," said the man. "I'll wait there for you."

The man then left the telephone booth.

But he was cautious. He loitered again at the
magazine stand at the front of the drugstore, and
this time he kept his eye on the telephone booth
into which Doc Savage had stepped.

Doc took his time about leaving the booth.
When he did leave it, he did so stern first, after the
fashion of a crab, so that the man would not be
able to see his face. He also kept his shoulders
rounded and changed both his stature and his walk
as much as possible. He got out of the store without showing the man his face.

He did note that the man had turned and was
following him.

THE fellow might not be suspicious, but at least
he was being extremely cautious. Doc Savage
turned toward a taxicab which stood at the curb.

He gave the man in the drugstore time enough
to come out and witness as Doc stepped into a
cab. The cab was parked, and the bronze man said
to the driver, "Here is five dollars. I am giving
somebody the slip. You know how dames are.
Wait a moment, then drive on. Don't look around
when I leave the cab."

Without turning his head and out of the corner
of his mouth, the driver said, "O.K., bud."

Doc Savage leaned back in the seat. He had
spotted the man by now, standing in the side door
of the drugstore.

Leaning back in the seat put the bronze man
out of sight of the watcher. Doc slid down in the
seat, got on the floor boards. When the cab started,
and the opening of the door on the far side was not
likely to be as noticeable, he eased the door open,
dropped to the street, made a scuttling run and got
behind another parked car. Fortunate timing and
the position of taxicab and parked cars kept him
from being seen.

The man who had visited the hospital was satisfied. He lit a cigarette, stood there for some time, then ambled down the street.

His hotel was not far away. The desk clerk of the hostelry was subject to a bribe. He sold out cheap. Five dollars.

The man was registered under the name of John Stone. He received mail under the name of Oliver Dillard. He liked to play the races, had a habit of coming in drunk. He had never had a visitor. He made many telephone calls, all of them to a girlfriend named Genie. Doc got Genie's number.

Doc Savage telephoned his headquarters and got Ham Brooks on the wire.

"Nothing new here," Ham reported. "Say, what's happened to Monk? He hasn't reported in."

Doc said, "Monk is in bad. They got hold of him somehow, and they are going to see what kind of a wild man he would make."

"Great Scot!" Ham exploded. "That's fantastic. Why?"

Doc said, "Get to the Jefferson Wilson Hotel on Fifty-fifth Street. I will meet you at a small restaurant at the corner west of the hotel."

"Right away," Ham said instantly.

"Is Miss Cushing with you?"

"Right here."

"Can you lock her up until I get there?"

"She won't like it."

"Let her not like it," Doc Savage said grimly. "I want you to watch this man in the hotel while I start other wheels turning."

"Right-o," Ham said. "Say, Doc, the Department of Justice has been trying to get hold of you on the telephone. I guess it can keep, whatever it is."

"It can keep," Doc Savage said.

Chapter IX
QUESTION OF GUILT

DOC SAVAGE met Ham Brooks on his arrival in the vicinity of the hotel. Doc gave Ham enough of an outline of what had happened for Ham to go ahead. What he wanted to know, Doc explained, was who came to the hotel to meet the man.

Doc Savage then rode a cab to his car, which he picked up and drove to his headquarters. He left the machine in the private basement garage which he maintained there, then entered the private elevator which lifted him to the eighty-sixth floor, where he stepped out into a corridor.

He stepped directly into the arms of three young men. Or, at least, he stepped against the stiffly outstretched arm of one of the young men and stopped.

"Mr. Savage?" asked the owner of the stiff arm.

He was a well-developed young man with a good jaw line and an eye that was not afraid, and at the same time not overbearing.

"That is right," Doc told him.

The young man produced his credentials. He was an F.B.I. operative.

"I am Swain," he said. "This is Carson and Roberts"—introducing his two companions—"who also are operatives."

"Won't you come in?" Doc suggested.

The door of the bronze man's suite of rooms—three great rooms, the smallest being a reception room, the other two scientific library and experimental laboratory—had been smashed open. The work had been done with a cutting torch, for the bronze-colored door was of armorplate steel. The cutting had been neatly and efficiently executed.

"We already have been in," said Swain dryly.

The reception room was the least distinguished of the headquarters arrangement. There were comfortable chairs, a great inlaid table of unusual design, and an ancient safe that was nearly the size of a box car.

Abba Cushing occupied one of the chairs. She tried to look at Doc Savage defiantly, but she was more frightened than defiant. She looked like a little girl who had been caught with a finger in the jam.

There were two more government men with the girl.

There was no loud talk and no accusations. But the conversation began and continued on a note so ominous that it did not need loudness.

Swain said, "I am sorry not to be able to meet you under more amiable circumstances, Mr. Savage. Unfortunately, it was not my luck to do so, and I might as well come to the two or three points we have to bring up."

Doc Savage nodded, but did not comment.

"First," said Swain, "my instructions are to advise you that each and every connection you have with the Federal Bureau of Investigation has been suspended. Not revoked, I was instructed to explain, but merely suspended pending clarification of certain matters."

Doc was silent.

Swain added, "I should further state that any attempt by you to give the impression that you are connected with the F.B.I. will constitute a crime. I say this because I have been informed that you attempted, within the past hour, to obtain the facilities of the telephone company by using your connection. This was not a crime because you had not, at the time, been informed of your suspension. But any further thing of that sort will be unfortunate."

Doc Savage asked, "Does an explanation go with this?"

"AN explanation," Swain agreed, nodding, *"and* an explanation, I hope."

"Meaning?"

"We explain. Then you explain."

Doc was silent.

"Is that agreeable?" Swain persisted.

Doc Savage said, "This interview seems to be starting off on a rather emphatic note. Under the circumstances it might not be advisable to make promises."

Swain said earnestly, "I can assure you this is not a pleasant or agreeable performance on my part. However, duty happens to be duty."

Doc asked, "Who explains first?"

"I do, if you wish," Swain said, smiling slightly. "First, there seems to be a rather mysterious epidemic of wild men. Very wealthy, very famous, or very important men in at least four different points on the Earth."

Doc Savage's eyes showed sudden animation. "Four?" he asked.

"Here in New York," Swain said. "In South Africa. In London. In Lisbon, Portugal."

"The Portugal instance is news," Doc advised him.

"You knew about the other three?"

"One of my associates is in South Africa, and another is in London," Doc explained.

The F.B.I. operative's face tightened. "Yes. We had noticed the coincidence."

Doc Savage saw the way the wind was blowing. He had suspected something of the kind. "I see," he said. "Can you tell me the type of men affected in Portugal?"

Swain nodded. "I see no reason why not. Augustez Goestal, the great reform leader of Portugal; Sir James Cousine, the English industrialist who is a citizen of Portugal, and one of the most wealthy men in the country; and Carlos Moste, the inventor and industrial organizer."

Doc Savage's voice showed emotion—thoughtfulness.

"A reform leader, an extremely wealthy man and an organizer," he said.

Swain said, "I see that the point has occurred to you."

"The point?"

"The three types of men have been the same in each case, here, in Africa, in England, in Portugal."

"Yes, they have that in common," Doc admitted.

For the first time the F.B.I. man was distinctly unfriendly.

"The other thing they have in common," he said, "is the presence of one of your associates in each instance."

"My fifth aide, Long Tom Roberts, the electrical expert, is in Portugal, if that is what you mean," Doc admitted.

"That is exactly what I mean."

ABBA CUSHING had been listening with growing concern. She had produced a handkerchief and was knotting and unknotting it nervously. There were moments when she looked as if she wanted to scream in remorse.

"Mr. Savage," Swain said, "these facts I have just mentioned to you have been drawn to our attention. In fairness, I will say that they have been called to our attention anonymously."

"'Anonymous,'" Doc Savage suggested, "is usually a word for trouble-maker."

Swain grinned. "Sure. Admitted. In this case the anonymous party gave a fairly sensible explanation. The party was giving us a tip, not proof. You are a very powerful and also respected individual. You could, if you chose, make a great deal of trouble for any informant. And the informant said that, therefore, it was more sensible to remain anonymous."

Doc Savage looked at the girl. He was thinking of Monk's report on what Ham had told him about the girl—that she always had a very logical explanation for what she did.

Abba Cushing leaped back, menacing everyone with the guns.

She seemed to realize that his thoughts were something of the kind. She grew more pale.

Doc asked, "The object of this interview is what?"

"There are two objects. Alternatives." Swain met Doc's glance levelly. "The first is to get from you a clear explanation of what this somewhat zany, but obviously sinister, matter of wild men is all about."

Doc made a slight gesture.

"At this stage of the affair, such an explanation is not possible," he said.

"That is too bad," Swain said. "Because that leaves us the alternative object."

"And that?"

"My boss is spending several days aboard an American destroyer which is going on patrol up in the direction of Greenland," said the F.B.I. operative. "He would be delighted to have you as his guest on the cruise."

"Another way of saying," said Doc Savage, "that he is taking me into custody."

"He did not put it that way."

"I can refuse."

"Not," said Swain, "very conveniently."

"This is hardly legal."

"Oh, yes, it is," Swain told him. "We have warrants, plus whatever in the line of charges you wish."

"On what grounds?"

Swain nodded at Abba Cushing. "Holding the young lady, here, a prisoner, for one thing. We found her locked up here. She assured us she was a prisoner."

Doc Savage looked at Abba Cushing. "You did that?"

She nodded miserably. "I'm beginning to wish I hadn't."

Doc Savage turned to Swain and asked, "Just what is the general nature of the department's suspicions about me?"

Swain replied frankly.

"We suspect—wrongly, we hope—that you are guilty, not of evil intentions, but of trying some rather terrible experiments on human subjects. We know that you are a scientist, and we know that you specialize in the unusual, the untried, the fantastic. Knowing a great deal about you, we sincerely believe that your objectives are good. But we are convinced that the methods in this case are completely illegal, both from a law and a humanitarian standpoint. Therefore, I do hereby inform you that you are in custody."

DOC SAVAGE turned to Abba Cushing and said, "That illegal experiment was your, or your father's, line of reasoning, was it not?"

"It was my idea," the girl said.

"So we gathered."

"This is also my idea," Abba Cushing said.

She jumped then, did something that no one in the least expected her to do. She dived at one of the F.B.I. men, and caught the fellow completely by surprise. She had evidently been studying him and had decided where he kept his guns, because her hands dived into his pockets and came out with, not one, but two revolvers. She leaped back, menacing everyone with the guns.

"I am a good shot," she said, "though at this range I do not need to be." She backed toward the door. "Come on," she ordered Doc.

Doc said, "It might not be wise to leave in this fashion. The F.B.I. is not a good outfit to trick."

The girl's voice was tight, but the guns were steady. "Come on!" she ordered. "I tried to make you a prisoner once. This time I'll get the job done."

Doc asked Swain, "What would you do under the circumstances?"

"I wouldn't get shot," Swain said dryly.

Doc followed the girl. She put a gun against his back, got him into the private elevator. She sent it down to the basement garage.

"Pick a fast car," she ordered. "It looks as if we will need it."

Chapter X
TOP WEST

AFTER Doc Savage selected the car, the girl drove the machine. She tucked her guns into a side pocket, and gave all her attention to the wheel. She seemed to have a definite destination, which proved to be the private garage in a townhouse in the plush-lined Seventies. A servant opened the doors at a signal from her horn and she drove inside. The servant, a man, showed no surprise at sight of Doc Savage. He went away.

"My home," Abba Cushing explained.

"Why did you just do what you did?" Doc asked.

She sat silent for a while, both hands on the steering wheel, staring fixedly ahead.

"My father is a strong character," she said. "He would have to be, to make the money he has made. But he is more than a machine for making money. He is a philosopher. One of the first things of philosophy that he taught me was to make sure you are wrong, then admit it and start undoing it."

"I see," Doc said.

Abba Cushing was thoughtful. "He has a quaint way of putting it, my father has. Admit, he says, and start again. He says not to leave out the admitting, because that's necessary. It jars your pride and makes you that much less likely to make the next mistake."

"You mean," Doc asked, "that you made a mistake about me?"

"I mean," said the girl, "that it is possible."

"Who set the Federal Bureau of Investigation on us?"

Abba Cushing stared at him. "Do you think it was me? If so, you're mistaken, and how! I don't know who did it. I haven't the least idea."

"Your father?"

She frowned. "I think not. He would have mentioned it to me if he had such an idea, I believe." She waved an arm at the place where they were sitting. "Matter of fact, I brought you here to discuss the matter with dad. I'll bring him."

She got out of the car, indicated Doc was to follow her, and escorted him to a comfortable room, where they were met by a servant, not the one who had opened the garage door.

"Your father," the servant informed Miss Cushing, "is not in."

"Where can I reach him?"

"I do not know, miss."

Abba Cushing grimaced. "I did so hope you and dad could get together. I'm sure this meeting would have a different result."

Doc Savage smiled pleasantly enough, then remarked, "But since he is not, it might be wise to be taking other steps. So if you will excuse me—"

"Oh, but I won't," Abba Cushing said, and picked up her hat, which she had removed and placed on a table. "I'm going with you."

"That is very kind of you, but you had better not."

"It isn't kind at all," she said. "It's selfish. I'm looking out for my skin. I stole a prisoner from the F. B. I., and in the line of crimes, that isn't exactly jaywalking. I think I did the right thing, because I think you will solve this affair to everyone's satisfaction. But until then, until you crack the nut, I do not care to sit looking at the inside of a jail."

Doc said, "But going with me might conceivably be dangerous."

"Conceivably. But interesting, though." She smiled slightly. "I was just going to say that you are probably an expert at keeping out of jail. If I go with you, I keep out, too. So I go with you."

Doc studied her for a moment. "You are not a young woman on whom an argument would have much effect, are you?"

"You read character, don't you?" she said.

ABBA CUSHING rode downtown with Doc Savage. They took one of the Cushing automo-

biles, a convertible coupé, which really belonged out on the country place, and which had a Connecticut license. This was at the girl's suggestion. She said that a guest had driven the machine into town, and probably no one would think about it.

When Doc Savage parked the car, she said, "We're in front of that newspaper office. You're not going in there?"

"Yes."

"Why?"

"To use a reverse-number telephone directory."

Doc Savage was inside the newspaper building several minutes. He came out hastily, got in the car and drove away.

Abba Cushing asked, "What is a reverse-number directory?"

"They are made up by the telephone companies," Doc Savage explained. "Most newspaper offices have one. Instead of listing the names in alphabetical order, it lists the names in numerical order. You look up the number, and the name is listed."

"Oh!"

Doc Savage drove uptown, then cross town to a section of rooming houses. He found a number, parked, and Abba Cushing followed him into the lobby of a small apartment house devoted to one and two-room apartments. Doc looked over the name plates on the mail boxes until he came to "Miss Genie Reaveman."

The place did not have a doorman. He went to the elevator.

"Girlfriend?" Abba Cushing asked, rather sharply.

"No."

"Who, then?"

"A man came to the hospital to either seize or kill the man he thought was R. T. Hooten. The man was scared into flight and trailed to a hotel. Ham is watching him, now. The hope is that the man eventually will lead Ham to someone higher up. In the meantime the man has been in the habit of making repeated calls to a girl named Genie at this address. This information came from the clerk at the man's hotel."

Abba Cushing seemed undecided whether to approve or disapprove of their objective. "You are after information, I presume."

"Exactly."

"Men," she suggested, "don't always tell their girls everything."

"Seldom everything, I suspect," Doc Savage said dryly. "But they boast."

"Boasting with a man," said Abba Cushing, "is what fanning his tail feathers is to a peacock. You may have something there."

Genie Reaveman was a small, mouselike girl who looked at them with wide blue eyes that were somehow scared. She asked what they wanted.

Doc Savage said, "We just came from the Jefferson Wilson Hotel where a fellow is registered as John Stone."

The small girl's blue eyes got wider and wider until they were bigger than it possibly seemed they could have been. Then, although she had given no noticeable impression of having her lungs full of air, she breathed outward a great, rushing breath, after which she sank toward the floor with her eyes closing.

DOC SAVAGE caught the girl before she could fall and carried her into a small apartment which was probably furnished with her own furniture, because it was the kind of furniture a mouselike girl like her would own. There was a studio couch. Doc put her on that.

Abba Cushing went to a door, found a kitchenette beyond, inspected it, then gave the bathroom a scrutiny. She shook her head to indicate there was no one else on hand.

Abba came back and stood looking down at the girl on the studio couch.

"I was going to get jealous, but I guess I won't," she said. "She's a bedraggled lamb, isn't she?"

Doc Savage was examining the girl. "She has fainted."

"Naturally," said Abba. "A girl like her would."

Abba began prowling around the apartment. She looked into drawers, opened boxes, dumped the contents of the girl's purse out on a table and pawed through the stuff.

She said, "Name seems to be Genie Reaveman, all right." She found a bank book, opened it and whistled. "She's been making money the last month."

Abba brought the bank book over and showed it to Doc. It had entries showing deposits of ninety dollars a week, each week for the past month.

"That's a big salary," Abba remarked. "Big for a girl, I mean. She must have something I hadn't noticed." She went into the kitchenette and came back with a glass containing four ice cubes. "I remember they did this to me one time after I saw a snake," she said. She poked one of the ice cubes down the girl's dress and rubbed the others on her face.

The girl opened her eyes, and they got wider and wider again, but this time she burst into tears.

Abba Cushing winked at Doc Savage over the girl's head. "We are the police," Abba said. "You had better come clean, young lady."

Doc Savage frowned, started to speak.

Abba interrupted, "I know you had orders not to say you were an F.B.I. man. But I think this girl should know it. She should know how badly she is up against it."

The mouse girl's sobs got louder. "I didn't know it was wrong," she declared. "I really didn't."

Abba snorted, "Not wrong? But you were able to deposit ninety dollars a week?"

"They only paid me a hundred," said the mouse miserably. "It doesn't cost me much to live. I was saving the rest. I … I'll give it back."

Abba Cushing laughed, said, "Never give a dollar back to a man, darling. It's simply not done."

This statement seemed to appeal to the mouse. She lifted her head, and even stopped sobbing. "I … I really didn't do anything so wrong."

"How much did your job include?" Abba asked.

"Mr. Stone—John Stone—was merely to call me up and talk to me as if I was his sweetheart," the mouselike girl explained. "I took it down in shorthand. Then I read what he said to the other man."

"Hm-m-m!" said Abba judiciously. "That just makes you the go-between. I imagine, as long as you are perfectly frank with us, there will not be such a mess. But, of course, you want to stick to the truth. How did you get hold of the other man, the one to whom you relayed the romantic talk?"

"Oh, I have his name, address and telephone number."

"What are they?"

"Mr. West. Mr. Top West. His phone is Wyoming 9-0711. He is at 37 Gourn Avenue."

Abba Cushing nodded understandingly.

"We have it that you knew most of what was going on," she remarked.

The mouse of a girl jumped violently, and her face blanched.

"Oh, but I didn't," she gasped. "That is what frightened me so. I was afraid I was doing something wrong. But I actually didn't know it."

"Didn't this Top West or this Mr. Stone explain what it was about?"

"No. I told them I was very curious. They told me that the hundred dollars a week was for my curiosity."

Abba Cushing looked at Doc Savage meaningly, then turned back to the girl. "Your life is in danger," Abba said. "You had better leave town. I have a place in the mountains to which you can go. Here." She wrote for some moments on a piece of paper, then showed what she had written to Doc Savage.

It was:

Miss Reaveman is my guest, and is to be treated as such for as long as she cares to stay.

Abba

Abba Cushing gave the girl the note, explaining, "I'll put the address on an envelope. You go there and stay until you hear from us."

The mouse of a girl packed quickly. They took her to the station and put her aboard a train.

"I sent her to dad's lodge," Abba told Doc Savage. "We can find her there at any time."

THE bronze man drove toward Gourn Avenue, where the mouse had told them they would find Top West, whoever he was.

Doc Savage was silent, but he was also appreciative of the talents of Miss Abba Cushing. The young woman had qualities he had not suspected. She had gotten information out of Genie Reaveman with much more skill, he strongly suspected, than he could have managed himself. Abba was a psychologist, which meant she had brains, though she was actually too pretty a thing to have those.

"In case you're wondering," Abba said unexpectedly, "I had never heard of anybody named Top West."

"I was not thinking that."

"What *were* you thinking?"

"That you have intelligence as well as beauty."

"My, my!" said Abba. "That was not a very flowery compliment, but coming from a man who is supposed to be proof against feminine wiles, I suppose I should be flattered." She was silent for a moment. "I think I am."

Doc Savage, who was uncomfortable, muttered, "For some reason, this Top West was using a very roundabout method of getting information relayed to him."

"Obviously, the sweetheart talk was a code," Abba agreed. "Imagine that! You know—this thing is interesting."

"It may be dangerous," Doc warned. "It probably will be. You had best let me drop you at home."

"Oh, I like it," Abba said, settling back in the seat. "My past life has been strangely devoid of excitement. It was dull. And already that dull past seems a thousand years gone. I realize I've been missing a lot."

She sounded as if she meant it.

Chapter XI
THE HERRING

DOC SAVAGE was silent during the latter part of the drive to Gourn Avenue. The address where they hoped to find Top West was a substantial but not pretentious block of straw-colored brick houses.

The bronze man drove on past, parked on another block, and walked back. He took his time and suggested that they have a cold drink at a yellow stand on the corner. Surprised, Abba Cushing did so. The orange drink they had was not bad,

"You're looking the ground over," Abba Cushing said. "You sure don't take any chances, do you?"

Doc Savage made no comment. He entered the building and examined a directory which showed that Top West had offices on the fifth floor. It was evidently not an extensive suite, because three other concerns were listed on the same floor.

Doc rode the elevator to the fifth. He did not enter Top West's door, which was marked with nothing but the man's name, and that in small letters. He went into one of the other firms, and found an operator and a PBX switchboard.

He told the telephone operator, "Checking your telephone. May I use your headset a moment?"

It was a natural request put in a casual voice, and the operator did not realize that the bronze giant could hardly be a telephone company employee. She turned over her board to him.

Doc called Top West's number, asked the male voice which answered, "Top West?"

"That's right," said the voice.

Doc said, "West, you were rather clever in giving the tip. But the Federal Bureau of Investigation is not partial to anonymous tips. How about telling the bureau just why you called their attention to Doc Savage?"

There was a kind of waiting-for-it-to-explode silence from the other end of the wire.

"You … er … have the wrong number," West said.

Doc asked, "Is this Top West?"

"Er … no. West, you say? No, no, this is Tom Hesten. H-e-s-t-e-n. Sorry," Top West said.

"Sorry," Doc told him.

"That's all right."

The bronze man hung up and told Abba Cushing, "Our Mr. Top West keeps his brain cut in."

Abba said admiringly, "You are a sly cuss, aren't you? No wonder we didn't get to first base fooling you." She followed Doc as he hurried for the door. "Did Top West put the F.B.I. on your neck?"

"Apparently, he did," Doc said.

The bronze man swung into the corridor, reached Top West's door and waited outside. He had been there not more than thirty seconds when the door burst open and a burly young man dived out, in the act of yanking his hat down on his head.

Doc put out a foot. Top West jumped the foot, which was quick thinking. He went half to a knee, however, and dived a hand for something under his coat. Doc Savage swung a short, chopping blow that was not a good one because Doc was off balance. It took some skin off Top West's forehead and pushed the man down and back on his knees.

Doc got hold of West's coat, out of which the man was trying to take something. Doc yanked and the coat came off until West tried to hold it on with his arms. They fought for a while as if West was a fish on a line, the coat being the line; then Abba Cushing became enthusiastic and tried to get into it, woman fashion, by kicking West. The result was that he suddenly let go his coat, grabbed her foot, gave a twist and nearly, but not quite, succeeded in using her for a shield. Doc took him by the neck; and shortly West made the motions of a man wanting to be peaceful.

WITHOUT saying anything, Doc Savage propelled Top West back into the office out of which the man had come, shoved him through a door on the other side of a reception room and down into a desk chair. Doc then searched a washroom and a clothes locker that was large enough to contain a man.

The furnishings were not elaborate and had seen use. Doc went through a desk drawer. The letters were mostly bills. They showed that Top West was a detective, one who was slow pay. Big pay, too, judging from the account book in another drawer. There were several cases entered, and the lowest fee was a hundred dollars, the highest five thousand, and there were three of those in the last three weeks.

Doc Savage asked, "Who paid you five thousand dollars a week recently?"

Top West gave a demonstration of why he was able to make five thousand a week. He took hold of himself as if he was a cowboy getting control of a horse.

In a voice that would not have excited a banker's conference, he said, "My money says you are the bird who just called up with that F. B. I. stuff."

Doc said, "So you put them on my neck?"

"Of course not." Top West leered. "Or did I sound too guilty for you to believe that?"

"Yes—guilty."

"O.K., my friend. I did. It was a job. I was hired to do it, and I was paid five thousand a week to do that. It was worth five thousand a week. It was worth more than that." He grimaced again, fiercely. "I worked too cheap. I was a sucker. Anyway, that explains who paid me five thousand a week recently. You asked that, didn't you?"

Doc Savage studied the man. Doc was no judge of women—he had no confidence whatever in his hunches and opinions in that direction—but he could tell something about a man's character. This man had plenty of character. He was strong. He was neither handsome nor a physical giant; he did not dress like a millionaire, neither was he shabby; he was not hard and he was not soft. But there was a dynamic quality about him that most men did not have.

"Any chance of your telling who hired you?" Doc asked.

"Not a chance," said West. "Protection due a client, and that sort of thing."

Doc said, "You sent a man to the hospital to get the man you thought was Hooten?"

"Sure! That was a pretty low trick you pulled, taking Hooten's place. Where is Hooten?"

"Dead!"

Top West became as alert as a cat at a mouse hole. "You do it?"

"No. He chased a subway train. He caught it."

Top West said, "Then you killed him. You made him a wild man. If he hadn't been a wild

Doc yanked and the coat came off until West tried to hold it on with his arms. They fought as if West was a fish on a line, the coat being the line.

man he wouldn't have been chasing subway trains. I know what he thought about subway trains; he thought they were big worms. He wanted to kill one."

"You seem to know a great deal about Hooten," Doc Savage said dryly. "I would call that an intimate detail."

West nodded. "I should know. I've been guarding him—my men have—for nearly a month."

"You were hired to do that?"

"That and some more."

"What more?"

"Get dope on you. Make sure you are behind this. Find out all I could about you. Find out, for instance, that you have three aides in the three cities where other wild men have turned up."

Doc Savage was silent for a while, his flake-gold eyes on West.

"Where," asked the bronze man suddenly, "is Monk Mayfair?"

West frowned. "Eh? Why ask me?"

"Something happened to him."

"Lots of things happen to you and your men, I've discovered," said West dryly. "How does that put the monkey on my back?"

"Your man who went to the hospital," Doc said, "knows who got Monk."

The effect of that statement on Top West was like a bomb with a long fuse. At first, he only smiled skeptically. Then he jerked violently, bolted upright and seemed to turn to steel. "Why, that damned slug!" he blurted. "I wonder if you could be right. I didn't hire him, exactly. He was recommended to me by my client. Do you suppose— But, hell, I couldn't be sucked in like that!"

Doc said, "We might go talk to the fellow."

West half closed his eyes for a while. "You know, you might have something there. I could have been whizzered on this thing." He came to his feet. "You said it. Won't hurt to make talk with this guy of mine—question mark."

THERE was a policeman at the front door of the Jefferson Wilson Hotel. There were two squad cars parked in the street, and the black bulk of an ambulance. While Doc was surveying the situation, the uniformed ambulance attendants came out of the hotel, lit cigarettes, entered their vehicle and drove away. They had not taken away a patient.

Abba Cushing said, "I think I can find out what this is about." She looked at Doc Savage. "At least, if the police get me, you can see what they've done and escape."

She got out of the car and moved forward. She mixed with the gathering crowd, and they lost sight of her. She was gone for much longer than seemed reasonable, and they were about to conclude

that she had been caught when she reappeared. She was pale.

"The hotel clerk is dead," she said. "He tried to stop some men who rushed in and seized Ham Brooks, who was concealed in the cloakroom off the lobby. The man who seemed to be in charge of the affair was the man Ham was watching." She turned to Top West. "Your operative."

West digested this with the fierce dignity of a cat that had just been kicked.

"Listen, butterfly, what are you pulling?" West asked.

Abba pressed a hand to her cheek. "Butterfly! The man I met near Mr. Savage's restaurant called me that. The man who said he was Mr. Adam. You are—or were—Mr. Adam?"

"I was Mr. Adam," West said fiercely. "Come on, butterfly, what are you pulling?"

"Pulling?"

"You are in on the game. Take off the mask and be one of the gang. You haven't got Savage, here, fooled, I'll bet you."

"I don't," said Abba, completely puzzled, "understand you."

"Your old man hired me."

"My—"

"Your old man. Your father. He's the guy who's been paying me that five grand a week."

Abba reached out and gripped the car door. "He is?"

"The eminent Mr. Cushing," said West grimly, "was so convinced that Doc Savage was guilty— so he said—that he said, 'Let's see that the F.B.I. knows about the strange coincidence of Savage and the wild men.' And so I tipped them off." He eyed Doc Savage. "Did that make trouble for you?"

"Slightly," Doc said.

"That," said Abba, "is an understatement. We're on the lam right now. I rescued us by grabbing an F.B.I. man's gun. I do not think they cared for that bit of Annie Oakley."

Top West turned back to Doc Savage. "Want a suggestion from the little man who fell in a hole? Let's go have words with Cushing."

"Let's do that," said Abba in a grave voice. "I'm sure dad is innocent."

"But you want to be *sure,* butterfly," West told her dryly. "Somebody has been pulling a red herring around in front of somebody. Let's see who."

Chapter XII
THE TERRIBLE THING

THE Cushing apartment, as Doc had noticed, had two entrances. One entered the front, off fashionable Park Avenue, where there was the doorman with the jackknife bow. The second entrance was to the rear, which gave into an old brownstone which was apparently a combined garage and servants' quarters. This had a connection by a private elevator to the lofty and elaborate quarters of the Cushings themselves, high up in the skyscraper apartment building that fronted Park Avenue.

Doc Savage, Top West and Abba Cushing entered by the servants' accommodations in the brownstone home and rode up in the small but excellent private elevator, seeing no servants on their way. The girl admitted herself with a key of her own and Abba remarked upon the absence of the help a little curiously. But the possibilities of what it might mean did not seem to dawn on her, although Doc Savage and West exchanged glances in the elevator, and they were very careful in leaving the lift, very cautious.

As soon as they were in the Cushing apartment itself, hardly had they crossed the doorstep, when Abba shrieked. It was a terrified cry she gave. She dashed forward, and sank beside the sprawled shape of a servant. She was there only a moment. Then she leaped erect, dashed away, running madly through the many rooms, and they could hear her crying, "Dad! Dad! What's happened?"

Doc went to the sprawled servant. He did the things a doctor would do on finding a man in that position.

"Dead?" asked West.

"Unconscious," Doc said.

"From what?"

"Head blow. Back of ear."

"How long?"

"Few minutes. More, possibly."

Abba Cushing came back. She was extremely pale, and completely speechless. She stood there looking at them, without words. Then she was seized with a nervous spell, during which she shook uncontrollably and drew her arms close to her and gripped the elbows with her hands as if she were very cold. The room was warm.

Doc Savage took hold of the unconscious man and administered harmless pain. This, the shock of the pain to the fellow's nervous system, caused the man to groan and twist and finally to open his eyes. The man took a few moments to organize his wits.

When he spoke it was to Abba Cushing.

"Miss Abba," he said, "something terrible occurred."

She was wordless.

Doc said to the servant, "Please tell us about it. And hurry."

"I am Spencer, the houseman," the servant explained.

"Yes?"

"I am not very good at fighting," Spencer added. "There were at least four of them, so they probably would have whipped me even if I had been a fighter. They came up by the servants' elevator, as if they knew the place. I heard them, recognizing that their footsteps were those of strangers. I am good at recognizing footsteps."

He stopped to moisten his lips.

"Once, I had trouble with my eyes, and was blind. I was blind for almost a year. Blind people get to notice such things as footsteps. But that is beside the point. There were four intruders, and they took me. One used a thing I think you call a blackjack. I remember wondering if it would hurt my eyes again as he hit me."

He tried to get up. The attempt was not successful. He must have been very dizzy, because he lay down again and gripped at the floor as if the room was turning over and over.

"They got Mr. Cushing. That is what they came for. They found him in the library. He fought them, but it was a brief fight. They came out, dragging Mr. Cushing."

West said, "Look, Goldilocks, I thought they hit you with that thing you think was a blackjack."

"They did."

"You see and hear things when you're unconscious, eh?"

"Oh, no. I'm not organizing my story very well." The servant sounded sick and apologetic. "The first blow did not knock me out. It stunned me. I could see and hear. I played possum, trying to get my wits back."

He looked at Abba Cushing like a faithful dog.

"When they came out with Mr. Cushing, I got up and tried to help," he told Abba. "I did my best. But they hit me again. I fell on the floor. But this time, too, I was not completely unconscious. I'll never forget what one of the men said then."

"What," asked West, "did he say?"

"He said, 'I wonder if this one will make as good a wild man as Monk Mayfair and Ham Brooks,'" the servant said.

"And then?"

"One of the men stood over me with what I think was another blackjack. And the next thing I knew, you aroused me."

"That's all?" Doc asked.

"All," said the servant miserably.

THEY left the Cushing apartment immediately. Top West approved of that. "The Federal men will come there looking for you and the girl," he said. "Wonder they haven't been there already."

Abba Cushing was still wordless, but her

speechlessness seemed to come from preoccupation rather than shock, because she led the way to her car with a step that was firm enough.

West looked at Doc Savage as they settled in the machine. "You wouldn't take some help from me, maybe?"

"Might."

"Apartment of mine. Nobody knows about it. I'm Mr. Dobie Johns at the place. Have kept it for years. A place to rest and a place to lay low when things get hot. By hot, I mean crooks. Crooks make it hot for me, now and then." He grinned thinly. "I'm not all skunk."

Doc said, "We might go there."

West was pleased. So pleased that he glowed.

He turned to Abba. "Snap the trance, butterfly. You're better off than you were. We know now that your father isn't guilty."

"I don't understand this," Abba said slowly.

"It's simple, butterfly. There's a third gang mixed up in this. First, there is your father and his party who are trying to help their friends, the three wild men. Second, there is Doc Savage here. Third, the parties unknown—the polecats who are responsible for it."

Abba asked, "Responsible for what? What are they doing?"

West considered the question. He grimaced.

"I still say it must be simple," he said. "What we do now is find the answer."

DOC SAVAGE sat at a telephone in West's apartment. Sitting there, he could see a vista of Bronx apartment fronts that were completely uninteresting except for the sameness of their wheat-yellow brick and the perfect uniformity in size of the windows, the sameness of the entrances, the alikeness of almost everything about the buildings.

Doc called his headquarters, and that made Top West's hair—West barked excitedly—stand on end.

Undisturbed by West's agitation, Doc did a thing that puzzled West. The bronze man whistled a code combination—long, pause, two shorts, pause, long, pause, three shorts—into the telephone mouthpiece.

This performance—it baffled West, until Doc explained it to him later—operated a sonic gadget which was connected to a combination relay similar to those used in commercial telegraph-relay offices. In simplified terms, the gimmick would connect the telephone line to any one of several gadgets in headquarters, depending on what combination was whistled into it. This particular combination hooked the telephone to a recording apparatus—the device recorded on a wire by magnetism—which would keep a faithful track of all reports telephoned to Doc Savage's office.

The recording device itself was equipped with a robot affair which, through the medium of a phonographic transcription, informed any caller that Doc Savage was absent—if he was absent, and had switched on the gimmick—but that any messages would be taken and recorded for the bronze man's future audition.

It was this recorded ledger of calls with which Doc Savage eventually got himself connected.

He sat there and listened.

What he heard was astounding.

Halfway through it, he beckoned Top West over and said, "You had better listen to this. It is the third report of the same nature."

West came over, wonderingly, and leaned close to Doc Savage's ear. One of West's fists, resting on the arm of the bronze man's chair, was made of corded sinew and full firm bone under smooth tanned skin. The man smelled clean and vital, almost like a young animal. The bronze man's sense of smell noted that, for it was one of his faculties that had been developed by scientific training.

The telephone recorder said:

"This is Denzil Bains calling from Paris, France, and reporting on the matter of the wild men. Up until last night there were no wild men in Paris. But last night and today, conditions changed. A wild man was reported running down the Quai d'Orsay hunting, he said, a wild woman. Apparently, he did not mean a wild woman in the usually accepted sense of the word because he turned out to be genuinely convinced that he was a caveman. Moreover, he proved to be a prominent politician who was cooperative with the Nazis. At first it was believed something had happened to him because of his Nazi leanings. But another wild man cropped up, more prominent than the first, and this one had no Nazi leanings whatever. The contrary, quite. In fact he was not long ago released from a concentration camp in Germany."

The rest of the report was garbled somewhat by wire trouble. Then it proved that the speaker was not Denzil Bains in person, but a friend who was relaying the information from a point in Mexico, where he had in some fashion received the information from Bains by radio. That concluded this report.

There was a pause while the recorder was passing through the preliminaries that preceded another long-distance call.

TOP WEST frowned at Doc Savage. "Who is Denzil Bains?" he wanted to know.

"An operative of mine, you might call him," Doc Savage said.

Actually, Bains was an ex-criminal "graduate" from Doc's unusual "college" in the upstate section.

West rubbed his jaw.

"You know, there're two ways of taking that report," he said thoughtfully. "The way it was worded, it could be a report somebody was making to you about progress. That would mean you are behind this thing. Or it might have been what you want me to think it was, just a piece of information."

Doc Savage's metallic features were remarkably sober. "It is worse than that."

"Eh?"

"Unless all the signs are wrong," Doc said grimly, "it is the beginning of a terrible thing."

The recording apparatus made the telephone say: "This is Jack Sheffing, Buenos Aires. The wild men have started cropping up here. They are not calling them wild men. They are saying that a number of prominent politicians and business leaders were poisoned at a banquet with something that has affected their minds. But the symptoms are the same as those Ham Brooks reported as identifying the wild men. So far, there have been five reported cases in Buenos Aires. All very prominent. This is Jack Sheffing, concluding report. Seventy-threes."

"Five!" Top West blurted. "Five! Great grief! Or did he say seventy-three?"

"Seventy-three," Doc explained, "is the telegraphic abbreviation for good luck, good wishes, and so on."

"Oh." West was profoundly silent for a while. "Are there reports still coming in?"

"Yes," Doc said. "That last one came in three hours ago."

The message receipt time was audibly recorded on the apparatus in Doc's office by a gadget which put the time on the end of each conversation in much the same way that the receiving time is placed at the end of a telegraphic communication.

They listened to two more reports. One was from Madrid, Spain. The other was from Berlin. They were similar to the others, and the sameness was unnerving.

Sitting there with the reports coming off the recorder in such a weird fashion, they got the feeling of a momentous thing beginning small and growing, piling up, mounting and darkening in ominous portent, like the gathering and frowning increase of a storm, a small black thing at first, then growing to a culminating, dread menace.

West pulled in a deep, shaky breath.

"'The terrible thing,' as you called it, is just that."

ABBA CUSHING had been fooling with the radio. She turned up the volume suddenly. "Listen to this," she said.

It was a commercial program to which she was listening, and the announcer was breaking in to say, "Ladies and gentlemen, repeating this special announcement: The Federal Bureau of Investigation has issued a special request that any citizen knowing the whereabouts, or able to ascertain the whereabouts, of the man named Clark Savage, Jr.—more often called Doc Savage—please communicate with the Federal Bureau of Investigation, the police, or your nearest radio station. This is an urgent matter. Doc Savage is not to be found in any of his usual haunts. Thank you. We now go back to the music of Ray Riser and his orchestra in the Blue Room of—"

Abba clicked off the radio.

"That," said Top West, "is what is known as having the crutches kicked out from under you, one at a time. That F.B.I. is nobody to monkey with."

Abba stared at him defiantly.

"I call it a challenge," she snapped.

"A volley, more like it," said West. "The kind they fire over your grave."

"That is a salute to the departed," Abba said.

"Same thing. We're going to be among the departed unless we have luck. They'll depart us for Alcatraz Island at the very least." He turned to Doc Savage. "Unless you have an idea, Mr. Savage. Have you?"

Doc Savage had been contemplating the radio without particular concentration.

"There is a chance, but not a very great one, that any one group of men could seize both Monk and Ham, and still prevent Monk and Ham from getting some word to me," the bronze man said, making what for him was a rather long and involved speech. "But the chances against such an eventuality are enormous, considering the amount of consideration and planning we have given to just such contingencies as this one." He shook his head slowly. "There has been no report of any kind telephoned to headquarters from either of them."

"Meaning?" asked West.

Doc said, "Go out and buy the late newspapers, will you? All of them. Better get both the early and late editions of all the newspapers you can."

West stared at Doc. "I don't see what good that will do," he said. "But from what I've heard of your methods, you don't do things without reasons."

He got his hat and went outside. Abba Cushing said, "I wonder if that lad is going to scram." She went to a window and watched. "He's getting newspapers all right, and he seems to be coming back," she said later. "I'm surprised, I am. I can't seem to feel like trusting that fellow farther than I could push a battleship."

West came in burdened with newspapers. "The newsstand owner thought I was nuts." He dumped papers on a table.

Doc Savage first sought out the most complete listing of radio programs. He checked the news broadcasts with a pencil, glanced on the other side of the sheet to see what news was there, then handed the page to Abba Cushing.

"Try not to miss a single news broadcast," he said. "In three hours, two stations broadcast the news simultaneously. By that time we should have a second radio."

"The idea," said Abba, "being to miss nothing. I get it." She seated herself in front of the radio.

Doc then went through the newspaper methodically, using the pencil to check each item as he finished with it. Top West watched, and finally rubbed his jaw, making neither heads nor tails of it.

From time to time, Doc cut out an item and placed it on the table.

He clipped an article about the wild men from each paper, such items about the affair in foreign nations as the papers contained. When these were on the table, he read them.

A news broadcast came on, and he got up, moved over to the radio, and sat there concentrating on what the newscaster had to say.

Top West, hearing nothing interesting in the radio newscast, walked over to the table and shuffled through the clippings. There was one item, he discovered, that had no connection with the others.

"Blazes!" he said. "What's this one got to do with it?" He turned the clipping over and saw there was nothing on the back but a meaningless fragment of an advertisement.

A startling thing happened then. The radio news broadcaster mentioned the item which West held in his hand.

THE announcer said, "And here is a new one down in Virginia. At Cypress Chapel, Virginia, this afternoon, a waitress bought a hog. Now there are hogs and hogs in Virginia, but it seems this one talked. Half a dozen persons testify to hearing the hog explain to the waitress that he was afflicted with the spirit of Blackbeard the Pirate. The hog demanded that his owner sell him to the waitress for fifty cents. The startled owner did so. The waitress has her hog. The hog has lost his vocabulary.

So now, everyone is wondering just what did happen. And we now know what happens to the spirits of radio announcers after they die. G'night, folks."

Top West snorted. He looked at the newspaper item again. "Tripe!" he said.

He was startled when Doc Savage got up from the radio and took the news clipping out of his hands. He could tell that the bronze man was animated by excitement.

"The perpetrators of this thing have a headquarters," Doc said.

"Sure, most everything has a headquarters," said West dryly. "A body has its brain, an engine has its carburetor, a beehive has its queen, a boy has his girl." He threw up his hands desperately. "Headquarters in this thing is wherever the spark plug of the thing is hanging his hat. So what has a talking hog got to do with it?"

"The talking hog," Doc said, "sounds interesting."

"It's a gag somebody pulled on that waitress," West declared.

"Sounds more like a gag on the hog's owner," put in Abba. "If he sold the animal for fifty cents." She wheeled on Doc. "Mr. Savage, isn't this very dangerous, your going out into the streets or the highways or however you're going to get down into Virginia?"

The bronze man was noncommittal on that point, but it hardly required an answer anyway. If the Federal Bureau of Investigation was seeking them it was no joke. No one had intimated it was a joke. Also, the city police, the State troopers and every town constable would be watching for them.

Doc asked, "Miss Cushing, have you a private airplane?"

"Yes." She looked startled.

"Would it be possible for us to use that plane to get to Virginia?"

"Of course," Abba said eagerly. "Gosh, we've got three planes. Dad has his big seaplane—his 'flying office,' he calls it—and a smaller and faster ship. I have my little cabin job."

THEY used Top West's car for the drive out of the city northward and up the Hudson into the section of impressive estates. The car was a small coach, and Doc and Abba kept down on the rear floor boards during the early part of the drive.

The Cushing estate was somewhat startling, because it was more impressive in its grandeur than the city apartment. It fronted the river; that is, there was a half mile of lawn and a curving drive down to the river and to the boathouse and hangar which were there.

Abba became puzzled as she stared around the cavernous innards of the hangar.

"That's funny," she said. "Dad's big plane is gone."

Doc Savage asked quietly, "Is it a ship of sufficient size for transatlantic use?"

"Yes, dad often uses it for that," Abba replied, apparently attaching no significance to the question. "Come on, we'll use my plane."

She climbed into the ship, which was one of the better comfortable and fast jobs being turned out for private use, and was equipped with pontoons. "I think I have charts of the route to Virginia. I flew to Florida not long ago, and used the charts."

Top West got into the plane, but not enthusiastically. He seemed to distrust either planes or female pilots; he did not say which.

"Five hundred miles to see about a talking hog," he muttered. "This gets me."

Chapter XIII
THE TALKING HOG

THE waitress in Cypress Chapel, Virginia, who had bought the talking hog for fifty cents was around twenty, looked remarkably healthy and had a sweet face. She probably did not weigh quite two hundred pounds.

She sat up on a cot in a pleasant parlor in a room over the restaurant—the place was a roadside restaurant, operated by her parents—and touched the bandage around her head.

She said, "The man, the little one, wanted to kill me. I'm sure of that."

Top West had a white face. He said, "Describe that guy again, will you, sister?"

"He was small. Not real little. Kind of grim. Dark face, mole on left cheek, twisted finger on right hand. And just covered with guns."

West suddenly doubled a fist and struck it against a palm.

"That," he said in a low, guttural voice, "is what I was afraid you said. That bird was—" He went silent, realizing he might say, and probably was saying, too much in front of the waitress.

The waitress demanded angrily, "You know the man? Then why aren't you telling this to the police? The man tried to kill me."

Instantly, without batting an eye, Top West lied, "We are investigators, kid. Did you ever hear of the F.B.I.? We didn't intend to tell anybody, but I guess you'll have to know. So keep it to yourself. We're a secret, see. Just tell us what else you know, and don't worry any more about it."

The waitress was satisfied.

"Well," she said, after trying to think of some more, "that's all. The little man just stole my hog and tried to kill me."

Doc Savage put in, "This man who struck you got the hog?"

"Yes. He grabbed the hog as he fled." The waitress nodded vehemently.

Doc Savage stood up and moved toward the door. "By the way, what kind of a looking man sold you the hog in the first place?"

"Oh, the funniest-looking fellow," said the girl quickly. "He looked just exactly like a big monkey, except that he looked kind of pleasant."

The girl then indicated that she was not exactly dumb. "The homely man was a ventriloquist. He threw his voice and made the hog seem to talk. It was such a funny-looking little hog—with awful long legs and great big ears—that I didn't mind taking part in what I thought was a joke of some kind. The hog was worth fifty cents as a pet, so I bought him. There were some customers in the restaurant at the time, and one of them worked for a newspaper in Elizabeth City. He said an item about a talking hog would make a good gag story. So that's how the story got in all the newspapers and on the radio."

Doc, with his manner casual, inquired, "Were there other men with this homely fellow when he sold you the hog?"

"Oh, yes; several men," the waitress said. "They came in a car. They were waiting for Charlie Davis and having something to eat while they waited."

"Who is Charlie Davis?"

"Oh, he rents boats to hunters. I think these men were hunters going into the swamp. They looked like the city hunters who go into the swamp a lot lately."

Doc asked, "What do you mean by a lot of hunters lately?"

"Oh, within the last year, we have had a lot of hunters go into Dismal from here."

Doc Savage opened the door. "Thank you," he said.

They went downstairs and outside. There were no facilities for landing a plane near the restaurant. They had left their ship on the shore of a lake about a mile away, back from the highway.

The moment they were outside, Abba Cushing exclaimed, "The man who sold the hog was Monk Mayfair! I'll bet he sold the hog deliberately."

Top West smiled grimly. "Sure, butterfly, that's it. Monk was with those guys, and the guys had guns in their pockets, and Monk knew they'd use them. The hog was Monk's pet pig, Habeas Corpus. Monk sold him to the waitress like that in hopes it would attract enough attention that Doc would hear about it."

"Charlie Davis, the man who rents boats," said Abba. "I wonder what he can tell us?"

CHARLIE DAVIS was a gangling chain of bones and gristle with a long mule face, one cheek of which had an enormous capacity for chewing tobacco. The first discovery they made about his character was that he was completely honest.

"No, I haven't guided any of them," he said. "They rent my boats. They don't want me along. They pay me good, but not good enough but what I've got some curiosity."

Doc Savage asked, "Have you done anything about your curiosity?"

Charlie Davis eyed the bronze man thoughtfully, measuring and weighing. Unexpectedly, Davis said, "I can tell you where they go. I can't promise you'll get in. But I think I can promise you'll have trouble."

"Why?"

"Swamp and man trouble," Davis said. "That's what you'll have. The swamp trouble won't be bad. Not to the kind of a man I can see you are. The swamp is no place for a fool, but mostly it's what its name says it is—dismal. You can go in and not come out—men have. There're poisonous snakes and mosquitoes and bears and bobcats and quagmires and mud with no bottom. There's no signposts, and everything looks alike, and you can get lost with your eyes wide open."

Davis paused and studied them with one eye narrowed.

"The man trouble might give you the real difficulty," he said. "Again, it might not. There ain't no fences. There are just guards. I didn't see if the guards had guns, but maybe they did have. I don't know. I was scared. I didn't see nothing to scare me. But I was scared. And the guards, they looked afraid, too. Never take chances with a man who is afraid. An afraid man is a desperate man. Nature put that in man when she made him."

"Then you take it these men go to a definite spot in the swamp?" Doc inquired.

"I take it that way, yes."

"Are you an easily scared man?"

"I dunno. Only fools don't get scared, I figure. But I don't go around shaking in my boots as a rule."

"But when you got near this place in the swamp, you shook in your boots?"

"Sure. Nearly shook 'em off. I ain't kidding, either."

"Thank you," Doc Savage said. "Could you give us a rough idea of where this happened?"

"I'll draw you a map. I won't go in with you."

"A map will be good."

Charlie Davis eyed Doc, somewhat strangely.

"I figure it will," Davis said. "Because you're Doc Savage. Oh, I know you, all right. I know the F.B.I., the police, and maybe the Army and Navy are looking for you. But don't get excited about me passing the word along. Do you remember a man named James Crowell?"

"The one who was crippled?" Doc asked, after considering for a moment.

"Sure. They said he would never be able to walk. For ten years he wasn't able to walk. Then you did one of those operations on him. He was as poor as hell. That was all right with you. You said if he felt he owed you anything, to give it to some hospital when he got it. Well, he got it. And he built one of the best hospitals in Virginia; he's still adding to it to pay off what he owes you, he says. He has never seen you since."

Charlie Davis grinned.

"Jimmie was my half brother," he said. "If you want me to go in that swamp with you, I'll go."

"Just make us a map," Doc said. "And thanks."

Chapter XIV
SINISTER IS A SWAMP

THE canoe was made of tin. Not exactly tin, but a sheet-metal alloy that, Charlie Davis had explained to them, had come from the float of a seaplane which had washed up on the coast a few weeks after the Great War began. They had gotten the canoe from Davis. Its hide was tough; snags would not puncture it. It was light enough so that they could pick it up and carry it. There was an outboard motor, a powerful light thing which they were not now using.

Dismal Swamp was around them. It was late evening, the sun an unpleasant flush near the horizon. The water was like coffee around them, dankly unpleasant with its odor of decaying vegetation. Top West thrust his paddle into a solid-looking bank—they were carefully traversing a narrow creek—and the paddle sank in the solid-looking crust, was gripped and held by amazingly black mud. West jerked angrily, yanked the bow of the canoe around into the bank. He swore, then looked at Abba and muttered an apology.

"I'd sell my part of this cheap," he said.

He seemed depressed. For the last two miles, which had been for some time because they were traveling slowly, his spirits had appeared to drop fast.

Abba was in the stern, strangely quiet. She had drawn her coat tight and buttoned it, although it was far from cold. She had taken also to drumming her fingers nervously on the control handle of the outboard motor.

"I'm getting the jitters," she remarked grimly.

Doc Savage's metallic features were without expression. He dug in his paddle, pulled the canoe ahead with powerful regular strokes.

After Doc had paddled awhile longer, his trilling sound came into existence. It was a weird sound in the dismal surroundings of muck and starved-looking trees. Roots of the trees were thrust down into the muck like fingers from which the flesh had been steamed.

West whirled nervously. "What the devil was that noise?"

Abba Cushing stared at him. "Say, you must be feeling the same way I am."

Doc Savage said quietly, "The same way all of us are feeling."

"Scared, you mean?"

"Yes."

Abba frowned. "That's queer. I mean all three of us feeling that way. We haven't seen anything yet."

The bronze man's mouth straightened slightly. He examined the map which Charlie Davis had drawn for them, glancing up and scrutinizing the surrounding swamp for landmarks. He thrust his paddle down into the bottom, brought up mud and examined it for color. It had a yellowish tinge that it had not had before. Charlie Davis had marked even such small things as this on the chart. According to the map they were not far from their destination, even closer to the point where they should desert the canoe.

"Miss Cushing," Doc said unexpectedly.

She jerked up as if he had screamed out that there was danger. It took a moment for her to get control of herself. "Yes?" she said finally.

"You remember the yacht in the East River?" Doc asked.

"The one that blew up? Mr. Hooten's boat?" She shuddered violently. "Of course, I remember it."

Doc asked, "Do you remember experiencing any unusual sensations whenever you were near the yacht?"

She was puzzled.

"Whenever I was near the yacht?" Then comprehension dawned. "Oh! Oh, yes, I do! It was this way! This fear!" She became even more pale. "But I don't understand that! I felt afraid around the boat. So did my father and the others. Terrified!"

"Did you," inquired Doc Savage, "feel this fear on other occasions?"

Her answer was not immediate. She tied her hands into tight knots for a moment. Then she nodded slowly.

"Yes, several times," she said. "I remember now. That is, it was this same feeling. I don't know whether that exactly describes it."

Top West swung to face Doc Savage. "You interested in something that just occurred to me?" West asked.

"About this sensation?"

"Yeah. About it." West sounded like a man who did not believe in ghosts, but who had seen one. "I remember having it several times."

"What occasions?" Doc asked quickly.

"Several. Also assorted, I would say. I don't know whether I can pin down to anything definitely the same about them. Any one thread that would connect these occasions, I mean."

West hesitated, glancing at Abba Cushing. "I felt this fear at your father's place, mostly. But not always there. I'm not even sure it was mostly there. And I noticed that your father and the others were feeling it at the same time."

"I do not understand this," Abba said in growing terror.

AFTER that, the "fear" grew rapidly worse.

And it came to them that the feeling was not exactly fear. Not fear in the true sense of the word at all. But the difference was not apparent until the sensation was much stronger, and Doc Savage pointed out that there was a difference.

It grew on them like atmosphere in a dramatic production of a horror play, except that it would have taken a playwright of powerful capacity and actors of enormous scope and conviction to produce such a thing. There was no feeling of staged melodrama about it, however. It was extremely real.

It was not physical in the beginning. At least there was no consciousness of its being physical. There was no weakness about the knees and tightness, or trembling, in the arm muscles in the beginning. In the beginning there was the consciousness, and nothing else, of something terribly not right, not as it should be.

Only in the beginning was it not physical.

Later, there were bodily sensations that were recognizable and plainly noticeable. Muscular and nerve behavior of pronounced nature, even of violence. Misbehavior was a better description.

An example: Doc Savage stopped paddling and placed a hand on the canoe gunwale. He watched the hand and the arm. The arm started trembling, very slightly at first, then more visibly and uncontrollably. When he began using the arm again the trembling stopped, but the sensation of weak helplessness was still in the limb.

Doc said, "This is not fear."

Abba Cushing nodded. "I was thinking that. It is more of a sensation of complete helplessness."

Doc added, "It is a symptom."

"Symptom?" Both Abba and West stared at Doc. "Symptom of what?" Abba asked.

Top West laughed suddenly and somewhat wildly. "Now, this thing really takes its head off. Before it was nutty. Now, what does it become?"

"Perfectly explainable," Doc said.

"Explainable? This thing? Wild men? And the way we're feeling?"

Doc Savage studied the thicket of swamp growth on the left bank. He turned the canoe toward a spot where there did not seem to be an opening, and there was suddenly another creek. It would have been almost impossible to find without the map. The water was such a deep-coffee color that nothing could be told about its depth by sight, and little more by sounding with a paddle because the mud bottom was so soft.

Doc said, "Did you ever work around an X-ray machine?"

"No," West said. "I've been X-rayed for broken bones and a bullet or two, though. Why?"

"Remember anything particular about the attendants who took the picture? About the way they worked?"

West frowned. "No. Except that they worked behind a shield of some kind."

"Yes. Behind a lead shield."

"You mean there's a connection here?" West demanded.

"Not exactly a connection. I mentioned it more as an illustration."

"Illustration of what?"

"The X-rays will burn you internally," Doc said. "They will spread over some distance. A very powerful X-ray machine will affect a photographic plate, for instance, at a distance of more than a block."

"You mean there's something like that affecting us? Making us feel that way?"

Doc Savage changed the subject.

"We are approaching the spot which Charlie Davis marked on the chart," he said. "And probably both of you should be warned."

"Charlie Davis warned us," reminded Abba Cushing.

"He neglected something," Doc said.

"What?"

Doc said, "Charlie Davis neglected to inform us that he was lying, that probably he was in league with the men we have traced here."

Top West's face went completely blank. "How … how—"

Doc said, "Charlie Davis said he had a half brother named James Crowell, on whom I once operated. I did operate on James Crowell who has since become very wealthy. But James Crowell did not have a half brother, something he doubtless believed I would not know, or would have forgotten, since the operation was some time ago."

Abba exclaimed, "Then we're going into a trap?"

Doc made no answer.

A VOICE out of the swamp, so close that it sounded almost in the canoe with them, remarked, "Now what are you going to do about it? That's the question."

Top West started to leap up and his hands sought a gun. There was an ear-splitting clatter, the gobble of a light machine gun, only a few feet away. West's mouth came open as if he wanted to scream and was trying and trying and couldn't. He seemed to be unhit. But he was as white as he could possibly be. He seemed paralyzed by terror, unable to move or even breathe. Finally, he toppled sidewise out of the canoe as stiffly as if made of wood, not bending a muscle. The water that was as dark as coffee splashed high, then closed over his body.

The concealed man's voice said, "Pull him out. I don't think he is hit."

Doc hauled West to the surface. A boat hook came out of the undergrowth, fastened to the canoe gunwale, hauled the light craft to the shore.

"Step out," ordered the voice. "You'll find the footing is solid. And there is plenty of ammunition left in this noise-maker."

Doc got out, hauled West from the water. Abba stepped on shore. The man with the gun was West's operative, the one who had, early in the affair, raided the hospital to get the man he had thought would be the Dutch financier, Hooten. There were other men with him, some of them with faces vaguely familiar. Faces that were familiar, Doc decided, because the men had helped shadow him at one time or another. One visage belonged to a newsboy who had been at work in front of Doc's headquarters building a week before. Another was a waiter in the restaurant where Doc and his aides usually ate. Here in the swamp, they were not newsboy and waiter. They were coldly efficient, grimly determined.

Yet, somehow, they did not give the impression of being criminals.

"We have a party all ready for you," one of them told Doc. "So get moving."

Doc said quietly, "This thing began as a party for me."

"I'd like to see you sidestep *this* one," the man said.

Doc studied the man. "You do not impress me as a criminal."

"I hope I impress you, though," the man said dryly. "Because this is one thing you are not going to stop."

Chapter XV
MAN OF DESTINY

The island was small, perhaps an acre in area. It was not high, and there was nothing distinguishing about it, except the growth of swamp vegetation which covered it and the size of these trees. They were great spreading trees, monsters that ran to width and not height.

The trees were all the disguise the place needed. That, and the fact that the buildings below had green roofing of the common composition variety. The roofing was not a permanent type. Neither were the buildings. They were built temporarily, and there were barrels sitting around, open at the top. The tops were covered over with a sealing of fragile but airtight stuff, similar to the fabric out of which light raincoats are made.

Their escort indicated the barrels.

"Gasoline," he said, "for a quick fire. Some chemicals, also, for fumes to keep anyone away."

Doc said, "For destruction of the place in case it is discovered?"

"That's right."

Abba Cushing screamed then. The scream did not seem so much terror as the culmination of anxiety. She pointed.

It was a plane, a large one. It lay in a creek under overhanging branches of a great tree, with the open water on which it had landed distinguishable beyond. From what Abba had said before, the plane was easily identifiable as the one belonging to her father. The ship the elder Cushing called his "flying office."

The chief of their guards looked at her, said, "Don't get excited. He's all right."

The exhortation not to get excited was not soothing in view of what they saw next.

Monk and Ham. They were in a great room. There was one door to the room and it was surrounded by heavy copper rods that were a high-voltage protective device designed to electrocute, perhaps not fatally, but at least distressingly, anyone who entered when the juice was on.

Monk and Ham were near the door. In lieu of chairs, a log had been placed on the floor, and Monk and Ham sat on this. They wore only their trousers. They were not bound or confined in any way. A man stood near them with a long thin stick which had a very bright red balloon fastened to the end. The balloon was about two feet in diameter. There was no recognition in the face of either Monk or Ham. Blankness only, and the blankness was horrible.

Doc Savage said, "Monk! Ham!"

Monk looked up and made a hideous cackling noise that was without meaning, but completely repellent under the circumstances. Monk then started to get to his feet.

The man with the balloon on the thin stick stepped forward and menaced Monk with the balloon. Monk recoiled as if it was something terrible, shrank back on the log in fear.

The escort laughed. "Silly performance, isn't it? But we did enough experimenting to learn how they react under almost every circumstance. They are afraid of large objects which look mysterious to their almost completely paralyzed minds. That balloon on a stick is such an object to their minds. It intimidates them, whereas a gun or a hand grenade would not faze them at all, because it would impress no intrinsic menace on their minds."

Top West said in horror, "They are wild men?"

"The word 'wild' is not a good one," said the escort. "'Men with a paralyzed mentality' is more exact. Still, the world seized on the term 'wild men' to describe them, and it is somehow apt. At least, it has plenty of popular appeal."

"What did it to them?" West asked.

"The same thing that is going to do it to you," the man said frankly. "Which is this gimmick over here."

THE "gimmick over there" looked about as simple as a television transmitter that had been wedded to the latest thing in linotype machines. At first glance it made about as much sense as that, unless one had a considerable knowledge of electricity and electrotherapy, which Doc Savage did. Then the gadget, without getting less complicated, showed that it had been carefully and purposefully put together in such an efficient manner that it would probably function well at doing whatever it was supposed to do.

Their escort said, "The electric hammer," indicating the mechanism.

"Hammer?" Doc asked.

"Well, that's as good a word as any. Better than most. The gadget induces nervous shock of controlled nature."

The expression that came on Doc Savage's features was one of extreme interest. "Controlled nervous shock," he said. He added skeptically, "You do not mean that."

"I sure do."

"Nervous shock," Doc Savage said, "has been to medical men something like an avalanche. The cause can be arranged, but after it is started, no one can tell where it will lead."

"O.K. You call it one thing; we call it another. What's the difference? The ocean is still made of water." The man shrugged. "Bring them over here, boys," he told his aides. "Get them ready for the treatment."

Getting them ready for the treatment—apparently this was going to be administered without the slightest delay and without explanations—consisted of stripping Doc and West of shirts and shoes. They did nothing to the girl.

Top West, looking puzzled, said, "What has become of that feeling—fear or whatever it was—that we felt awhile ago? It's gone now."

"You mean that sensation you had while you were in the canoe and getting near the place?" the man asked.

Doc said, "Also the sensation Monk and I had while on board that yacht in the East River."

Their captor nodded. "Sure. There was one of the machines on the yacht, too."

"In operation?"

"Sure. You only get that feeling while the machine is working. It's got quite a field. You feel it even some distance away. Like an X-ray machine, the boss says. Or the experiments have shown, rather."

"Boss?" Doc Savage said instantly.

Very carefully, without a change of expression, the man said, "Boss? Who said anything about a boss? Oh, just then you mean? I meant the guy who built the gadgets for me. He's boss of the machine shop. We all call him boss."

"That," Doc Savage said, "is a waste of breath."

"What is?"

"Your declaration that there is no boss."

"But there is. I just told you. In the machine shop—"

Doc Savage said quietly, "The owner of the brains behind this affair has been evident to me for some time. I think he knew it, or suspected that I would soon find out. So he arranged this chase here to at least get me out of my city hunting grounds into those here in the swamp, with which he figured he was more familiar."

The other man stood there with narrow eyes for a while. He was impressed. Also thinking. He grunted audibly, then said, "Keep him here, you men. I guess he knows more than we figured."

The man went away and was gone for a few minutes. Then he came back and said, not particularly to Doc Savage, but in a more general tone, "The vote seems to be that we no longer carry on the pretense." He grinned at Top West. "How about it, chief?"

"I don't see any sense in it either," West said.

The men who had been holding West released him and he stepped forward.

West pulled down his sleeves with an unconscious return to neatness. He put on authority as a man puts on a coat.

"I don't see how I sucked you in," he told Doc Savage. "You know, you had me scared stiff half the time."

ABBA CUSHING looked at Top West with white, wordless rage. But not with surprise. She was not surprised, her manner showed. She had at no time been fully convinced that West was of lamblike innocence, so she was not particularly astounded now.

West added proudly, "I did a good job of acting, don't you think? Back there in the swamp, just before I got you into the trap, I mean. I thought maybe I was overdoing it. I am not an actor, you know."

Doc Savage made no comment.

The bronze man's silence seemed to irritate West, who was warming up to the job of showing that he was the intellect behind the affair.

"It was slick! Might as well admit it!" West snapped.

"The acting?"

"Yes."

"The acting," Doc said, "would have been a poor job for any vaudeville ham."

West darkened. "Yeah?"

"If the rest of the scheme demands no more intelligence than that," Doc Savage added, "there is probably nothing to worry about. The thing will stub its own toe and finish itself."

West became more indignant.

Abba Cushing watched the expression on West's face, then warned Doc Savage, "The man is an egoist. You are kicking him where it hurts."

West snorted. "Hurt me? Egoist, am I? I'll show you something, you two!" He jerked his head angrily. "Come on into another room, here."

Doc Savage and Abba Cushing, surrounded by guns, walked through a long tunnel affair that was simply a roof and walls over a path connecting to another building, which was larger than the first. It was a hive of bustling activity.

"Oh, what on Earth!" Abba exclaimed. "It looks like a newspaper office!"

A news-association central-bureau office would be a more fitting description. A relay office into which came news reports by wire, telephone, radio and teletype, from all parts of the world.

Or the headquarters of a general in command.

That was it.

A man, a young man with an intelligent face, came up and asked West, "Would you care for the reports from Rome, sir?"

West nodded, and was handed a sheet which bore typing. He scanned this, hesitated, then handed it to Doc Savage.

The typing read:

GENERAL GIO MARTINI A VICTIM AT HOUR THIRTEEN NAUGHT FOUR STOP ONLY OTHER MAN CAPABLE ORGANIZING STABLE GOVERNMENT CARLON PINELLA WILL BE VICTIM BEFORE NIGHT OVER.
PARKER ROME

"Gives you some idea," West said.

Doc told him, "I take it that this means that you have made more wild men?"

"Yes. But you shouldn't persist in calling them wild men. That isn't what they are."

"Then you have more of the machines? One in Rome, for instance."

"We have," said West, "more then fifty of them." He waved suddenly to indicate the young men at work in the room. "This is the nerve center of our organization. From here we keep in contact with our men throughout the world."

Doc Savage had surmised as much. The thing was very complete, with a dozen sets of radio short-wave apparatus, probably using highly developed beam-projection aerials so that they would not easily be discovered by direction finders.

"A large organization," Doc said dryly.

"Very complete," West agreed.

"Took brains," Doc said, "to get it together."

"Thanks."

"Took money, too. Lots of money."

"Sure!"

"More of both," Doc said, "than most people would be willing to throw away."

"It's not," said West, "thrown away."

"The stake must be large," Doc said.

"It is."

"A lot of money, probably."

West shook his head quickly. "You know better than that. You said once we didn't look like crooks. You were right. There isn't enough money in the world to get us into this thing we're in."

"More money, and more brains," Doc said, "than you have."

West became tense. "Yeah?"

Doc said, "You are not behind it, West. You are just a fellow disciple in the thing, like these others here."

West swallowed. He seemed wordless.

Doc added, "You might as well produce Cushing, who is masterminding it."

Raymond E. Cushing, dignified and venerable, composed, fully in command of himself and the situation, came from behind a nearby screen where he had been listening.

"This is too bad," he told Doc Savage. "I feel it is my destiny to see this thing through to the end. That necessarily means you will not be permitted to stand in our way, to use a somewhat hackneyed way of putting it."

Chapter XVI
THE WILDEST MAN

ABBA CUSHING tried to leave then. Not to escape; that was not in her mind. What she wanted

was to get out of sight of her father, to get away from the awful discovery that had confronted her.

Cushing made a quick gesture, said, "Abba, please! Come back here." And when she did not stop he told one of his men, "Get her. Bring her here."

The girl came back without resistance.

Cushing said, "Abba, you should have known this earlier. I thought, at times, that you suspected it. And on a number of occasions I was on the verge of telling you everything about it."

Abba said nothing. She was as pale as she would probably get. The bottom had gone out of things.

Cushing said, "Abba, this is a tremendous thing. It is destiny. It is a solution—a quick and somewhat violent one, but is worth that cost—of the world's problems."

His daughter seemed to have no words.

Whirling on Doc Savage, Cushing said, "This is largely your fault, damn it!"

Doc seemed surprised. "My fault? In what way?"

"The first three subjects of our experiments," Cushing said, "were Irving Eenie, R. T. Hooten and Miner Thomas. These men were selected for two reasons. First, their characters were not as lily-white as the world believed. Second, each was a representative type."

Doc Savage put in, "What do you mean by representative type?"

"Psychological types."

"Yes?"

Cushing said, "A financial leader, a political leader, and a religious or sociological-reform leader. You noticed I picked, in the beginning, one of these types in each country for my experiments."

Doc Savage was an interested listener. "What would making wild men out of three different types of men prove?"

"Nothing initially," said Cushing, "except that all types were subject to mental unbalancing by my apparatus." He smiled slightly. "There was to be more to the experiments. But, unfortunately, you stuck your big nose into it."

"What else was there to be to the experiments?"

"Further treatment with the machines," Cushing explained, "has a most desirable result. The will power of the victim is weakened to such a point that he will take a suggestion and act upon it."

Doc Savage made a quick, somewhat angry gesture. "That is impossible. Do not try to tell me otherwise."

Cushing frowned at him. Then Cushing shrugged. "Oh, all right. It was simpler than that."

"How simple?"

"Victims of the machine recover," Cushing snapped, "but they are like men who have had a nervous breakdown. They are easily terrified. Threat of further exposure to the machine easily persuades them to do what you wish."

"You were, then, going to weaken these men, then terrorize them into doing what you wished?"

Cushing was becoming irritated. "Put in unkind words, that is it." He scowled at Doc. "Furthermore, I am doing just that."

HE was doing it, too. Just how thoroughly, Doc Savage realized when two more young men from the radio equipment interrupted with more messages. Cushing, with a grim kind of glee, ordered the messages read aloud. One was from Egypt, and another from Japan.

Cushing had selected the leading nations of the world, probably not more than a dozen of them— twelve nations could swing the rest of the world to their way of thinking, as had been proved by war—and was systematically getting control of their political, business and sociological leaders. The man was a genius. He was not, in the greedy sense of the word, a crook.

Doc Savage, watching the man revel in the growing success of his fantastic scheme, turned over in his mind what he knew about Cushing. The man was extremely wealthy, a self-made man. Cushing was a man who had been fabulously clever in the amassing of money, and also very lucky. He had acquired wealth at a very early age. Cushing had genius, undoubtedly.

He was also a man of paradoxes. There had been an interval in his life, shortly after he became wealthy, when he had given tremendous sums to charity and to worthwhile enterprises. He had squandered millions, not all of which had done good. Then he had suddenly drawn the purse strings tight and, so far as anyone knew, had never given another cent to charity.

Shortly after that was the period Ham Brooks had mentioned in his investigation of Cushing. The revolution in Central America. The revolt laid at the door of Cushing's sugar company. Cushing had placed supposedly broadminded Central American politicians at the head of the new government. These had turned greedy and became as bad, or worse, than any other set of politicians.

The revolution indicated a quirk in Cushing's character.

The man thought he had a destiny to reform the world.

This, then, was another reform by violence on a broad scale.

Doc said, "Why did you frame me, Cushing?"

"You mean select my subjects for experiments in London and South Africa and Portugal, where your aides were at the time?" Cushing asked.

"Yes."

Cushing frowned. "That was an unfortunate necessity. For two reasons. First, you were sure to investigate this affair of the—shall we call them 'wild men?'—when it came to light. You would investigate it because it was up your alley. You like such things. You specialize in them. That is true, is it not?"

"Yes. The second reason?"

"A group of my wealthy friends," said Cushing, "insisted on calling you in when Hooten was made a victim of the machine. To prevent that I had to make them think you were the one doing the harm."

"I see."

Cushing grimaced. "Unfortunately, it worked too well. The friends began insisting that we seize you and make you repair the damage."

Doc Savage was silent a moment. "That," he said finally, "explains all but the blowing up of the yacht."

"I had one of the machines on the yacht," Cushing said. "It had to be destroyed."

"The idea," Doc suggested, "wasn't to destroy me also?"

Cushing became white. "I am not a murderer."

"You are something." Doc studied him. "You are something rather fiendish. The best thing for you to do would be to take a treatment from one of your own machines."

Cushing was grimly silent.

"Who," asked Doc, "invented the gadget?"

Cushing said, "One of my employees. An old fellow. He came to me with the thing. I saw its possibilities. So did he. He is working with me."

"Reform," Doc said, "is the object of the whole thing, I presume."

"Exactly."

"It is terribly wrong."

"Reform is never wrong," Cushing snapped.

The bronze man shook his head slowly. "It is not a thing for one man to take into his hands and try to force by violence upon the rest of the world. That has been proven. Many of the great wars of our day and the past have grown out of that sort of thing. Reform, any reform that is lasting and genuine, must result from the slow development, the molding of the minds and the way of life, of all the people as a whole."

"That," said Cushing, "is an opinion."

Doc said nothing.

Cushing said, "Look. You've got an out on this. You can either help me or be neutral."

"No."

Cushing beckoned his men. "Put him in the machine!" he said.

THE gadget had a table. A tilting table covered with leather, like the tables under X-ray machines in large hospitals. In fact it was a table taken from such a device, as indicated by the name plate of the manufacturer.

The tubes above the contrivance were not like X-ray tubes, not in shape, although they were metallic after the fashion of modern X-ray tubes. They were larger, and there was a multiple battery of them, apparently two tubes of each variety, arranged in the shape of an arching canopy. There were also, in addition to the tubes, large electro-magnets, evidently for the bending and deforming of emanations from the tubes. The mechanical part of the apparatus seemed to consist of a shutter affair, similar to a heavy Venetian blind, operated by a motor so that it could be opened and closed at high speed many times a second.

Doc put up his first real fight when they were strapping him on the table. The fight was not successful. He did succeed in doubling himself into a knot and stumbling back a pace or two until, almost covered by foes, he was forcibly returned to the table and strapped there.

As soon as they had him on the table, one of the men wrenched his coat back in place—a button was now missing from the coat—and forced him flat on the table. The straps were put in place.

There was nothing dramatic. No pseudoscientific mumbo jumbo of flashing fire and shooting sparks. The apparatus, at first, was noiseless. Later, there was a brisk rattling as the shutters opened and closed. They were a kind of shield, apparently, and their object was to shut off the emanations like the shutter in a motion picture projector to enhance their shocking effect. An interrupter.

The treatment lasted about five minutes, which was a long time under the circumstances.

Doc Savage was completely limp when they lifted him from the table. They put him in a chair. Then they stood around, waiting.

In a puzzled voice Cushing said, "His two men, Monk and Ham, were also unconscious when taken from the machine. That's strange. None of the others were that way."

Monk and Ham sat on their log, guarded by the man with the silly-looking balloon on a stick. They did not say or do anything, except to look idiotic.

Doc Savage sat up finally. That was after fully twenty minutes. He sat without moving in the chair for another five minutes.

Then Doc looked at Monk and Ham.

He said, "This foolishness has gone about far enough, do you not think?"

Monk and Ham began looking perfectly sane. They got off the log.

"I think it has," Monk said. "And right now I'm the wildest man around here. I'm itching for action."

SURPRISE has the qualities of an opiate, if sudden. And, too, there was the effect of the machine, its unnerving emanation which, although the machine had been shut off some time, was still productive of some aftermath which manifested itself in the form of uncertainty. The fact that Doc Savage and his aides had not been affected by the apparatus, which obviously they hadn't, was dumfounding.

Doc Savage went for Cushing. Getting his hands on the man was easy. He not only got Cushing, he was able to start for the door with the man.

"Get away!" he shouted to Abba, who had stood pale and distraught through all of it. "Get to the plane!"

The other men, the men who were Cushing's helpers in his gigantic and complex scheme to force some kind of reform on the world's political leaders, tried to save the situation. They rushed Doc.

Monk Mayfair began howling. He liked to howl when he fought. His best fights were his most noisy ones, he always claimed. The bellowing uproar he could make was something out of prehistoric times.

Monk hit two men and left them flat. He went on and tangled with a third fellow who was half Monk's size, but who in a twinkling had Monk on the floor. Immensely surprised, Monk began trying to get his hands or feet, preferably both, on the little man. The little man was an experienced atom.

Ham got a chair. The same one Doc had been occupying. Lifting the chair, Ham made for a man who had gotten the idea, a good idea under the conditions, of switching on the machine.

Ham smashed the chair into the apparatus. The result was only slightly less hell than a battle. Sparks and electric fire a yard long came out of the gadget. Two tubes exploded like shotguns and hurled out some kind of vapor that was as hard on the lungs as tear gas, but which did not affect the eyes. Simultaneously, there was a loud explosion in some other building, evidently caused by the short circuit.

Doc Savage was fighting now. He was armed with nothing but his fists, and handicapped by the necessity of hanging on to Cushing. The latter speedily became impossible. The foes were too many.

Abba Cushing tried to help Doc. It must have been a hard decision for her. It was a choice between her father and the bronze man. Probably she saw it also as a choice between the right or wrong of what her father was trying to do and the bronze man's principles. She tried to help. She did not do much good.

Men got between Doc Savage and Cushing. They separated them.

Ham yelled, "Doc, we've got to get out!"

That was true. If they could get out and reach the plane themselves they would be fortunate. Cushing had been taken away from them. So had Abba. Two men had grabbed the girl.

Doc said, "Break for the plane."

He added something else, in a much louder voice. A voice that everyone heard, even above the noise of the fight.

"Cushing!" Doc shouted. "We have protection against your brain-shocking apparatus! You saw that! It did not affect us!"

They fought their way out and to the plane. There was no fight to it after they were out of the building. It was a race, with no one in their path.

The plane, the big private ship belonging to Cushing, was tied with two lines which terminated at the cabin cleats, where they could easily be cast off. The ship was already sitting with its nose toward the large lake in the swamp where it had landed.

Doc started one of the plane's motors. The other would not fire. It was cold. The one motor gave him trouble, but he managed to get the plane down the creek to the lake. He let the plane float there, making no effort to take off.

"Talk about bum fights," Monk muttered. "That was one. We got licked, what I mean. It makes me wilder than I was."

Ham stared at the water, then at Doc Savage.

"Doc, why aren't we taking off?" he demanded. "We had better get away from here and take a fresh start at getting this thing stopped."

Doc Savage made no effort to put the plane in the air.

"There is a good chance," he said, "that it is already stopped."

Ham blinked doubtfully. "You mean that Cushing will think there is a protection against his gadget? That's fine if he thinks there is. But suppose he finds out the truth?"

"There is no one," Doc reminded, "to tell him that bit of truth."

WHEN Cushing came out to the plane he came alone in a small boat, his shoulders slumped and rowing listlessly. He was not armed; he held up his hands to show them this. "I want to come aboard," he said.

"This a surrender?" Doc asked.

Cushing climbed into the plane. "What can I do? I'm licked. The whole success of my plan depended on there not being any protection against the apparatus."

"It did not affect us," Doc said.

Cushing was a collapsed man. "Yes, and that's why I am here. I'm licked. All you have to do is cable men you might figure would be my victims, and tell them to take cover until you could get whatever you used into their hands. Then I couldn't do a thing to them."

"That," Doc told him, "is logical."

Cushing leaned back and closed his eyes. "I've told my men how it stands. They agree with me. But they are like I am in not understanding how you found a preventative so quickly. We experimented for months and we found no protection against the device. Yet, you discovered one almost immediately."

Doc Savage looked at the man thoughtfully. "How about your convictions as to the right and wrong of what you were doing? Do they still stand?"

Cushing gathered enough spirit to compress his lips. "I'm afraid they still do."

"In that case," Doc said, "we will have to send you to a certain institution which we maintain for men whose ideas are injurious to society. At this place, you will undergo an operation which will wipe out your past, after which you will be trained to think differently."

Cushing held his head in his hands for a while. The result of his thoughts was to bring forth an admission. "I think I would almost welcome that," he muttered. "I've been a reformer the wrong way. I never seem to be able to think of a damned way of doing it except by violence."

MONK went back to the island alone. That was in case there should, after all, prove to be a trap, which there wasn't. He made sure the apparatus was demolished. He also found his hog, which he considered almost equally important.

He reported back to the plane, "I saw a bunch of radio messages they were sending to their organization. They are calling off the whole thing."

Ham got Monk aside, asked, "You figure we better tell Cushing why the machine didn't effect us?"

"Why not? It was that pill, shaped like a button, Doc gave us. Why not tell him?"

Ham stared at Monk incredulously. "Don't you know what the pill was? And you a chemist?"

Monk scowled. "You casting reflections on my mentality again?"

Ham burst into laughter.

"Your mentality casts a reflection all its own," he said. "Wait until you find out what those button pills were made out of."

THAT was all the satisfaction Monk got until they reached New York and everything was satisfactorily settled.

Monk came into headquarters wearing a strange expression on his homely face.

"Is Doc in?" he demanded.

"Not right now," Ham explained. "He is down in Washington again, trying to persuade them that we should be in the front lines, fighting. I bet he gets the same answer—that the country needs his brains more than his brawn. He'll come back as mad as a hornet."

"I wish he was here." Monk rubbed his jaw. "A man was just found downstairs. You know those big modernistic ceiling chandeliers that light the lobby? He was in one of those. He was dead."

Ham stared. "That sounds crazy. Is that mentality of yours reflecting again?"

Monk scowled.

"Or maybe those button pills are taking effect on you again," Ham added. "They were just a strong hypnotic, you know. Stuff that the doctors give patients to quiet their nerves. The pill was just a heck of a strong dose that numbed our minds until Cushing's apparatus wouldn't affect us. Served the same effect as an anaesthetic before an operation; only this was on our nervous systems, not our bodies."

"Then there wasn't any preventative. It was a trick?"

"Yes."

"I wish," Monk said, "that Doc was here."

"Why?"

"Because," Monk said, "that man in the chandelier climbed into the chandelier hunting a vampire. I think Doc would be interested in a thing like that."

The mystery of *The Fiery Menace* is related in Volume 51 of *Doc Savage*.

THE END

Coming soon in DOC SAVAGE #62:

Doc, Monk and Ham journey to the Indo-China jungles to solve the strange enigma of *The Flaming Falcons* in a novel expanded from Lester Dent's original 1939 manuscript. Then, what is the bizarre connection between *The Two-Wise Owl* and the murder of Ham Brooks' brother?

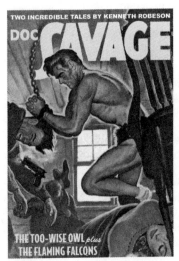

978-1-60877-091-5

BONUS: Supersnipe, "the boy with the most comic books in America," gets into mischief on the set of a *Doc Savage* movie in a classic tale from the Golden Age of Comics!

978-1-60877-092-2

HOW TO WRITE DOC SAVAGE by Will Murray

Lester Dent at his typewriter

Lester Dent once said, "I make no claim of writing literature. I write dime novels, clean stories with plenty of excitement, and I have a lot of fun writing them.

"I write mechanically, to a formula, a story blueprint. A writer's yearbook—*Writer's Digest Yearbook* for 1936—published my mechanical plot formula for a 6,000-word short detective story. Over two hundred writers wrote in that they had sold their first story by writing it to the formula."

This was the famous Pulp Paper Master Plot, which launched a thousand writing careers—and remains in use even today!

Pulp writers often worked from mechanical aids. Many were devised for this purpose, ranging from dime novelist William Wallace Cook's famous *Plotto* to *The Plot Genie*. One ingenious concept consisted of a deck of cards that could be shuffled and dealt out to make a story. Cards included protagonists, antagonists, villains and plot complications.

Lester Dent's Master Plot may have been the most effective of them all. His core concept could be boiled down to one prime directive.

Mort Weisinger described it this way: "Lester Dent, alias Doc Savage, says that the secret of filling up the entire issue of his magazine is 'to get someone in a tight predicament and then let Doc Savage, the hero, do his stuff.'"

Dent told his Doc Savage ghostwriters, "Keep somebody in trouble all the time, keep everybody in trouble as much of the time as you can."

"Trouble" was one of Lester's favorite words, as far as writing is concerned. But he reserved a different word for his big bronzed hero, Doc Savage.

The key ingredient was one Lester told anyone who cared to listen, like Billy G. Smith, a young Doc fan when Dent came to La Plata, Missouri in 1936:

Mr. Dent was asked to address the high school on 'How to Write Fiction Novels.' I could scarcely contain myself! The secrets of how to write Doc Savage stories! I was about to be disillusioned!

His formula for adventure yarns, and here I think I can recall his exact words, was "give your hero plenty of grief. When the reader thinks the sun is about to shine, hit your hero with another bucketful of trouble."

Dent's friend, newspaper columnist Cal Tinney, once asked Dent, "How do you do a story? And he said, 'I set down to the typewriter, with a bucket of grief on the floor by my chair, and as I move along, I just throw grief— I throwed grief on Doc Savage.'"

A newspaper woman, attending one of Lester's famous talks, also reported the Dentian formula in Lester's own words.

In the first line, walk your hero in, then reach in a pail of grief and take a good handful and swat him with it. He squares off and fights back. For the second part, pile on more grief, and bring in some struggle and physical conflict. For the third part, do the same thing some more. For the fourth part, do the same thing some more, until he doesn't have a chance— Now you've reached the place where, in the old melodramas, the hero is tied in a shack on a hill, and around the track the train is coming—Whoo! Whoo! Whoo!

Then the hero has got to extricate himself through his own ingenuity—it can't be by an act of God. Don't have lightning strike the shack for instance. He's got to do it himself.

But there was more to writing Doc Savage than the imaginary bucket of grief.

Mort Weisinger expanded on the Dent approach when he said, "Dent had a formula he used for every one of his novels. He claimed you should always have an exotic locale, and the mystery should be: who did it and the motivation. Why did he do it? And a unique murder method. How did he do it? And in every book a unique treasure."

One of Dent's ghostwriters, Ryerson Johnson, remembered that Dent was always focused on finding new and original treasures for his heroes to hunt.

"A current newspaper item, a spurt of imagination—anything—was enough to spring a plot," Johnson recounted. 'It often started with 'something of value to be attained.' 'Can you think of any new treasure Doc can go after?' Les would sometimes ask me. 'Something nobody would think of. The farther out, the better. I get the treasure, I've got the Doc....'"

Every Dent novel was a treasure hunt. Ordinary treasures did not cut it. His editors would not stand for the commonplace.

"Buried treasure stories, you know, are pretty old stuff among the pulps," Lester once explained.

"These treasures ran the spectrum," Weisinger recalled. "I remember one novel where the treasure was—bat shit! Guano droppings. It was used for fertilizer—a very valuable fertilizer. There were caves of the stuff. Thousands of tons of the stuff. Since time immemorial bats have been feathering the nest, so to speak."

The story behind the Master Plot was told by *Writer's Year Book* editor Aron M. Mathieu, who considered it one of the two most valuable how-to articles he ever ran:

Most published articles have interesting histories behind them. This one might interest some of you. Lester Dent sent us a modest little six-page article just about the time this magazine was going to press. The last line of the article mentioned his master plot formula; the famed master plot that has fed every Lester Dent story for the past several years.

We wondered if Mr. Dent would share that formula with the fraternity. We phoned his hotel in New York. "Sorry, Mr. Dent has gone to La Plata, Mo." We phoned the village postmaster at La Plata. "Sorry, Mr. Dent is on his yacht, the *Albatross*." "Where?" "Off Miami someplace; my goodness, why?" The long distance operator in Miami, a student of human nature if there ever was one, asked us a question: "How long has Mr. Dent been on his yacht?"

"Why?" We were glad to ask this for a change.

"Well, you see if he's just bought a yacht he's on deck running up flags, and then running them down again."

"Oh."

"But if he's had it for a while, he's below listening to his radio. If you want, I'll have the police put out a call for him on short wave."

We demurred.

The operator coughed, letting us know she knew we were a plain sissy.

To invade the privacy of an author anchored God only knows where by belching into his radio: "L-e-s-t-e-r D-e-n-t, Lester Dent call Miami police station. Yachts at sea off Miami, flag the *Albatross*. Owner wanted by police."

What a rummy we've turned out to be, we thought, as we gave the operator, who was by now politely sneering at us with her conversational coughs, the go ahead.

About two hours later a startled voice called us from Florida and asked what the hell we were up to. It seemed that every yacht off Miami caught the call and began signaling the *Albatross* while the rest of that busy little city came down to the wharf to see L-e-s-t-e-r D-e-n-t, a man obviously wanted by the police.

We explained demurely. And of such stuff are authors made that Mr. Dent agreed to send along his famed formula, although he added, with a touch of homespun: "I hadn't ought to."

It's a pretty fine thing for an author to share such a hard-won secret with his competing professionals, so if you like this piece, we have a mild suggestion to make. Buy a copy of *Doc Savage* on the newsstands and if you like the lead story, tell the publishers so in a letter.

In his Master Plot article, Lester revealed:

Framed over this typewriter, on a bulkhead of my schooner now anchored off a bay in the Caribbean while we attempt to raise a Spanish treasure, is an object which tends to make the convictions mentioned appear to be facts—or an unexpected hallucination.

The object on the bulkhead is a formula, a master plot, for any 6000-word pulp story. It has worked on adventure, detective, western and war-air. It tells exactly where to put everything. It shows definitely just what must happen in each successive thousand words.

No yarn written to the formula has yet failed to sell.

Dent instructed writers to:

DEVISE:

1—A DIFFERENT murder method for villain to use.

2—A DIFFERENT thing for villain to be seeking.

3—A DIFFERENT locale.

4—A menace which is to hang like a cloud over hero.

What was unique about the Master Plot was that it divided the traditional three-act story structure into a four-part formula.

When hour-long television programs came into existence in the 1960s, this unique structure was rediscovered by scriptwriters who had to work around the reality of four commercial breaks per episode. But Lester Dent pioneered the idea.

When it was published in *The 1936 Writer's Year Book,* the Master Plot brought in sacks of mail from

seasoned beginners and veterans alike, all of whom praised it for helping them sell more pulp stories.

"And that," Lester later complained, "was the

most awful thing I ever did. I got 780 letters from fellows who said they tried my formula and sold their first story—and that was building up a hell of a lot of competition for myself!"

The formula was reprinted in the annual *Writer's Market* every year clear into the 1940s. Writers evoked it often.

In a 1947 article published in *Writer's Digest*, pulp adventure writer Walt Sheldon described his own approach to producing pulp:

> I kind of do it by ear now, but one of the biggest helps I ever had was an old WRITER'S DIGEST article called "The Pulp Paper Master Plot" by Lester Dent. It had everything, but for some reason left out the idea of an emotional problem.
>
> Dent divided a story into four parts with a lesser climax and surprise at the end of each and a whopping climax at the end. I've sold them with three or six such parts, or even without a conscious attempt to divide them in any way. But I've had *surest* success with those old Dentian movements. Allegro, andante, scherzo and finally allegro with oomph.
>
> So now you manipulate your narrative. You put it into parts, movements, not to be confused with chapters. To get your climaxes in the right places, you use cushion material—background, explanation, atmosphere, scenery, action details.

In 1956, long after the pulp magazines for which Dent wrote had folded, *The Mystery Writer's Handbook* reprinted the 20 year old formula. For this, Lester penned a new introduction.

There, Dent called the Master Plot "a howling success and a great failure." He went on to recount the reaction he received from his old *Doc Savage* editor, John L. Nanovic:

> But what knocked me over was the attitude my favorite pulp editor had about it. This was back in the thirties. I was not as hard-nosed as in these days. Still, I was not easy to knock over. My favorite editor was irked. He got me on the carpet. "You insulted your readers," he said. "Surely you were joking. That stuff about searching Eloise, that was ridiculous." "Yes, sir. You're right," I'm sure I said. "I hope none of your readers see that," he said. "They will believe that you insulted their intelligence, and they will all quit you."
>
> "Yes, sir. I'm sorry. You're right." One always tells an editor he is right, the oftener the better.
>
> What bowled me over was that I had been dumb enough to forget to genuflect when approaching the subject of how a story is created. I had forgotten to treat the abstract art of plotting with respect. I had cavorted.
>
> I had already found out you could sell the same story over and over. I had already sold this one some four hundred times. This editor had already bought about a hundred of them. However

it was all right, because I went on and sold him the same story over and over again about two hundred additional times. I recall him complaining only once…

Lester went on to explain the art of storytelling, and retelling:

> There may be an editor here or there who won't buy a formula, or contrived, story. They don't stick around long.What they want is a story with the bones of the formula so cleverly covered that it isn't standing out like the bones in a starving cow. With a little practice it is not hard to cover the bones.They want a yarn that starts with a situation that precipitates the characters into conflict, jumps into the story quick, has as few characters as possible. They want the desires built strong; characters must be torn between them. The protagonist must be forced into a corner where he must make a final decision, and let there be no doubt anywhere in the yarn which character is the most important.
>
> If you can rig yourself up a story skeleton which ensures all this, and sell it over and over by putting a little different flesh and clothes on each time, it simplifies things.

The Master Plot was a great aid to writing, but even Lester had his construction problems, especially when doing his Doc Savage outlines. The Shadow's Walter Gibson remembered this vividly.

> Les Dent wrote a very breezy outline because his stories weren't as complex. He would bring in different things that happened but, every now and then, he'd find himself out on a limb. Something that he'd figured on wasn't jelling well enough; he had to beef up the story at some part.

That was because Lester was writing adventure stories, which often sprawled across continents, and relied on unexpected twists and turns.

Another Missouri Doc fan, John Yauk, recalled, "He wrote so damn much I never could figure out where all the words came from. A prolific writer, you know. One time I asked him, 'Where do you get all of your ideas for all these weird stories that you write?'

Dent told him, "Well, it's just a cultivated sort of a thing. There's nothing inspired about it. You just start making up things."

"First, he'd make up a situation, you know," explained Yauk. "There's a man on top of New York's Empire State Building, we'll say. And you go on thinking from there. How did he get up there? Well, he landed in a balloon. What was the balloon doing up there? Well, the balloon was this. You just go on from there. And finally you wind up with a story."

Lester Dent made it sound easy. For him, it was! •

Lester Dent (1904-1959) could be called the father of the superhero. Writing under the house name "Kenneth Robeson," Dent was the principal writer of *Doc Savage,* producing more than 150 of the Man of Bronze's thrilling pulp adventures.

A lonely childhood as a rancher's son paved the way for his future success as a professional storyteller. "I had no playmates," Dent recalled. "I lived a completely distorted youth. My only playmate was my imagination, and that period of intense imaginative creation which kids generally get over at the age of five or six, I carried till I was twelve or thirteen. My imaginary voyages and accomplishments were extremely real."

Dent began his professional writing career while working as an Associated Press telegrapher in Tulsa, Oklahoma. Learning that one of his coworkers had sold a story to the pulps, Dent decided to try his hand at similarly lucrative moonlighting. He pounded out thirteen unsold stories during the slow night shift before making his first sale to Street & Smith's *Top-Notch* in 1929. The following year, he received a telegram from the Dell Publishing Company offering him moving expenses and a $500-a-month drawing account if he'd relocate to New York and write exclusively for the publishing house.

Dent left Dell to pursue a freelance career, and in 1932 won the contract to write the lead novels in Street & Smith's *Doc Savage Magazine.* From 1933-1949, Dent produced Doc Savage thrillers while continuing his busy freelance writing career and eventually adding Airviews, an aerial photography business. Dent was also a significant contributor to the legendary *Black Mask* during its golden age, for which he created Miami waterfront detective Oscar Sail. A real-life adventurer, world traveler and member of the Explorers Club, Dent wrote in a variety of genres for magazines ranging from pulps like *Argosy, Adventure* and *Ten Detective Aces* to prestigious slick magazines including *The Saturday Evening Post* and *Collier's.* His mystery novels include *Honey in His Mouth* (recently published by HardCase Crime). In the pioneering days of radio drama, Dent scripted *Scotland Yard* and the 1934 *Doc Savage* series.   —Will Murray

Thrill to the adventures of the greatest superheroes from the Golden Age of Pulp Fiction in double-novel trade paperbacks, available at bookstores, comic book specialty shops and directly from SANCTUM BOOKS; P.O. Box 761474; San Antonio, TX 78245.